'T̶... ...enjoy this book. P̶... ...ls London and
Sy̶... ...norrifi̶... due date. ...ploration of di̶...nt kinds
of betrayal'   *Literary Review*

'Norman is an innovative stylist: the fast-paced narrative,
fluently rendered in translation by Ian Giles ... A sense of
intimacy that is almost claustrophobic, especially at the roller-
coaster climax'   *Financial Times*

'In this taut, engaging and fascinating thriller ... the writing is
crisp, the action fast paced, the plot and psychology convincing
and the subject matter both credible and contemporary ...
Andreas Norman will be one to watch'   shotsmag.co.uk

'An engrossing, and occasionally thrilling, examination of
minor and major betrayals that fans of Henning Mankell will
certainly find enjoyable'   crimefictionlover.com

'With a credible plot and believable characters, this is a high-
tension thriller of dirty tricks and calculated revenge'
                                                    Choice Magazine

'A powerful indictment of contemporary espionage techniques
in the West's ongoing conflict with terrorism ... This propul-
sive, thought-provoking thriller will leave readers pondering
the bedeviling eternal question: should evil ever be done so that
good may result?'   *Publishers Weekly*

Andreas Norman is a former diplomat who worked for the Swedish Ministry for Foreign Affairs. For several years he was a member of the Ministry's counter-terrorism unit, working with partners across the globe. *Into A Raging Blaze*, Norman's debut novel, anticipated the Edward Snowden revelations, received international acclaim, and was shortlisted for the 2015 CWA International Gold Dagger Award. Rights for *Into A Raging Blaze* and *The Silent War* have been sold to several countries and both are currently being developed into a major television series. Andreas Norman lives in Stockholm, Sweden.

Also by Andreas Norman

Into A Raging Blaze

THE
SILENT WAR

Andreas Norman

Translated from the Swedish by Ian Giles

riverrun

First published as *De Otrogna* in Sweden in 2017 by Albert Bonniers Förlag
First published in Great Britain in 2019 by riverrun
This paperback edition published in 2020 by

riverrun

an imprint of
Quercus Editions Ltd
Carmelite House
50 Victoria Embankment
London EC4Y 0DZ

An Hachette UK company

A CIP catalogue record for this book is available
from the British Library.

PB ISBN 978 1 78429 729 9
EBOOK ISBN 978 1 78429 361 1

10 9 8 7 6 5 4 3 2 1

Typeset by CC Book Production
Printed and bound in Great Britain by Clays Ltd, Elcograf S.p.A.

MIX
Paper from
responsible sources
FSC® C104740

Papers used by Quercus are from well-managed forests and other responsible sources.

A cold November rain has drawn in over Brussels during the morning and is pattering onto streets and squares, thudding onto car roofs, splashing and rippling as if pounding out its command of the city. Bente Jensen has no umbrella but doesn't care about the wet. She walks resolutely past a couple huddling together under an umbrella and an older man in a sodden jacket who is trying – in vain – to shelter from the rain by holding a newspaper over his head. She notes them and everyone else around them with small, rapid eye movements, glancing at reflections in windows to catch glimpses of what is happening beyond her field of vision. She assesses everything that passes her, looking for patterns and deviations, and she trusts nothing.

Her brisk walk is the final stage in a long sequence of planned movements that have been taking place on this rainy, grey morning. The man she is meeting has contacted her over the course of the last week in a series of brief, factual emails. He calls himself 'B54'. A strange cover name, she thinks, as she weaves her way along the pavement. She and her technical staff have tried to trace the emails, but all they have come up with are impenetrably encrypted servers and digital dead ends. The man clearly knows how to cover his tracks. He is familiar with specific details of British intelligence work that imbue him with such a great degree of credibility that she has decided to meet him.

There is the gallery, renowned for its photography exhibitions. She can see the grey façade and the large windows facing the street.

She pulls open the narrow door and finally escapes the rain. Her clothes cling to her. She is standing in a large hall. The quiet is so absolute that she can hear tiny dripping sounds as water drops languidly off her onto the floor.

She has been wondering why B54 wanted to meet her somewhere like this. But now she understands. It is secluded and there are presumably multiple escape routes. It has been well chosen.

On the walls there are a number of large portraits of faces. Everyday, anonymous faces – like huge passport photos.

A man with curly grey hair and wearing a corduroy jacket appears in a doorway, and she catches sight of an office behind him. 'Welcome,' he says warmly, handing her a programme. Then he sits down behind a white table set slightly to one side.

She is alone in the hall. A woman who had been standing in front of one of the large photos a few moments ago has vanished into an adjacent room.

Yet she feels watched. She can't escape the feeling that the photographs are observing her, reserved and dismissive, as if wondering what gives her the right to stand there staring at them. She has seen the expression before, on other faces: a hesitant defiance at being observed, documented and questioned. The flyer says the man responsible for the photos is world famous. She has never heard of him, but she seems to understand his pictures.

Then she spots a faint annotation in the programme margin: *Top floor.*

The man who handed it to her has disappeared.

She walks across the floor, taking deliberately leisurely paces, careful to adopt the plodding slow-motion gait of a gallery visitor. She walks around a screen and enters another large room. There are four people spread out around the area: a young couple in dark clothing, a single man in an anorak who might have been the person she was seeking if he hadn't been one of her own operatives who had previously been stationed there as planned. And the woman now standing, engrossed, in front of a new portrait. She is dressed practically, in a raincoat and trainers, and is clasping a dripping umbrella in her hand. She too has just come in from the rain.

It is impossible to say whether the woman is a scout from a hostile intelligence agency, or whether she is cooperating with the man that Bente is about to meet, ready to raise the alarm should the meeting go south. Or perhaps she is just a woman in a gallery. Even after two decades on the job, determining whether a person behaving normally is hiding another, secret identity remains the hardest part.

Only at this point does she become aware of a low, pulsing sound that has been present in the room all along: a dark hum, almost mechanical in nature. The sound is coming from a staircase that disappears up to another level.

She wanders up the stairs, taking care not to appear too eager in her movements, and emerges into another large room. Silver-grey rays of daylight slant through the skylight above.

In the middle of the room is an enormous cube, like a room within the room.

The sound is coming from inside the cube. It is powerful,

filling the entire space. She recognises the booming sound of a helicopter rotor. She looks back towards the stairs: no, the woman has not followed her.

She approaches the smooth surface of the cube and lifts the dark felt curtain covering its entrance.

Inside the cube, all is darkness and flickering shadows. A film is being projected onto a large screen – a forest by night, illuminated by a searchlight, as if from a helicopter. The circle of light sweeps across the treetops, which are swaying and shaking in the downdraught from the rotor blades. The sound of the helicopter fills the darkness.

'Hello?' she calls out quietly, although just loudly enough to be heard through the din.

When no one answers, she fumbles her way to a bench and sits down.

Someone is behind her. She can feel them as a close presence just behind her back, and she turns around.

'Hello?'

Very close to her left ear she can now feel the light movement of someone's breath.

'Thank you for coming,' a man whispers.

She attempts to distinguish the nuances of the voice through the blaring racket. Someone young, she thinks. Speaks British English with an educated tone: an academic. He is frightened.

She feels a hand rapidly pushing something into her jacket pocket.

'Wait!' she shouts.

The felt curtain across the entrance to the cube is pulled aside, and she just has time to catch a glimpse of a man with a pale, flabby face and dark hair.

She runs towards the stairs. Her footsteps thud as she hurries down. Her lookout is already in the outer hall, and he turns towards her and points. She rushes to the narrow door and gazes out at the façades beyond, dark with rain. He is gone.

In the car on the way back to the office she pulls the small object from her pocket. It's a memory stick. It rests, like a dark scarab, in the palm of her hand.

Three Weeks Later

Bente Jensen can already hear the loud buzz of voices as she climbs the wide marble staircase at the Hotel Metropole. The Swedish Embassy's reception started an hour or so ago. She hugs Fredrik's arm and they smile at each other, engulfed by the lively noise as they emerge into the ballroom. Later on, she will reflect that this was one of the happiest moments for a long time.

They are late. The traffic on the way into Brussels this evening was terrible. She had stood in a hurry in front of the mirror, making a final check and re-applying her lipstick before hurrying down to the boys, who were watching a film in the living room. She was eager to get away, and rushed through telling them that there was food in the fridge and that if they needed anything they should just call, before giving each of them a hasty kiss and leaving them, safe in their home.

'It's good that I came along, isn't it?' she said in the taxi, and Fredrik smiled at her, teasingly waving the invitation in front of her as if she were a cat. She kissed him. He had initially offered to go alone. He knew that she disliked events like this, he had said. But of course she wanted to accompany him since he had been honoured with an invitation.

Nordic Business. In the darkness of the taxi, she fingered the thick, exclusive stationery with the embossed Swedish coat of arms. *His Excellency the Ambassador*, it said in a courtly style, *is hereby delighted to invite ...* On the line below it said: *Mr and Mrs Fredrik Jensen*. For once, he was the most important member of their family.

In the ballroom, it is so noisy that they have shout to hear each other.

'Do you want a glass of wine?' Fredrik bellows, while pretending to knock back some imaginary wine and getting drunk. She laughs and sneaks her arm around his waist.

They are a couple in the midst of the throng, just like they used to be before she got a job so secret that she started declining invitations to dinners and events. It's a long time since they have gone out, just the two of them. They ought to do it more often.

She is overwhelmed by the desire to kiss him again. But she hesitates. She has fallen out of the habit of pursuing impulses like that, uncertain how to pull him towards her and press her mouth against his, here, in front of other people.

Fredrik looks good in his suit. He is conservative when it comes to shirts, and always chooses white or pigeon-blue, which he usually orders online when he has nothing else to do. But this evening he is wearing a pale-pink shirt. It must be new, she thinks to herself. It suits him. It makes him look surprisingly glamorous.

She is wearing a cocktail dress that Fredrik gave her two years ago but which she hasn't worn before tonight. There are rarely occasions in her life that call for her to wear a pearlescent creation in chiffon, with pleats, and she had hesitated for a long time. But as if responding to some internal form of civil disobedience, she eventually chose it precisely because part of her insisted on wearing something more discreet. Once she had overcome the sensation of being dressed up, rather than overdressed, she felt happy. Just before they left, she looked in the mirror and thought to herself: a woman's body is her castle. She is filled with a happy feeling of insurrection. And love. Yes, love too. Because she has chosen the dress that Fredrik gave her as a present on their wedding anniversary.

It strikes her that she doesn't have her phone with her. 'Have you got your mobile on you?' she shouts to Fredrik. He nods. Well that's fine, the boys can call him if they need anything.

He is gazing around the room, looking for someone he knows, while she sips her wine and hopes it won't take too long, because she feels a little sorry for him and she doesn't want to feel like that. She is proud of Fredrik. She likes the fact that he is so handsome this evening, and is pleased for him that he has been invited to this embassy party. For herself, she is satisfied standing here with him; she doesn't care about all the other people, but if he needs to feel validation, then she hopes it happens soon, before he gets into a bad mood.

Fredrik has caught sight of a colleague. She follows in his wake and is introduced to a tanned man with a booming voice, who shakes hands with them with vociferous cordiality – it is obvious he doesn't know Fredrik more than superficially. It transpires that the man is a middle manager for one of Fredrik's corporate clients. The men fall to discussing a merger. Listening to them talking about the joining of two companies is interesting because Fredrik hardly ever talks about his work. But after a while Bente realises she is not part of the conversation: the other man is completely ignoring her and Fredrik is so busy directing his full attention towards the middle manager that he barely notices when she leaves to fetch them each a new glass of wine.

She plots a course out of the room. She is halfway across when she glimpses a familiar face in the midst of the throng.

Jonathan Green.

Apart from Bente, few know who he really is: MI6's man in Brussels. She hasn't seen him in more than a year, but he looks the same as ever: the same boyish countenance, the same mop of red hair and the same unblinking blue eyes. He catches sight of her.

She quickly slips behind a group of suit-clad backs, retreating through the loudly talking guests. She most certainly does not want to meet Jonathan Green here. The Brits are close partners of Sweden, and Swedish resources regularly contribute to the work of the British foreign intelligence service – but since B54 contacted her, everything is much more complicated. She can't be seen together with someone from MI6.

How odd to run into Jonathan Green here. Then it occurs to her that he is officially listed as the Senior Trade Attaché at the British Embassy. Of course, that isn't accurate – he is a spy – but he is here this evening in his trade role. The chatty guests surrounding him have no idea what a skilled and ruthless man, with at least three false identities, hides behind that smiling façade.

To see him in this glittering, merry ballroom, when she knows what he is hiding, makes her feel ill at ease. Over the last three weeks, she and her colleagues have reviewed the material she was given at the art gallery, and what she has seen has changed everything. She has tried to explain to Stockholm that future cooperation with the Brits is out of the question after this, but they haven't responded.

Jonathan Green is enormously capable but also something of a cold fish. She will always see him as the enemy. When she was the new Head in Brussels, he had managed to turn the head of Swedish Counter-Terrorism against her – he had turned

10

everyone against her – and had made them demand that she submit to MI6. Green had the power to influence others. He had harmed her and, deep down, he had shaken her self-confidence.

It is precisely these random meetings that make her worry about ambassadors' receptions and dinners. Fredrik doesn't understand that she constantly has to be on her guard when surrounded by the observant, social animals that inhabit the world of diplomacy.

At the drinks table, she ends up next to two men engaged in an animated discussion about the other guests in French. Fortunately, they ignore her. Or rather, they don't even notice she is standing there since she is not *attractive* or beautiful in any conventional sense, and because they don't perceive her as an important person. It entertains her to listen to them, because they are so keenly aware of who amongst the guests is worth talking to, and who is a nobody. They are career diplomats at the French Embassy – probably graduates of the École Polytechnique or the École Normale – and have a bright future ahead of them in French state administration. These assured, skilled and exquisitely arrogant predators are so foolish, and simultaneously supremely slick. To them, she is invisible and that suits her down to the ground.

She knows many of the guests present, even if they don't know her. If only they knew how many hours of their conversations she has listened in to over the last few years. In fact, if she is not mistaken, she has even listened to these Frenchmen.

She reaches for two glasses of white wine and hears that they have moved on to Syria. Everyone is trying to find the answers to the same questions: what will Assad do, which elements of the opposition will function as partners after the war, what do the Russians want and what on earth are the Americans actually up to? They talk about rebels and Islamists – she hears one of the Frenchmen mention Islamic State using the term 'Daesh', from the Arabic, *to trample*.

All these men and their embassies, she thinks to herself with a smile. They are scared to death of being infiltrated; yet for many their secret wish is for precisely that. He who is not being bugged is not worth listening to. And who doesn't want to be heard? Who doesn't want to be loved?

When she returns to where she left Fredrik, he is gone. As if by magic, he and the middle manager he was speaking to have vanished into thin air. She surveys the room of faces.

Perhaps he has gone to the men's room. For the first few minutes, she sips her wine and amuses herself by watching nearby guests. But after five minutes, the wait is beginning to drag. She puts down the glasses of wine. Perhaps he has found someone else to talk to and become so absorbed that he has forgotten she went to fetch wine for them. It has happened before. After eight minutes, she has the feeling he won't be coming back. Hesitantly, she leaves her spot on the floor and does a lap of the room. After fifteen minutes her absent-minded pondering has grown into perplexed irritation. A hollow absence flows between all the unfamiliar faces – all she can see is the absence of Fredrik. She ends up standing in the middle of the crowd like a spare part.

Where is he? She leaves the ballroom and quickly walks down a corridor until she reaches a door, but it is locked. She turns around and heads up the wide marble staircase to the next floor, but all she finds is an empty breakfast room.

She had hoped for a pleasant evening together with him, and now she has to wander around looking ridiculous as she searches for her worse half. The festive atmosphere which had been seeping into her just a little while ago has been subsumed by cool anger. She has already begun to formulate her righteous criticism, polishing up some of the wording she will direct at him, when she catches sight of some double doors one floor down that she hadn't noticed previously.

Chilly evening air wafts in through the open doors. There are clusters of guests standing in the cobbled inner courtyard in the dark of the evening. So this is where the smokers have set up shop. She slowly walks the courtyard perimeter, shivering in her flimsy dress.

She catches sight of three men and a woman standing to one side, talking cheerfully. When one of the men leans forward she sees his face. It's Fredrik, and then, in a moment of flat, confused denial, she wonders why he is standing there with that woman and the two men. He appears to be telling them something funny. The woman laughs enchantedly: they are in the midst of a lively conversation. It is clear they know Fredrik, but Bente has never seen them before. Perhaps they are colleagues.

She heads towards them and just catches sight of the woman leaning towards Fredrik for a farewell kiss on the cheek before quickly disappearing into the crowd.

Fredrik doesn't notice Bente until she is standing right in front of him. He obviously hasn't been looking for her; quite the opposite, in fact: he looks surprised, as if he has completely forgotten that they came here together. She feels embarrassed, ridiculous even, when he loses his thread in the middle of telling a lively anecdote to the other men. 'Darling,' he exclaims, giving her a slightly distracted look, before hastily introducing her to the men, who immediately seem to want to leave them alone. 'Be in touch,' they say to Fredrik, while smiling at Bente.

13

'Where did you get to?'

He explains that he ran into some people from work and nods in the direction of the men. She says she has been searching for him for a long time.

'I looked for you,' he says evasively.

He reaches out a hand and touches her arm. 'Darling . . .'

He shrugs his shoulders as if to excuse himself and says that surely no harm has been done. She holds her tongue and looks around the courtyard without actually seeing anything except shadows. A dull sadness runs through her veins when she hears him say, 'I was only gone for a few minutes,' in the tone of voice reserved for moments when he wants to appear sensitive and a little wounded in order to make her feel controlling, and to get the better of her by insinuating that she limits his so-called freedom – this is one of his favourite stratagems when they row. A tremor, almost imperceptible, runs through Bente; they are close to stepping over a line. Then she decides not to make a scene – he clearly isn't planning on apologising. She takes his hand and notices how he immediately relaxes.

Jonathan Green is shaking the hand of the energetic, greying man in the chalk-stripe suit, whose name he has already forgotten, and repeating how pleasant it has been talking to him. This is not entirely true: he remembers nothing of what the ageing man has just said, except that he is a manager at Crédit Lyonnais.

When he thinks no one is looking, he allows his face to relax. The smile melts away. He looks around, but Bente Jensen has already disappeared into the crowd. He surveys the ballroom with the fatalistic feeling that a seemingly insignificant, but ultimately catastrophic mistake could happen. Has he been careless?

14

He looks at his watch.

He makes his way through the guests with a determined stride, without pausing to greet anyone, so that no one is tempted to stop him. Two hours of small talk with management consultants, financiers and bankers is more than enough. The effort of appearing interested has formed a grey cloud of exhaustion inside him. What's more, it bothers him that Bente happened to see him, since she is the only person in the room who knows who he actually is. Ever since he took the post as Senior Trade Attaché, he has been exceedingly careful to wear the mask that the diplomatic role calls for – a lie that has to fit him like a universal truth. Knowing that the Swede is out there in the ballroom and can see through his charade makes him feel uneasy.

They are still working out how such a junior analyst could have gained access to so many sensitive documents. The thought that the Swede has them and is familiar with vast swathes of their work in Syria makes him feel out of sorts. *Semper Occultus* – always secret. Well, not so *semper* any longer, he thinks to himself bitterly. If he had his way, he would simply approach her and force her to give him everything, but that's not how it works. He will resolve the problem by other means, and if everything goes according to plan, then the leak will soon be under control.

He is out of the scrum. The smile that has been frozen on his face for hours finally gives way to forbidding seriousness.

Fifteen minutes later he pulls up outside the British Embassy in his car. The building looms like a dark fortress above the sparse traffic on Rue de la Loi. He squints at the light of the coldly bright entrance, and holds up his pass – but the guard has already recognised him.

All is quiet on the fifth floor. He wanders down the deserted corridor, the air-conditioned peace calming him. This is where MI6 has its Brussels bureau.

He grew tired of Brussels long ago but still likes his office. He also has an official workspace, which is attached to the trade delegation. The ambassador likes to acerbically point out that the trade delegation is based on the third floor, and that if he is meant to be pretending to be the Senior Trade Attaché then he actually ought to play the role. To avoid unnecessarily irritating the ambassador, he makes the journey down two storeys once a week to his official office to reply to emails about business lunches and other pointless frivolities, before returning to MI6's office.

He looks at the time.

Standing by the window in his office, he traces the glittering stream of traffic flowing around the roundabout at Place Schuman. If everything goes according to plan, he will soon be able to say that the leak has been handled and that the danger has passed. But the Swede is aware of the House. He could tell when he saw her at the reception: she knows. It bothers him that she looks at him that way – as if he has a burden of guilt on his shoulders. As if *he* is guilty.

A minute or so left to go.

Barely a month ago, he thought his time at MI6 was over. The leak was a disaster, but he has taken responsibility and attempted to minimise the damage, as London knows. But it has been a dreadful month ever since that wretch stole the documents that he shouldn't even have known about, let alone shared with the Swedish Security Service.

How could a young Brit betray the confidence that becoming part of Her Majesty's Secret Service involved? He has never encountered such self-indulgent blind faith in morality. So awfully disloyal. Putting yourself above the system just because some things don't suit you is treachery, he thinks. It's lucky he didn't recruit the conscientious arse; that would definitely have meant curtains for his own career.

He knows what they have been saying back in London over the last month: Brussels leaks like a sieve. An office of incontinence. Even if he manages to deal with the leak, there will be many who remember him as the station chief who made a mistake. This vexes him deeply.

Hercules, he thinks. That operation is an opportunity for him. If it ever happens. It has been quite impossible for Robert to get anyone to make a decision over the last month. The leak has paralysed everyone. Everyone knows how Parliament would react if they ever heard about the House. Damn hypocrites.

Personally, he despises the House, but he doesn't believe that entitles him to object to what goes on there. His own personal views and thoughts are one thing; his loyalty to his organisation is more important than his own values.

The phone rings, piercing the silence.

'Hello?'

'Jonathan, old boy.'

Robert's familiar baritone reaches him through the receiver. He can hear the hum of the city in the background: London.

Robert sounds short of breath – as if he is walking upstairs – as he says that he is looking forward to Jonathan coming to London. Then it goes quiet. He hears his friend close a door and seamlessly change tone. He no longer merely speaking with his friend Robert, but also Robert Davenport, Head of the MI6 Middle East Department.

'They want to revive Hercules,' he says, purring like a cat.

17

'The powers that be have given us the nod. So how are things in Brussels? Have things started to resolve themselves?'

Jonathan sits down in his office chair; he is finally able to give Robert the good news that he has been wanting to share all evening.

'The leak is under control,' he says. It feels wonderful to finally be able to say it. 'We have infiltrated them. It is only a matter of time before I have confirmation. If everything goes to plan, we will be able to eliminate all leaked documents over the weekend.'

'Good, good . . .'

It is gratifying to hear how relieved Robert is.

'And what about you?' he says. 'I mean . . .'

'We've dealt with him.'

'Dealt with' is an unpleasant term. He is tempted to ask what exactly they have done with the analyst, but he stops himself. No, he doesn't want to be involved, and as soon as he has that thought he feels relieved. To hell with the analyst.

They talk about Hercules.

'So we have an operation?'

'I hope so,' Robert exclaims jovially. 'The final obstacle is Paddy. The Minister of Defence is still worried about the leak. Same old story – it could cost the Minister's job. But if the leak has been eliminated then that's marvellous. That means they have reasonable grounds to deny any and all knowledge of the matter. They don't want to hear a word about the House. You wouldn't believe how many times Paddy has called in the last week and been *concerned*.'

They laugh.

The Minister's advisor, Paddy, has been constantly *concerned* for three weeks. For God's sake, imagine how easy everything

18

would have been if the Ministry had simply never found out about the leak, he thinks to himself. They would never have heard about the House, and Operation Hercules would already be complete. Robert liked to say that Ministers didn't need to know everything, and he was inclined to agree. It would be better if the politicians gratefully accepted the information provided to them by MI6 without giving so much thought to the methods behind espionage.

'A meeting?'

'On Sunday. Just Paddy. He is prepared to discuss the operation with us again.'

Robert sighs deeply in the same way he has been sighing in recent weeks. The fact that Robert has secured a meeting about Hercules at the Ministry of Defence is truly good news – the bad news is Paddy. Paddy the Bouncer – the Ministry's very own doorman. This man has made a shining career out of saying no. But perhaps he can be persuaded if the Prime Minister has expressed interest in the operation.

'I need you in London, Jon.'

Jonathan smiles, because there is nothing he would like more than to leave Brussels to travel to London.

'I can be there tomorrow.'

Robert insists they have dinner. No ifs, no buts. He interrupts Jonathan's polite objections in his usual loud manner. He will collect Jonathan at his hotel at six o'clock and won't entertain another word on the matter.

Bente coaxes the high heels off and massages her sore feet. Maybe she should have said that seeing him standing there with his colleagues and directing attention at them that he should have been giving her made her feel jealous. She knows she is exaggerating, but it can't be helped. The thought that there are people who know Fredrik but are complete strangers to her, and who make him forget her, blossoms in her mind like a dark flower.

They had been planning to go to a bar afterwards for a drink, but in the end they hadn't. Both of them had been tired. They joked about how they were no longer party animals.

On the way home they didn't talk about it – because what exactly was it that had happened? Nothing. She told him about the snobby Frenchmen and they laughed and talked about the diplomats, the other guests, the Hotel Metropole and what a magnificent building it was. Then they sat in silence.

'What are you thinking about?' he had asked her, and she had responded evasively.

But she could have said: 'I'm thinking about how we belong together. That it's difficult not knowing whether I can trust you as much as I should.' But opening up like that scared her and she had remained silent.

They have lived in Brussels for five years. She is not happy. This isn't some deep insight but more of an objective under-standing that has emerged. She will never be on good terms with this untidy, rainy city. And she can't understand how to speak French – the sounds seem to slide around in her mouth and make her feel stupid when she tries to pronounce them.

Time has passed so quickly while also seeming to last an eternity. It is strange to think that in future just one sentence will encompass the myriad of events that has passed in five years.

The boys are asleep. She can see the traces of their evening together: the dirty plates on the coffee table, leftover grilled chicken, glasses and a bottle of pop. Everything seems to be in order. She can't put her finger on when it happened, but her boys need her less now – soon they'll need her less than she needs them.

But she is worried about Rasmus. He is in secondary school, but doesn't see the world like other children of his age, and he has an anxiety that pulses through the entire family and can make them lose their footing. Down the years, they have discussed medicines and therapies with a string of paediatricians, and she wonders whether any of them work. They struggled with his last school and now, finally, he has moved to a new one. But his outbursts have got worse recently. Over the last few weeks he has been behaving oddly. He turns away from his parents, furiously retiring into his shell in a new way that frightens her. It is going to be a tough winter and spring. A new year of screaming and fighting with his big brother.

She hears Fredrik open the bathroom door. Quickly, she gets up and turns off the light so that the dark conceals her.

Sometimes she can see the boys watching her and Fredrik, as if they are only just understanding that their parents are separate individuals, with their own mysterious lives that began long before they were even born.

She presses herself softly against Fredrik as he lies beside her. She carefully runs her hand down his stomach and feels him react. He grows between her fingers and it makes her feel assured. She likes being able to make him breathe more deeply, to make him go hard. Then he is on top of her, and she is wet. Perhaps it's the relief that he wants her too that excites her. She meets him with her hips and lets him enter her while wrapping her arms around him, because she wants to push away all disappointment, she wants to be taken, not tenderly, no, not with comforting affection, but powerfully and unconditionally. And then it happens: rhythmically, further and further up the bed until they turn to face the ceiling, united in their lonely lament into the darkness.

It is gently drizzling outside. Bente is lying in bed, calm and comfortably at ease. There is a mild sense of happiness in waking up on a Saturday morning and knowing that this is her home and that she has a day off with her family. No work, or at least not before lunch.

All their weekends begin in the same tranquil way: Fredrik cooks breakfast which they eat together, whereupon they all lose themselves in their respective newspapers and devices.

She hears Fredrik rattling about in the kitchen. She can hear the boys in Rasmus's room and for once their voices are soft and calm. She likes lying there listening to her family. She likes that Fredrik sorts out breakfast at the weekend and is so painstaking when he cuts up grapefruit, scrambles eggs, slices different breads and puts out sandwich fillings. It is a resolute love. She can't understand what made her so glum the evening before.

Fredrik is already dressed when she descends to the kitchen. *My husband.* She is only wearing her dressing gown and she is tempted to open it slightly to make him touch her. 'Did you sleep well?' He nods, then shouts upstairs that breakfast is ready.

She often reflects that a family is a unit built on trust and a sense of kinship. It is unspoken ties, and the silent commitment to give each of the others a specific place in one's life, that hold them together.

The soft thudding of boys' feet can be heard on the stairs. Rasmus lumbers forward sulkily and slumps into his chair, helping himself to a slice of bread and some scrambled egg.

'Good morning, Rasmus.'

The boy mutters.

Shortly afterwards, Daniel appears and sits down wordlessly.

They eat. Rasmus eats his scrambled egg, while Daniel prefers yoghurt. Bente considers Daniel: almost grown-up, yet still a child. The boy grunts affirmatively when she asks whether they had a good time the evening before. She smiles at Fredrik across the table. They have shared so many of these quiet, meaningful glances over the years, but this morning Fredrik is reading something on his mobile and doesn't notice that she has turned to him. She looks at her boys. She can still remember when they were just the same height as the table they are now sitting at, so lanky and tall.

Rasmus is tense. He is due to play with his football team and is hurrying to eat his scrambled eggs even though there is plenty of time. He is anxious and wants Fredrik to double check that his trainers and kit are ready.

The football trainers are important: Fredrik gave them to him last week and he loves them. He has declared that they are 'epic' because they have a ribbed rubber trim on top that improves ball control.

Fredrik ruffles his hair but this merely annoys the boy. 'Stop it,' he says loudly. Fredrik immediately withdraws his hand. Contact like that can unleash anger that easily escalates into a roar. Rasmus is a sensitive child and they have to interpret his state of mind and weigh up each and every word and touch to avoid exposure to a blind rage that never seems to end, until it suddenly vanishes as if it had never been.

'You've got plenty of time, Rasmus,' Bente says.

Rasmus looks at her suspiciously, and promptly asks what the time is. But she isn't wearing a watch. Does Fredrik know what the time is? Worry oscillates between them. The boy continues to nag them. What time is it? How long will it take to get to the recreation centre? Daniel glances morosely at his little brother. The anxiety brings everything to a halt for a brief few seconds, then Fredrik stops taking an interest in his mobile and says that it is 9.35, and that it will take twenty minutes to get to football.

It bothers her that Fredrik can't see as clearly as she does that Rasmus needs routine and predictability. Reality confuses him and he requires support to structure it. It is typical of Fredrik to fail to notice that the boy was on the verge of a tantrum.

Personally, she likes order. Why shouldn't food packaging be arranged in the cupboards so you can read the labels? But Fredrik's mind doesn't work like that. Neither Fredrik nor Rasmus put things where they belong. So it is up to her to keep things in order and create a safe, calm environment for the boys.

Fredrik is lying stretched out on the living-room sofa. He is leafing through one of his silly men's fashion magazines that he is so keen on. Has he seen her mobile? She doesn't know where she put it down, she says.

Fredrik hums and haws without interest. She left it at home when they went to the reception the day before. Or did she have it with her? She had drunk more wine than usual, but she normally remembers these things.

He lowers the magazine and looks at her.

'Didn't you put it on the hall table, like usual?'

'I usually do, but it's not there.'

She always leaves her phone to charge on that table. But it wasn't there yesterday; she can't picture it in her memory.

'Can you call it?'

Fredrik puts away the magazine and reaches for his mobile. She can hear the ringing on the line. She listens intently.

Yes, now she can hear it: a low, rumbling noise. It's coming from somewhere in the kitchen, or perhaps the hall.

'Call again,' she says, walking slowly out of the living room.

The whirring is once again audible. From the hall. No, the porch.

She rummages through the outer garments. The sound is nearby now, it is coming from one of the coats hanging there.

In the middle of a ring, it stops. But she can already feel the phone's slender, rectangular shape. Relieved, she picks it up and can't help checking it. Other than Fredrik, no one has called.

Only then does it strike her that the mobile was lying in Fredrik's jacket pocket.

'It was in your jacket.'

He looks at her across the top of the magazine. Well, perhaps she put it there instead of in her coat, he suggests, before reading on.

In his jacket? No, she didn't put it there. But then she feels uncertain, because his jacket and her coat are a similar colour and are usually hanging side by side in the hall.

The doorbell rings.

When she opens it, a woman clad in a gilet and cap is standing on the step. She looks sporty and healthy. Around thirty years old, medium blonde, well-to-do.

'Hi,' says the woman in Swedish, using a pure Skåne dialect filled with warmth as if they were friends.

She returns the greeting. The woman is vaguely familiar, but Bente doesn't know her. They smile at each other. The woman looks at her attentively.

'Perhaps I could come in?' the woman asks, tilting her head to one side.

There is something slightly compelling about the situation, because even though she doesn't know the woman, it is hard to say no unless there is direct hostility, and the woman seems normal, and most definitely not threatening.

'Of course,' she says, stepping a little to the side.

The woman comes into the porch and then continues into the hall.

'What a lovely home you have.'

Bente comes to a stop, with a floating feeling caused by not knowing what the woman wants, or why this stranger has come into her house.

Outside on the gravel path, a boy wearing football kit appears. And in that moment, she joins the dots of reality, understands, and calls over her shoulder:

'Fredrik!'

Once Rasmus and Fredrik have left, the whole house is still. She loves this silence. It is as if it is healing the rooms and restoring them to their original condition. She descends the narrow stairs into the basement before stopping in the small space outside Daniel's closed bedroom door. A guitar. Daniel is playing a chord, but stops. She continues quietly past his door, taking care not to disturb him.

She takes a quick shower. The sauna is up to temperature.

The heat is powerful and all-encompassing when she steps in. Her pores open, and after just a minute beads of perspiration cover her back and run between her breasts. This is her solitary ritual at the weekends: the sauna, followed by a couple of hours' work.

Sometimes, when Rasmus is screaming, she can't stand it. That's when she comes down here. She knows that Fredrik is better at dealing with their youngest, he has more patience and can continue speaking in a calm voice when she would long ago have shouted at the boy to pull himself together. Fredrik knows his boys, he has always known what sizes they wear, what they do and don't eat, and he can handle Rasmus. When the boy is screaming he can sit down next to him and simply wait until it is possible to talk. The screaming drives her mad; she can barely deal with it any longer. As she sees it, they have an unspoken agreement: he talks to Rasmus and she stays out of the way or keeps Daniel company. Sometimes she takes a sauna.

They built it a year ago, but only Bente uses it. Here she can be herself again: it is her own steaming territory.

She thinks about the week to come. As Head of the Section for Special Intelligence, SSI, or just the Section as it is referred to in the field, she is responsible for one of the most secret, best protected Swedish intelligence offices in the world. But even the Section, which has recently acquired a major tranche of intelligence about the war in Syria straight from the hands of one of MI6's own operatives, still has to battle against cuts. She has to sing for her supper.

There is a wonderful tingle as she breathes through her nostrils. The sweat runs down her cheeks in swift small droplets.

Three weeks have passed since that rainy Saturday when she met the Brit, B54. She needs to know Stockholm's view on the documents provided to her by the British leak. All she has had so far is a brief email from Roland Hamrén, Deputy Head of the Security Service, who acknowledged her report about the contact with the Brit and in a few long-winded sentences asked her to wait.

She assumed that Stockholm would rejoice over the documents she had found. They are so rich in detail, she has never read anything like them. Together, they provide a thorough overview of Islamic State and its structure, but above all a unique picture of how the British operate in the Middle East. Those who can interpret the material can understand how MI6 recruits its agents in war zones, which resources the Brits have in Syria and Iraq, how they are mapping Islamic State in order to eradicate its leaders. The senior people in Stockholm ought to be in raptures, which is why their silence worries her. They have asked her to wait. But what are they waiting for? No one is replying to her emails, and management always seems to be in meetings when she calls. The silence indicates sensitivity. She hasn't done anything wrong, and it annoys her that her train of thought is even drawn that way, but it is unavoidable; their silence is making her thoughts anxiously twist themselves into tight ropes.

She showers and loads the washing machine. There is the pink shirt, together with the other dirty laundry in the basket. She picks it up and reflects that it suits Fredrik. She quickly holds the fabric to her face and discerns the fresh, familiar scent of Fredrik's aftershave. Then she goes back up the narrow basement stairs, back to the light.

The weather has brought clarity to this November day. High, chilly air movement is tearing apart the cloud cover and opening

28

up the sky. A persistent headache radiates across the crown of her head. She is airing rooms and wiping down surfaces. These chores give her a deep sense of satisfaction. Sunlight streams across the floor and everything is glittering.

After tidying the kitchen, she reads the news on her mobile, skimming through it restlessly and fixating on facts and figures.

This is how she catches sight of a short notice from Reuters with a link to a British newspaper. The story is modest: a thirty-year-old employee of the British Foreign Office has been found dead in a flat in north London.

She clicks on the article.

Daniel says something to her that she doesn't understand. He repeats the question and she looks up, disturbed. What does he want? He asks whether there is any Coke in the house. She tells him to drink water, it's healthier, before returning to her device.

The man had worked in public administration for three years and was back home for a brief holiday staying with his parents. According to the preliminary police findings, no crime had occurred and the man had taken his own life. The article includes a photo of an ordinary redbrick house. The door was locked from the outside, it says.

Daniel sighs theatrically and vanishes into the basement.

No signs of a struggle, the article says; an odd-sounding statement. It is as if it were sagging beneath the weight of something unsaid. He was a happy guy, says an interviewed friend, he was going to be a father in a few months' time.

On the British newspaper's website, she finds a picture of him. The face is out of focus, as if death has already begun to dissolve his features, but she recognises him. It's him, she thinks in surprise. It's B54.

*

Bente goes upstairs to her study and although Daniel is down in the basement she closes the door. She crouches in front of the safe and enters the code that no one except her can know.

Inside the small cube of reinforced steel are the few objects from her secret life that she keeps at home. The two small shelves hold her lead-lined computer, three false passports and her service weapon: a Glock. Next to the weapon is the small black USB stick given to her by the Brit. She pulls out the computer, inserts the memory stick and opens the documents.

She has read them so many times that she already knows parts off by heart. But now the lines of text shimmer with a new and sombre import.

There are more than one thousand files. Several of them are top secret reports from British sources in Raqqa – to all appearances well-hidden, infiltrated sources close to Islamic State. The British code word for IS is Hydra, and many of the documents seem to relate to an operation known as Hercules. What stands out is a number of photos of a house built in the traditional Ottoman style. There are no notes about the house or its address. There are, however, photos of a cobbled courtyard that appears to be part of the house. There are also pictures of a basement and other rooms.

Her analysts at the Section have reviewed the photos, enlarged them and examined every pixel in the dark rows of windows around the inner courtyard to see what is hiding behind the shadowy panes of glass. They have analysed the robust wooden door standing ajar, and tried to distinguish the room that can be seen in the gap. They have scoured the cloudy sky for flight trails and other details that might reveal where the house is. The architecture suggests it is a Turkish building, especially given the windows, the shape of the roof and the appearance of the roof tiles. Another cue is a silhouette glimpsed in the far distance: a mountain ridge. This means they are certain the house is somewhere in eastern Turkey. Given that the documents relate to the war in Syria, the house may be in the town of Reyhanlı, on the border with northern Syria, or more likely in the slightly larger town of Antakya, a few miles further into Turkey. It is obviously a location the Brits want to keep secret, because there is no address to be found anywhere in the documents. But many of them refer to the location as 'the House'. Simply 'the House'.

There are another ten or so photos which are much clearer. They are photos of a row of men, captives, referred to as *clients* in the documents. The pictures are supplied with British Intelligence's brief notes and remarks: names, dates, prisoner numbers. Then there are other photos that seem to be a form of documentation: each showing a man whose face has been beaten to a pulp, date, name, prisoner number. They are dreadful photos. Some of the numbers correlate with other pictures: a man with a swollen face reappears several times, a man with an exhausted expression that might be found in an antiquated medical reference work under the heading 'madness' is photographed five times. There are also notes here that they have been able to interpret as codes and abbreviations used by the American military.

Apart from the pictures, there are hundreds of reports that all refer to conversations conducted at the House. Most are analyses of interrogations where the focus is on various terrorist groups. Bente is familiar with many of the names and places mentioned. Many of the reports discuss al-Qaida, and later reports Islamic State and the al-Nusra Front.

But the files that make her most uneasy are ten or so tables. These include a list of Arabic names, prisoner numbers and two dates: probably the date they arrived as prisoners and the date they left the House, along with a column for notes about their medical condition. Many of the tables are several years old, but there are also some that are brand new. When they reviewed the documents, there was a clear pattern: the first tables are from the period 2001–2009, and then there is an interval followed by some tables dated two years ago, in the autumn of 2014, and later. By all accounts, prisoners – *clients* – were taken there during the War on Terror, with prisoners returning once again two years ago after a hiatus.

She can see that prisoner 154-3 has diabetes. Another has high blood pressure. These clinical documents come from the heart of a deadly bureaucracy that she is not meant to have the slightest insight into, and several of the documents have been created by one Jonathan Green. The first time she saw the name, she thought she had misread it. She couldn't see how he had anything to do with a facility of this kind in south-eastern Turkey. But it struck her that he had been posted in Damascus once upon a time, and that it was likely the same Green. The other person to have signed many of the interrogation reports is Robert Davenport. She knows of only one Brit with that name – the Head of the MI6 Middle East Department.

B54 had good cause to be careful. Still, he had obviously not been careful enough.

Never before had anyone so directly contacted her, and it worried her. She had alerted Stockholm, because to the outside world she was merely a business owner with a start-up making custom databases. Anyone who knew more than that might pose a threat to her entire operation.

But the man turned out not to be a threat. He was a professional, but with friendly intentions. He had asked whether they would like information about British activities in Syria. After a few days' silence he returned and answered her control questions. Yes, he was a British citizen. Yes, he was an analyst in British Intelligence. He refused to give his name, but promised he had information that they, as close partners of Great Britain, ought to see. They also ought to inform their politicians, in his view. His tone was bombastic. She didn't trust him, because the Brits might just as easily be doing this to see how she and the Section reacted. It might even be Stockholm testing her to assess how she, as Head, would deal with that kind of contact. But during the week that she was in contact with the Brit, it became clear to her that he was serious, acting independently and because of an inner conviction, as he had said. He took care to point out that he was no traitor, even if that was how everyone would see it. He didn't want to provide any information except about the House, in which the code name Hercules appeared repeatedly. He promised to give them more information as soon as he could. Then, after a few days' silence, he asked to meet.

And now he was a brief news story, a cursory death notice. The article implied he had hanged himself. But who hangs themself just before they are going to be a father? she thought to herself. What sort of son was completely healthy but let his parents come home to find him hanging lifeless? No, it didn't add up.

She calls Mikael, her right-hand man. He answers sounding out of breath. He laughs.

'Sorry,' he says. 'Just a moment.'

He has been out cycling the country lanes all morning and has just got home, he explains while still gasping a little. Cycling, how amusing! She didn't know he cycled. While he catches his breath, she tells him the news.

33

'Are you certain it was him?'

'Yes, I'm certain.'

He falls silent, breathing heavily.

'What does Stockholm say?'

'I haven't heard from them.'

Mikael thinks it can wait. They have a teleconference with Roland Hamrén scheduled for Monday about the British leak; can they find out more about the dead man before then? Perhaps an analyst can run some searches on the story, but nothing more than that.

A shrill shout can be heard from the street. She asks Mikael to call the on-duty officer and ask them to keep an eye on the news, then hangs up. She shuts down her computer and puts it back in the safe along with the small memory stick, before locking it carefully and then checking the handle anyway. May the secrets she stores there never trickle into their home.

Something is wrong, that much is obvious from the voices. Then Fredrik comes in the front door. His voice is muffled, and Rasmus is responding with loud, angry replies.

When she appears in the hall the boy is standing there in his full kit, muddy and raging. He squeezes past and stamps up the stairs.

'What's happened?'

Fredrik looks tense. Rasmus got angry during the match and ended up in a fight. He doesn't want to talk about it.

She can hear Rasmus crashing around upstairs, throwing things in his room. It is as if the boy is carrying an impermeable darkness within him. A wild frenzy that can be unleashed by nothing at all and sweep them all along in its wake. And now it has happened again.

Rasmus is in the bathroom, huddled up on the toilet seat with a despondent, wretched expression, as if he has just returned from the battlefield. She coaxes his shoes off his feet. Show me, she says. Reluctantly, he pulls off his jersey. On the side of his ribcage she can see a large, ugly bruise. He grimaces. He has been struck there. She says nothing else, but helps him to undress and leaves him. A little later, she finds him in his room, straight out of the shower and looking melancholic. There is no point in talking to him, not when he has that tough, withdrawn look. When he looks like that, he refuses to talk to anyone; it is as if he tries to annihilate everything around him with silence.

Daniel is sitting on his bed practising chords on the guitar. She knows it is better for Daniel to avoid being at home when his little brother is angry. Because Fredrik is going to talk to Rasmus and the boy is likely to throw a tantrum.

'Come on,' she says.

Daniel looks up.

'Why?'

He sullenly fingers the strings.

'You can get some driving practice,' she says.

She likes being in the car with Daniel and seeing him behind the wheel of their large car; it makes him seem strangely grown-up. He drives safely, with considered movements, and she can see that he manages to absorb what is going on in the mirrors.

She has always thought that they are alike. When he was little, he was able to learn entire rhymes off by heart, he observed things and saw connections; she got the impression from early on that he understood what the adults were talking about.

The sun is shining. Everything is glittering.

Is it unnatural to love one child more than another? If it's wrong, she still can't change it. If Rasmus died, she would carry on, but if Daniel disappeared, then everything would come tumbling down for her.

The sun transforms the damp road into a blinding white ribbon. She is forced to squint to discern the road and the oncoming traffic.

'You need your sunglasses,' she says.

He is driving a little too fast, and is very close to the cars in front. Everything is being corroded by the dazzling light.

'Slow down,' she says. 'Pull over here.'

He mutters and slows down. They pull into a lay-by.

He doesn't have his sunglasses with him. She opens the glovebox and roots around, finding Fredrik's glasses. He can borrow them, and she takes her own. Out of the corner of her eye, she sees Daniel quickly lean forward towards the floor and when she turns to give him the glasses he straightens up.

The world is presented in mild shades of green.

'What's that?' she asks, but he simply shakes his head: nothing. But she can sense it at once, the suppression, something unsaid.

'What do you have in your hand?' she asks.

He looks at her quizzically.

'What did you find?'

He opens his fist. In the palm of his hand is a pearl earring. She picks up the small piece of jewellery. It is beautiful, a genuine pearl with a delicate setting of white gold. She has pearl earrings, but this is not hers.

'Was it here in the car?'

'Yes,' he says.

'Give it to me,' she says.

*

36

The store stretches out in front of them in long, straight rows. She knows where things are, how the shelves are arranged. Daniel walks quietly beside her. She dispatches him in various directions. She loves doing the shopping, not for the sake of the food, which doesn't interest her at all, but because the structure of the shop appeals to her. Here, everything has a function, and there is care in ensuring that everything is in the right place and in orderly rows. If she didn't work in intelligence, she would be quite satisfied working in a supermarket, maybe as the purchasing manager, or perhaps in charge of ensuring the shelves were stocked and that supply lines were functioning. She likes to fantasise about having a job like that as she slowly fills the trolley with what a family needs for a week. It gives her a calm sense of satisfaction. But today, she is struggling to concentrate on that feeling, with her hand repeatedly sliding into her trouser pocket to touch the cool, smooth surface of the pearl.

Fredrik is lying on the sofa with his eyes closed when they get home. She unpacks all the bags and then goes to look in her jewellery box upstairs in the bedroom, but just as she thought, there is no pearl earring like it. She can't remember whether the football mum who rang the doorbell this morning had earrings like that. Perhaps. Sitting next to Fredrik on the sofa, she pulls out the piece of jewellery and shows it to him.

'Do you know who this belongs to?'

He looks at her sleepily.

'No . . . Isn't it yours?'

'No. It's not mine.'

He lifts himself up and she wishes that he would kiss her, would run his hand over her T-shirt and touch her breast. She wants to feel his intention, that he *wants* something. But nothing like that is going to happen; he looks exhausted, lying half reclined on the sofa. He has borne the brunt of Rasmus's fit of rage.

'What's the name of the woman you gave a lift to the football this morning?'

He yawns. 'Elisabeth?'

'Perhaps this is her earring,' she says.

She looked good. Elisabeth. Fit and slim, with the kind of spirited charisma that she knows Fredrik finds attractive. A woman like that might very well make a pass at him. She can see them together in the car, him joking with her, her nervously touching her ear lobe and thinking about how she'd like to sleep with him, and then the earring falling.

'What exactly happened at the football?'

Fredrik makes a parrying gesture. There was a fight. He doesn't feel up to telling her more.

This response awakens a piercing irritation in her. Isn't he taking his son's problems seriously?

'Rasmus kicked another boy and was sent off.'

Reluctantly, he explains how it began. Rasmus scored, but the referee disallowed it since he had already stopped play because one of the other team's players had been fouled. Rasmus couldn't accept the referee's decision and started fighting. He struck an opposition player. Then he chased the lad across the pitch until he caught up with him and kicked him to the ground.

Late in the evening, when the boys are asleep and Fredrik is watching TV, Bente goes up to her study. Sitting at the family computer, she logs into various social media.

She has several accounts to enable her to follow Fredrik. She also follows the boys, logging in now and then to see what they are saying, which pictures they are posting, keeping an eye on them – it's no stranger than her occasionally going into their rooms to look for cigarettes or anything else that might suggest they are keeping secrets from her that she ought to know about. She cares about her family and wants to know what they are doing.

Her own accounts are obviously fake. But 'fake' is a naive description given the context, because who presents their true self via these kinds of sites? A clever, funny, successful, smiling, flattering self, perhaps. But a true self? Fredrik's Facebook profile is probably as close as you can get, as he posts indiscriminately and seemingly without any ulterior motives. He is clearly unaware of the privacy settings, since his account can be seen by around two billion users.

She examines Fredrik's pictures. He has posted some new photos of himself and the boys from when they had coffee at Grote Markt a week ago. There are also some new photos of people she doesn't recognise, all wearing suits. Colleagues, perhaps. In one of the pictures, they are sitting around a table, while in another they are standing by a bar.

She enlarges the picture and looks at a woman standing next to Fredrik. No earrings. She clicks through to the woman's account but finds no photos of her wearing pearl earrings.

Bente has forbidden him from posting photos of herself or mentioning her at all. The thought of it is terrifying, because pictures like that could jeopardise her entire professional life. But sometimes she wishes that she was in a picture too, that she could be together with him even there.

Elsewhere, she finds two short tweets from Friday: #NordicBusiness. He is holding the camera up to take a selfie. Two men are in the photo and she recognises one of them from the embassy reception. In the dark, she also glimpses a third person, presumably the woman with them, but she is turning away and her face isn't visible, only some of her hair and one ear. She zooms in and on the ear there is an earring. But it is hard to see; it might be a pearl or it might not.

With a pang of shame, she realises what she is doing: she is investigating. But it is out of love. No harm has been done. And it can't be helped, the pearl earring is worrying her.

The subdued sound of the TV can be heard from downstairs.

She turns off the computer and goes to the bathroom. Apart from the sound of the TV, it is so quiet that she has the feeling that Fredrik is no longer down there. Perhaps he has fallen asleep. The silence beneath the sound of the TV is like condensation in the air, an ominous tranquillity.

The clear morning light slants onto the parquet, fading the images on the TV as if the bright weather is trying to dissolve everything taking place on the box. During the night, the Assad regime has carried out air raids over northern Syria. Two men appear from a collapsed house supporting a third with blood on his face and shirt. They barely avoid tumbling to the ground under the man's weight as they stumble across the strewn chunks of concrete. A man hurries past with a child in his arms. A boy. The boy is injured, his face dirty. The sequence is shakily filmed.

Jonathan turns off the TV and goes into the bedroom. He has to continue packing. Kate appears behind him in the doorway. He folds a white shirt into the bag.

'When are you going?'

'The flight is in three hours.'

He says it as if the trip were a burden, to ensure she doesn't notice how keen he is to get away. In some ways, he wishes things were different, that he missed Kate when he was gone from home. But it hasn't been like that for a long time. Things were different before Brussels, when she still had her job at the bank.

He starts to fold a second shirt.

The Kate standing behind him is someone else entirely from

the cheerful, outspoken woman he ended up next to at a seminar on international finance in Oxford, the happy and candid and beautiful woman with clear opinions. He admired her, but that was a long time ago.

'Is it for work?'

'Yes, it's work.'

The first posting in Amman had been an adventure for them, and Damascus too. He remembers the young, open couple they once were.

Perhaps it was when they returned to London after the Damascus years, perhaps that was when it changed, he thinks to himself. The doctors said it was inexplicable. It wasn't a surprise – they had been trying for a long time.

She so longed for children. So did he, but for him it wasn't the same thing. He wonders whether that grief within her has ever healed. She became a different Kate, thoughtful and taciturn. Something between them hardened.

'Send my love if you see anyone I know.'

'I'll make sure I do.'

He knows that it is a sacrifice to live with him, to move from country to country. It is partly because of him that she didn't secure the career she had dreamt of in the world of banking. Now she is involved in every imaginable charity project. He is glad she has found a way to move on, but he is sick of the fact that she always has to talk about the most unfortunate, as if she can think of nothing else. She exaggerates, and he knows he can't say that without riling her, and what's more, it is as if she blames him for all the world's evils. She is loyal, a faithful wife who has given up a lot, yet he is unable to muster more than tepid sympathy for her.

He folds another shirt.

This afternoon he'll be with Frances. He longs for her so much that all he feels is anger towards Kate, as if she is in the way. Beautiful Frances, so sharp and playful. Since they began seeing each other in secret, he has been unable to look at Kate without being irritated by her. It vexes him that she thinks she knows what's best for him, for them, when she hasn't got a clue.

All at once, he can imagine Frances naked and he closes his eyes, desire running through him like a tremor. She has become such a natural focal point in his life that he sometimes forgets that Kate is completely in the dark.

'How long will you be gone?'

'I'm not sure. A few days. It depends.'

She knows that he can't provide an exact answer to the question and yet she asks it, and it annoys him. It is as if she no longer cares about their agreements, he thinks, but on the other hand neither does he. Usually he makes up one excuse or another to escape to London, but on this occasion he actually has a legitimate reason.

They never talk about his work or his travels. That whole world is an unspoken presence that occasionally breaks through the surface of daily life, before once again sinking. Kate respects it. She knows that when she married him she also married MI6. His 'I do' involved a check of her and her finances and employment and friends and family: everything was assessed to discover any dependencies, vulnerabilities or threats.

'They're bombing Aleppo to bits.'

'Yes, it's awful.'

He knows what she wants, but he isn't willing to have that discussion now. Kate has spent the entire morning on the phone with volunteers. She is raising money for refugees and the cash is flooding in. She is naive to think that he might be able to be part of her work. Perhaps she just wants them to have something in common, but it doesn't work, he thinks.

Of course, he knows more about Syria than what they say on the news. He reads the reports that come in via London and knows everything there is to know about the escape routes from Syria and the situation in Schengen. That's what she wants him to say something about. But does she really think that he can tell her what he knows? The fact that she even tries to get him to break that silence is just stupid. He has no right to give her that information, not even if it could save lives. Sometimes he wonders whether she has forgotten what 'secret' actually means. If he were to tell Kate the things he actually knew, Kate would presumably mention them to a few volunteers, who in turn would call people in their networks to tell them about the situation around the borders, to provide warnings of air raids, to provide situation reports that only those with secret information could be aware of, and all those conversations would, without a doubt, be captured by signals intelligence and be traced back to him.

The bag is stubborn when he tries to close it. He tugs at the zip. It reluctantly gives in and its resistance makes him unreasonably annoyed. He sits down heavily on the bed. Only then does he discover Kate is no longer there.

When he takes off he feels deeply happy. The plane is lifting him away from the heavy gravitational pull of Brussels, up through the clouds, towards heaven. He is free. An hour later, when he emerges from the gate at Heathrow, he is in an excellent mood, full of expectation, as he always is when London is close.

Although he wants nothing more than to get to his destination, he consciously saunters through the airport, stopping in a shop and observing the other passengers from the flight hurrying past him across the gleaming, newly polished floors.

He recognised one of the men on the flight. A Swede. Presumably someone from the embassy who was at the reception the day before, so there is probably no danger, but he wants to be sure. The only thing you can rely on is your methods; everything else just leaves space for guessing and worry – cracks through which the paranoia can seep in.

He catches sight of himself in a small mirror on a table with make-up on it: a serious face, with short, curly red hair and sharp blue eyes. No one takes any notice of a man like that, but if they knew who he was, he reflects with satisfaction, they would be impressed. Perhaps even frightened. He does a lap of the shop, impulse-buying a bottle of burgundy that he knows Robert likes.

At the luggage carousel, he watches the bags passing by at a languid tempo, as if they were deliberately moving slowly. All he wants is to get to the hotel. In the taxi, he tries to avoid getting worked up over the slow-moving traffic. The city is unfolding around him. Saturday afternoon is a wonderful time in London, as Londoners cut loose and join the weekend throng outside pubs and shops. He loves this dirty, overpopulated city.

Frances closes the door to his hotel room and kisses him. He slips one hand down inside the waistband of her suit trousers, reaching down towards the mound between her thighs and sliding his fingers down, stroking her. The excitement at finally being together with her and seeing her taking off her clothes with unrestrained, impatient movements grows into a feeling of pain, a desire that approaches violence. He has wanted her for so long that the yearning has begun to turn into an ache, and now that she is standing naked before him, he is almost tempted to bite her round shoulder to avoid bursting with his own need. Quietly and purposefully, they come together again. For a long time they stand, breathless, like two wrestlers entwined in an even match. Then she frees herself and lies on the bed.

For once they have plenty of time. It is a Saturday and Robert is at the office; he won't be picking up Jonathan for another four hours. But Frances is impatient. It surprises him that she doesn't want him to stroke her. She usually loves the lingering foreplay, but not now. With an assertiveness that is unlike her, she sits astride him, parts her legs and grips his cock to guide him in. She does everything with silent fervour. It surprises him and makes him feel slightly detached. He watches her strained, concentrated face. He is too close. Wait, he whispers. Wait. But he isn't in charge of what happens. She wants him like this; she is in command.

'Harder,' she says.

He grabs her hips. In that moment, the pleasure is so great that it feels like he might be obliterated altogether. It is pure love, pure destruction. He could never explain to Kate what happens in those moments, except that he has never experienced it with her. When she comes it is with a drawn-out cry. She has been longing for this too, he thinks.

Then it is over. The proximity abates. They lie beside each other quietly on the bed, two separate, distinct bodies. After having been so close to him, she withdraws into her thoughts, which disappoints him, although he doesn't want to admit it.

'What is it?' he says, reaching out his hand.

She lays her head right next to his face and looks at him without saying a word. Her eyes are shining.

*

46

He is flattered and a little concerned that Robert is actually going to pick him up at the hotel later that afternoon. His friend's message only arrived half an hour after Frances left, and it worries him.

Standing outside the lobby he catches sight of a cream-coloured Mercedes flashing its headlights. He looks, but doesn't recognise the car, and then sees Robert waving from behind the windscreen and laughs in astonishment. Now he understands why Robert absolutely insisted on collecting him from the hotel. My God, he thinks, the car looks like the favourite toy in a Chinese billionaire's automobile collection. He himself knows nothing about cars, but the sleek chassis, with its aggressive, streamlined shape and wide tyres, both impresses him and awakens a childish jealousy.

'Marvellous to see you again, old boy,' Robert bellows cheerfully as Jonathan gets into the passenger seat beside him.

The engine starts with a sultry purr.

'What a car,' he says, making sure he sounds impressed. 'Is it new?'

Robert hums affirmatively. 'Brand new, bought it last week.'

Robert loves luxury with a rare degree of intensity. Unlike most people in the field, he is uninhibited when it comes to material things; he has a voracity that many find vulgar and unsuitable for a spy of such high station. What they don't understand is that it is precisely Robert's garish style that makes him ideal for MI6, because who would think that the jovial man in the expensive cashmere suit cruising along in his customised Mercedes Sport Edition with a fat watch dangling from his wrist was one of the most important defenders of the realm?

As they head into the evening traffic, Robert talks with exhilaration about the car's performance. It has seven-speed transmission, a V8 engine, and can do nought to sixty in 4.6 seconds. Facts like this mean nothing to Jonathan, but he can feel the power of the car as Robert softly accelerates adjacent to the river and sweeps into a tunnel. He passes his hand over the car's pale leather upholstery and elegant detailing. He never usually thinks of cars as something to enjoy, but sweeping through the afternoon traffic in Robert's car is fantastic. He envies his friend for so shamelessly allowing himself to buy a luxury car, as if it were a toy.

The car hurtles onwards as if in close convoy with the vehicles around it.

Robert pats him heartily on the arm.

'So the situation is under control?'

He nods. 'Yes, absolutely.'

His body is still buzzing from the pleasant sensation of time spent with Frances, and he must be careful not to relax too much.

'What do you think about Paddy?' says Robert after a while.

He says what he has been thinking for a long time. They must convince Paddy that Hercules is a solid operation. That the methods to be used will be unimpeachable, and British. So British that even the British Minister of Defence will be able to sign off on the operation. This means they won't be able to use the House.

'I propose that we promise not to use the House,' he says. 'You know how Paddy will react. He objects to the House.'

Robert glowers at him.

'Paddy is a namby-pamby.'

'Paddy wants to minimise risk. He wants to ensure he has the Minister's back. If we insist on the House, he'll say no, you know that.'

He knows that he is right; the operation won't be approved if they go against Paddy.

They race onward, changing lanes. This is how Robert drives: too fast and with fine margins. Jonathan tries to relax.

'I want you to interrogate Pathfinder,' says Robert.

'I'd be happy to. But it would have to be a normal interrogation.'

'Yes, yes, a normal one.'

Robert has always defended the House and the special methods used there. Personally, Jonathan has often doubted whether they are as useful as his friend asserts. Deep down, he is relieved that the Minister of Defence so strongly dislikes the House. He also wants nothing more to do with the place, but he'll never admit that to Robert.

There was a time when he, too, thought the House worked for good, when everyone thought that. But things are different now and he doesn't want to get involved in that kind of dirty work again, not ever.

It is strange how different they are. Robert has always been unaffected by that sort of thing. It is as if his friend can always see a greater purpose. In a way, he admires Robert for this. He can't stomach it himself.

Robert takes an exit. The tyres screech on the curved ramp.

Slow down, he wants to say. But he knows there's no point when his friend is in this kind of dogged mood. Oh well, he thinks, drive us to our deaths if you must.

They are heading out of the city on the M4. It is in completely the wrong direction, but he says nothing.

'Bloody hell, it's all taking so long,' Robert sighs. 'For a while, I thought we might not have Hercules. It has to happen now, otherwise the rebels will sell Pathfinder to someone else.'

'It'll be fine, just as long as we get Paddy on board.'

Robert turns on the radio and the rich sound of strings envelops them.

The motorway rises above the endless scrubland and crash barriers as they mount a flyover. They are gliding along past treetops in a park that vanishes beneath them as office blocks suddenly tower beside them like shards of glass.

He is unprepared when the car's engine gives a roar. The acceleration pushes him backwards into the soft seat. What are you doing? he wants to ask. Robert leans back with a broad grin on his face.

Their speed increases. As they enter a prolonged curve at Brentford, he can see the speedometer showing 110. They fly towards the summit of a motorway bridge and sweep past other cars as if they were stationary. He unconsciously presses his foot into the floor, as if attempting to brake. A shooting panic is close to getting the upper hand and he wants to shout at Robert to stop, stop for God's sake. But he clenches his teeth and stares out of the windscreen with the sense that he is encircled by his own imminent death.

'One hundred and fifty-five,' Robert laughs.

Robert slaps him merrily on the knee and laughs loudly. 'You weren't afraid, were you?'

Then he feels the force of the brakes. They are still tearing along the road, but more slowly now. And, as if exhaling one enormous breath, the world regains its normal, inert form.

He discovers that his left hand is holding tightly on to the door handle. Slowly he straightens his fingers. Robert is jubilant. 'What a *car*!'

It is so typical of Robert to have taken a completely unnecessary and insane risk. He has never understood why his friend does it. Bloody idiot, he thinks, and is almost tempted to ask him to turn around and drive him back to the hotel. But then he hesitates. He doesn't want to ruin the evening, even if he is shaken up – it is important to ensure Robert is not in a bad mood, because he needs him. Then it is as if he's been infected with his friend's high spirits. Perhaps it is relief at avoiding a pointless demise. There is something comical in the whole thing: Two Senior Spies Killed in Car Crash – he can see the newspaper headlines now.

'Your driving ... Jesus Christ!'

The atmosphere between them softens. They are friends; he wishes that it could simply be that way.

'Admit it,' says Robert. 'You're jealous of my car.'

Jonathan admits it with a smile. He is very jealous.

He spears the tender beef with his fork and slices into the meat. A beautiful, perfectly aged cut. It is lightly browned outside and a delicate shade of red inside. He lifts the chunk into his mouth and chews, taking a sip of wine, grateful for the warmth spreading through him, courtesy of a substantial aperitif and two glasses of red. Each time he is here, he is struck by how wonderful their flat is and that it is becoming increasingly unbearable for him to visit their home and pretend nothing has happened.

He had wanted to decline the invitation, but this wouldn't have been possible without awakening suspicions. Robert would be affronted and Frances would ridicule him and call him a coward the next time they were together.

Robert cannot stop talking about their holiday villa in Tuscany. It is finally all done, and his friend is so pleased that he doesn't care that no one else is as interested in all the details as he is. Jonathan nods and hums appreciatively at the right points in Robert's lengthy description of the bathroom, its roll-top tub and tiles, as well as the fantastic, untreated Carrara marble in the kitchen.

'You've done such a beautiful job, darling,' says Frances, placing a slender hand on her husband's back. In that moment, she stretches her torso so that her chest strains against her white blouse, which is unbuttoned with careless elegance, exposing her beautiful collarbone and tanned skin.

She is so calculated in her movements. Jonathan feels himself growing hard.

'Yes, you must visit,' says Robert.

'Naturally,' he replies, reaching for his wine glass. 'Kate loves Tuscany.'

He glances at Frances. Beautiful, intelligent Frances, with all her money. Perhaps Robert bought the villa in order to feel like he could have something of his own. Jonathan remembers when his friend found the place, the same summer that he and Frances started seeing each other.

He cuts off a piece of meat.

'Yes, you really must come,' Frances says with a smile.

She is enjoying this, he thinks. Evil, beautiful woman. He is possessed with a strong desire to kiss her.

Three years ago, he kissed Frances for the first time on the terrace one floor up. It was at the party to celebrate Robert's promotion to Head of the Middle East Department. He remembers how hopeless it all felt. He had already fallen out of love with Brussels then, and it wasn't easy to return to London to congratulate Robert on securing a job he himself had been dreaming of.

He remembers that evening and how she watched him with the same gaze as she does now. They caressed each other with their eyes. He had been thinking of her for a long time, perhaps ever since that evening eight years ago when a beaming Robert had introduced Frances to him and Kate in a Beirut bar. Beautiful, lightning-fast Frances. Many a time he had tested life with her in his thoughts.

He got drunk that evening. He ignored Kate and was heading for the kitchen to find more wine when he found Robert and Frances there. He remembered their row. How she bent her head and how Robert grabbed hold of her arm, hard, brutally, and how she struggled free. Perhaps it was then he made up his mind. He found her on the terrace. He couldn't remember what he said, only that he thought: to hell with caution. Then he kissed her.

And the joy he felt when she responded, when her lips met his, her arms wrapped around him; that joy was greater than anything he had ever experienced before.

The biggest risk I've taken in my life, he thinks.

Robert asks Frances to fetch a new bottle of wine.

She ought to be the woman in his life, not Robert's. He can still feel her hands and mouth like a trail of heat on his body.

Then he notices Robert watching him. His friend has a baffling sense for the unspoken. Behind the bluff façade is a highly attentive person, making Jonathan nervous.

'I don't know what the matter is with Frances this evening.'

'She's delightful,' Jonathan says.

They fall silent. He knows that all Robert wants to talk about is the operation, the plans. But Frances can hear them from the kitchen, so instead they discuss the wine they are drinking. It is from a vineyard near their villa, Robert explains.

We've known each other for twenty-five years, he thinks to himself as he listens to his friend describing an Italian vineyard in Montepulciano that they found during the summer. He can still see his old tutorial partner at Oxford in that middle-aged face. Robert was always the eternal charmer. They got on well because Robert liked to talk, while he was quieter and preferred to listen. When they went running, Robert would always be ahead of him over the middle distances, because his friend didn't know about running, he just sprinted till he threw up. Robert pulled him out of his shell and showed him another way to approach life. Robert took risks, lived intensely in the here and now, fought and bragged and cheated, but could also be tremendously empathetic, and read others with uncanny precision. It was as if Robert had discovered a path to his own form of freedom, and it fascinated him.

Personally, Jonathan was thorough and headstrong. He always worked the hardest of them all, but it was his friend that everyone admired. They were recruited to MI6 together and rose into its clandestine firmament like two shooting stars. Before long he was in Amman, and Robert in Cairo. Then they both ended up in Damascus.

Robert laughs.

'You're very thoughtful this evening,' he says.

'I was just thinking about Damascus.'

Frances returns with a new bottle of wine.

'By the way, Robert, did you mention that you've applied for the post of Deputy Head?'

Robert is startled and looks at her angrily. It is clear that he had had no intention of saying anything about it.

'The job, yes. My superiors asked me to apply.'

Jonathan tries to seem nonchalant, but this is difficult to take. Management asked him to apply? Presumably they haven't even considered himself. It is as if Robert senses his strong position and can't help saying:

'It's a real honour. The job hasn't even been advertised.'

'Well done,' he says. 'You would make a perfect Deputy.'

Perhaps this is why Robert suggested inviting him over, he reflects. He wishes he didn't have to sit here at the table, listening to Robert's self-satisfied boasting.

'You're always a step ahead.'

'Oh, my champions,' Frances says in exhilaration. 'My race-horses.'

Robert laughs and asks her to stop; his tone is cheerful but the undertones are sharp. Jonathan hopes they will quarrel once he leaves. That thought lingers, just like the thought of being alone with Frances again soon.

They raise their glasses.

Their superiors like Robert; he can't understand how his friend does it. His own efforts are often more sterling, but it is still Robert that everyone admires. In Damascus, it was Robert, rather than Jonathan, who broke the record as the youngest station chief ever. Then he was chief in Beirut, while Jonathan was toiling back home in the corridors of Vauxhall Cross. It wasn't fair, but Robert understood how to make the apparatus of state work to his advantage; he always managed to make friends with the right people, to be seen on the right occasions, while all Jonathan did was work hard and stubbornly in the hope that he would eventually receive recognition for his valuable input. Brussels was a triumph. Brussels was an important posting. He was ahead of Robert. But a year later Robert became Head of the Middle East Department, a position that Jonathan envies to this day.

They finish eating. He focuses on the plate: the fig salad is delicious, but the small salad leaves are cumbersome to eat using a fork and he is unable to transport them efficiently to his mouth without them clumsily falling off it.

Frances leans forward and kisses Robert on the cheek.

She has never been a good girl. It is too tempting to taunt him and toy with her husband, too great a pleasure for her to abstain. She has always been phenomenal at playing social games. So smooth and sharp. No one can be as crushingly charming as Frances. As Press Officer for the Home Secretary, she charms and tames even the sulkiest of journalists. She would be a hopeless housewife, he thinks.

'How is Kate these days?'

He replies that Kate is well.

She knows exactly how Kate is and wants to mess with him. The thought of Kate at home in Brussels fills him with despondency. He could leave both her and Brussels; it would be easy.

'It would be lovely to see her,' Frances says pleasantly, and he meets her look and decides to fuck her harder than ever the next time they meet.

He can discern the Shard and the other skyscrapers in the city against the dark sky, like distant giants. A dirty pink haze stains the cloud cover. It is cold, the breeze blowing straight through his jacket up here on the roof terrace. He shivers and drinks a mouthful of brandy.

Robert is standing to one side and is on his mobile.

They have stood here so often, gazing across London and talking about how to crush its enemies, Islamic State. Daesh.

Ever since the terrorist group swept into Syria and Iraq, he and Robert, as well as vast swathes of MI6, have developed a huge apparatus for mapping the terrorists. He is responsible for giving IS its internal code name, Hydra. He was very pleased with it: an apt name for a monster with many heads. They knew a lot about the Hydra, but they still couldn't say for certain where the monster was hiding its heads, its leaders.

But then Pathfinder turned up. A man who they had rapidly come to realise could provide them with outright victory, the chance to chop off all of the Hydra's heads in one fell swoop. He remembers the jubilant call from Robert, how the entire Middle

East Department had simmered with determined delight. The man who, without knowing it himself, had become a priceless gem within British counter-terrorism, was a taxi driver in the town of Raqqa in northern Syria. After IS took over and made Raqqa their capital, the man became a driver for various IS leaders. This man knew all the names and addresses they needed.

The man was given the code name Pathfinder to remind them of his significance. Then Hercules had been born – the operation to get the driver out of Syria and make him tell them everything. But the man was in Raqqa and trying to capture him there would be suicidal, even for the most skilled specialists.

Then, by chance, the silent war turned in their favour. While driving, Pathfinder had run into an ambush set by some rebels east of Aleppo. They took the driver hostage and transported him to Idlib.

It took a few days before MI6 found him again, a captive of the Ahrar al-Sham Brigade, a larger Islamist group that controlled large parts of Idlib province. They began listening in on the rebels' satellite phones and were able to track him as he was moved between houses in northern Syria by night.

The entire Middle East Department worked frantically to create a chance to reach the rebels and get their hands on Pathfinder, because no one knew how long the rebels would continue to hold him hostage, or whether they would kill him or sell him on. He could not be allowed to disappear. Barely a month ago they had been on course to establish proper contact with the rebels.

Then the leak had happened. Management became anxious, Ministers concerned, all decisions were put on hold and Hercules was checked mid-step ...

Robert ends the call and stands next to him, leaning heavily on the balustrade.

'That was my assistant,' he says. 'He just got another update on Pathfinder. He is alive. We can hear the rebels talking about him. They're moving him again tonight.'

Robert stops, raising the bottle of brandy and sloshing more into both their glasses. He also has bad news, he says.

'Paddy wants to postpone tomorrow's meeting until three o'clock.'

They both think about Paddy. Paddy changing the appointment is not a good sign. But what can they do? They can only hope they manage to persuade him tomorrow. They change the subject and talk about the Ahrar al-Sham Brigade. As before, the plan is to make contact with the rebels through an intermediary.

'Vermeer is ideal,' Jonathan says.

'Yes, he's the right man.'

He hopes the agent he once christened with the code name Vermeer won't cause any fuss. He is the right man, with the right contacts. He is looking forward to meeting Vermeer. Handling an agent is a special pleasure.

Vermeer first, at the beginning of the week. And if it all goes to plan, they will have Pathfinder out within the week. Ahrar al-Sham are Islamists, basically their enemies. But they have negotiated with enemies before. If the first contact is made through Vermeer, it may succeed; they trust him.

'We are playing a historic role,' says Robert, who is pursuing a different train of thought. 'We have to understand our significance for the Middle East. Look at the bastards in Islamic State: they know their history. They remember that we made the maps; they hate the Sykes-Picot Agreement as much as their fathers did. We must demonstrate that we are worthy of their hatred.'

Jonathan smiles; it is rare to hear his friend speaking in such lofty terms. Robert must have got smashed during dinner, because he is now in the festive mood that he often ends up in when he drinks, and that always makes Jonathan think that Robert would have made an excellent politician.

'They're barbarians,' Robert says. 'We'll show them what happens when you challenge Great Britain. Isn't that right, Jon? We'll crush them.'

Barbarians: it has been a long time since he heard that word. He suddenly feels a sense of devotion to this man, as to a brother. If only they could be more open with each other. If it wasn't for Frances, he thinks.

He shivers; it really is cold. He wishes he could go downstairs to Frances in the snug warmth of the flat and be the one to show his friend to the door and wish him goodnight, before being drawn back to Frances.

'What have you got against the House, Jon?'

Robert is still stuck in his clash of civilisations, and wants to look him in the eye. But the booze has made his friend's eyes watery and unfocused. It is stupid and pushy, but Jonathan plays along.

'You know what I've got against the House, Robert.'

He has explained to his friend: he abhors physical violence. Violence is necessary in many situations, but rarely in intelligence work. He has had enough of it.

'You're always so cautious,' Robert says.

'I often have good cause to be.'

'You worry too much, Jon!'

The same old thing when his friend gets drunk: friendly and irritable in unpredictable measures. He looks at Robert and wishes he could show everyone who the real brain behind Hercules is.

Bente is standing in the hall with her coat, waiting for Fredrik and the boys. She is ready first, despite being the least keen to go. She had forgotten that their neighbours had invited them for coffee this Sunday. When Fredrik mentioned it at breakfast she couldn't help sighing: was that today? She had been looking forward to a peaceful and secluded Sunday. She had imagined the boys would run along to their friends' and that she would get to stay at home, that the day would remain idle. Now it was as if the whole Sunday were being broken in half.

Fredrik had nothing against meeting friends and neighbours at the weekend. He liked the company, even with people they barely knew. The good-humoured chatter seemed to energise him – she couldn't understand it. What was the point of meeting people to chit-chat idly? She felt nothing but drained by that kind of thing.

But Fredrik was always so disappointed when she stayed at home. This morning he had said: 'Please come. You don't have to love them.'

Which was true. The people they are about to meet mean nothing to her.

Petra and Mats have organised a gathering to welcome a new Swedish family that have just moved into the area. What does it matter that they are Swedes? she wants to interject. But she acquiesced, and now she is standing here, waiting.

Mats and Petra have a large, newly refurbished kitchen and Bente is in the middle of it, together with the hostess and her girlfriends. The coffee has been decanted into a thermos; the cinnamon buns Petra baked are covered by a cloth in a basket. It is perfectly pleasant, but she doesn't belong here.

She surveys the open-plan setting. Mats and Petra really do have a tasteful home. It strikes her that they have the same white oval table with chrome legs in the kitchen that Fredrik bought, and she reflects that perhaps he bought a table like that because he wants the same kitchen as Mats and Petra. Perhaps Fredrik wants their lives to be more like this, she thinks.

The boys are nowhere to be seen. Daniel has vanished with the hosts' daughter, and Rasmus is in the back garden with a group of other children. She can hear Fredrik's characteristic cackling laugh from an adjacent room.

Mats and Petra set the tone amongst Swedish expats. Petra is chair of the Association for Expatriate Swedish Women, while Mats hosts gentlemen's dinners that Fredrik usually says are 'very agreeable', without going into any further detail. She can see that Fredrik admires Mats, that he would like some of the jovial self-confidence that Mats possesses. Fredrik likes to say that Petra is so beautiful. And Petra certainly is a warm, lovely person, and submissive, too. She works out to look good and always gives prominence to her husband, who is mediocre. Petra is probably the kind of woman that Fredrik sometimes wishes she was.

She sips her coffee and listens to the other women. Standing beside her is the recently arrived Swede, Elisabeth, who turned up at the door the day before.

'Isn't it great that the boys are on the same football team!' Elisabeth exclaims, with an enthusiasm that is also a shield, Bente reflects, and which conceals the sharp attentiveness she discerns beneath the woman's cheerfulness.

Once again, she is struck by how fit and good-looking Elisabeth is, and how she greets everyone with the kind of adroit friendliness that stems from a sunny disposition. She apparently works at the European Commission. Fredrik knew that Elisabeth and her husband were new to Brussels; he must have met her without telling Bente about it. She wouldn't be surprised if Fredrik flirted with Elisabeth.

She pulls back her blonde hair: her ear is adorned with a small diamond. A pearl earring would also suit her.

Fredrik could fall for Elisabeth, she thinks. Or Petra. He would probably happily sleep with either of them.

She leaves the group for more coffee. Elisabeth follows her with an inquisitive gaze, she notices, while the host tells them about the American school, how good it is, how it is the *obvious* choice, the others assenting.

From a short distance, it looks like all three of them are trying to look like each other, which they are presumably not consciously aiming to achieve. Back home in Sweden they might not socialise, but abroad it suddenly becomes crucial for all Swedes to spend time together, as if nationality were the most important thing. She is the one who has never followed that unspoken rule. She keeps her distance. She knows that the other women think she is serious and annoyingly solemn, and they probably say that Bente is gloomy and 'a bit odd' when she is out of earshot. What they don't understand is that she can't let them know who she truly is. She doesn't want to, either; the mere thought of a deeper friendship with these people seems pointless.

She lingers by the coffee thermos and relaxes for a moment. Fredrik is standing next to the elegant sofas in the living room, together with Mats. This is a different Fredrik to the quiet man who spent the entire morning reading the newspaper. He is lively, as if transformed into another person.

The pearl earring is in her pocket and she rolls it between her fingertips. Then she decides to take a flyer and returns to the women.

'Look,' she says.

She holds up the earring. The women lean in curiously. 'What a lovely pearl,' Petra says.

Bente explains that her son found it. 'Is it yours?' she asks Elisabeth.

'Mine?' Elisabeth smiles in surprise, fine furrows appearing in her smooth, creamy forehead. No, it isn't hers, she says.

The other women don't recognise the piece of jewellery either. They smile, because, of course, everyone is having a good time. They inspect the earring as if it were an unusual insect. She tries to interpret their reactions. But they are all behaving so tamely and politely, without any sign of anxiety. As if to test them and potentially generate a stronger reaction, she says it was lying outside the house.

'Here?' says Petra. 'Outside our house?'

The women look at the earring more carefully. You might need to have a word with Mats, says one of them cheerfully to their hostess, laughing loudly without noticing that Petra is upset, and they continue to provoke her, saying that there are lots of beautiful Swedes here, *ooh là là*, until Petra says she is going to make more coffee and walks off to the kitchen counter.

'It really is a beautiful piece,' says Elisabeth.

The others remain irresolutely quiet.

Bente excuses herself and seeks out the bathroom. The cool seclusion is pleasant as she sinks down onto the toilet seat.

When she returns, it is obvious they have been talking about her because they quickly change the subject. But she doesn't want their cloying company and continues on towards the living room, and then out onto the decking.

It feels wonderfully fresh to get out of the house. The afternoon sky has slowly darkened, and she can finally say that it is time for them to go home. The men are standing in a group on the lawn, like statues. As she crosses the garden, she decides never to return here.

Fredrik is standing with the other men and smoking. 'Already?' he replies. 'It's not that late.'

'Would you like to stay for dinner?' Mats says.

Fredrik is about to answer, but she beats him to it. 'This evening isn't so good, but perhaps another time,' she says, managing to sound sincere. Mats is on the verge of saying something but changes his mind and nods, flicking ash onto the grass.

The disappointment is sketched tightly on Fredrik's face. He wants to protest, but he also doesn't want to cause a scene in front of the others. But he still can't help himself and spreads his arms, exclaiming, as if joking:

'You're so antisocial, Bente!'

Mats and the other men chuckle. She can feel her face reddening. But it ought to be Fredrik who is ashamed, not her. A clear and piercing rage runs through her like a blade.

'You can stay if you like,' she says quietly.

But then it is as if he withdraws. 'No, perhaps it is time,' he says valiantly, whereupon Mats reflexively falls into his role as host and says:

'It's so nice that you could come!' He places a hand on Fredrik's shoulder, as if to give him support: a silent understanding between men.

His unspoken accusation hangs on the air between them. She knows he thinks that the evening has been ruined and that it is her fault. They order pizza and eat together like proper families are supposed to. She turns to the boys: 'Did you have fun?' They sense discord and hurry to finish eating.

That evening, she and Fredrik watch two episodes of a TV series. It is dramatic and well-made, trivial but entertaining, and it changes the atmosphere between them. When they turn off the TV she manages to sound easy-going when she says she talked to their new neighbour Elisabeth today. She seemed nice, she says. By the way, she adds as an aside, the pearl earring wasn't hers.

He looks at her, puzzled.

'Why did you ask her about the earring?'

'It's not mine, and Elisabeth and her son went with you and Rasmus to football yesterday.'

The pearl chafes between them. He shrugs his shoulders.

'I don't know whose it is, darling.'

Her silence weighs against his words. She gives him a stare usually reserved for the interrogation room and remains silent, waiting.

'I don't know where it came from,' he repeats.

He shows no signs of lying. It is difficult to lie. The membrane between a fabricated and a true course of events is brittle and can easily split.

66

She opts to believe him and kisses him. He smiles and they meet in another kiss. She decides not to think about the pearl earring for the time being; she just wants to feel that they are close to each other. She tugs hard at his belt, pulls open his trousers and kicks her underwear off impatiently. She runs her fingers through his hair and clenches her fist, searchingly, and notices that he responds a little half-heartedly. Between her legs she is warm and urgent. She feels his cock, wrapping her fingers around it, and opens up, trying to guide him in. But he is flaccid; it won't work. She quickly crouches down on her knees and takes him in her mouth for a bit, and now she can feel him growing, and it is easier. For a few dogged minutes she thrusts herself against him, huddled over and silent. He sits still. She feels a violent desire to hit him, to awaken pain in him – he is sitting too still, as if he were waiting for her. Move, she thinks. Be with me. She wants to trust him. She wants to know that he wants her. She moves more rapidly, more spasmodically. It feels good, but she wants him to touch her more and so she guides his hands onto her buttocks, wishing he would squeeze them, digging his fingers in deep, but his hands are so very smooth and powerless. And then she feels him come. It happens quietly: he draws breath and gives a sub-dued groan. She would have liked it to be wilder, harder, but she is glad they did it, even if she didn't quite make it all the way.

A sound. They freeze, listening. She lunges for her trousers and pulls on her blouse with just enough time to fasten two buttons as she quietly hurries upstairs. Rasmus is standing in the middle of the dark landing.

'What are you doing?' he asks suspiciously. His eyes shine, as if he has recently woken.

'Sweetheart,' she says, leading him back into the closer dark-ness of his bedroom, 'you need to sleep.'

'It sounded like someone was hitting you,' he says.

She perches on the edge of the bed with an arm around his narrow shoulders, and tells him that no one has done her any harm. He doesn't need to worry. She and Dad are fine. No one is hurting anyone.

After a long walk he ends up at the Tate, where he drinks tea in the half-empty restaurant, surrounded by tourists, then wanders back to his hotel, where he lies on the bed watching the news. The logo whirls around the screen to magnificent electronic music. A globe of communication barrelling forward. Nothing about the analyst, the dead traitor. Robert shouldn't have silenced him so definitively. What's done is done, and must be dealt with.

While buttoning his shirt, Jonathan thinks through what needs to be said to Paddy McGuiness, the Minister of Defence's perpetual advisor and naysayer. The opposition to be conquered. The anxiety to be pacified. He presses the cufflinks through the small slits. Then he selects a deep-red tie, ties it in a double Windsor knot, adjusting it as he examines himself in the mirror. The red nicely complements his graphite-grey suit. A suit of armour; now he is ready.

Twenty minutes later he is approaching the Ministry of Defence, that granite monument to Britain's lost empire. He steps up to the navy-blue door through which he has passed on so many previous occasions. 'The Catflap' is what they call the tucked-away side entrance to the Ministry offices, intended for those who prefer to make a discreet arrival.

Inside, there is a dark hallway. He ambles along beneath the vaulted ceiling. Robert is standing at the foot of a broad staircase.

They hurry up the stairs, through a heavy wooden door and into a light corridor, where their footsteps are absorbed by thick carpet. The air is still, in the way that is only possible in an unoccupied building.

These are the offices of the Minister of Defence. On a Sunday, the rooms they wander past are deserted, but during the week the decisions emanating from here concern the defence of the United Kingdom and its international actions, the controlled use of death.

Jonathan hears muffled voices.

Two men are standing in the middle of the corridor that they turn onto, engaged in a muted discussion that stops abruptly as Robert and Jonathan approach. Their faces turn towards them, apprehensive. Then the men recognise them. One of them listlessly raises a hand by way of greeting.

'Robert,' says Paddy. 'Give me a minute.'

They step to one side. Robert's face contorts into a contemptuous mask. Being left to wait by Paddy is a bad sign.

A trickle of nervousness oozes out of Jonathan's armpit and is absorbed by his shirt. Hercules has to happen, he thinks. He can't bear the thought of seeing all the work they have done being laid to rest this afternoon. Only now does he realise that he has been taking it for granted that everyone, including Paddy, could see what a victory this operation could be. But now that he can see Paddy standing with his secretary, he is struck by quite how real the risk is of the operation never seeing the light of day, and it upsets him. He is already out of favour, thanks to the leak in Brussels, and he doesn't have many opportunities left to save his career. Without Hercules, those chances are zero; of that much he is certain.

Paddy disappears through a pair of double doors with his secretary, leaving them standing in the corridor.

'Bloody fool,' Robert mutters.

Calm down, is what Jonathan wants to say. Robert is too tense, as if he might lose his self-control at any moment and storm after Paddy. The advisor is engaging in small-scale psychological warfare; there is no need to lose one's balance over such pathetic attempts at mastery, and it annoys him that Robert cannot keep his cool. Jonathan stands by a window. Outside are the well-tended Whitehall Gardens, illuminated in shades of autumnal yellow.

It is a relief when the secretary reappears after a few seemingly unending minutes, smiling apologetically. 'Please, come in,' says the young man, watching Robert anxiously as he blunders past.

Paddy is standing by the tall French doors, outlined by the daylight cast through them.

'Come in, come in,' he says loudly but not particularly enthusiastically, and he approaches them slowly. They shake hands.

Jonathan contemplates Paddy's broad shoulders and muscular arms that don't quite fit into the dark-blue suit. Paddy the Bouncer. Perhaps this security advisor would have been happier standing outside a West End club denying people admission, Jonathan thinks as he sits down on the visitor sofa beside Robert.

'Thank you for taking the time to meet like this on a Sunday,' Robert says with surprising warmth.

Paddy nods absently, massaging his temples with his coarse fingertips and squinting at Jonathan.

'So, Jonathan,' he says. 'Are you watertight in Brussels now?'

'Yes,' he replies lightly, 'the leak is under control.'

'Very good,' Paddy mutters, not the least bit impressed.

That's exactly how the Ministry sees it, Jonathan reflects. A matter of incontinence; a tired, incompetent body leaking secrets of state. He hates the thought of Paddy and everyone here in London talking about him like that.

Paddy is in a bad mood, as if vexed by having to be here with these spies on a Sunday. He glowers at his visitors.

'So, Robert. You think the time has come for Hercules?'

Robert nods seriously, as if he has great sympathy with the advisor's scepticism. It is splendid theatre when Robert calmly explains what he has already told Paddy at three other meetings: how important Operation Hercules is in the battle against Islamic State, how crucial Pathfinder is to it all.

Paddy listens impatiently.

'We're ready,' Robert says, holding up a hand to forestall Paddy, 'despite the mishap in Brussels.'

'Mishap?' Paddy cries out, exposing his blunt teeth in an acerbic smile. 'It's a bloody catastrophe.'

'And as a result of what happened in Brussels,' says Robert, 'we've decided not to use the House. We won't be using those methods, Paddy. Apart from that, the operation will go ahead as planned.'

Jonathan looks at Robert. Are they closing down the House? It is a pleasant surprise but it astonishes him: he had thought Robert was against it. But his friend has the right idea. He is engaging in damage limitation and calming Paddy down, ensuring he feels confident enough to approve the operation.

'Good,' says Paddy. 'We don't like that facility.'

The honourable Paddy is lying. He doesn't care about the House and has always appreciated the information extracted from its clients. What he doesn't like is the risk that his Minister will have to take public responsibility for the House. The wrong people getting hold of the right information and beginning to ask questions is what Paddy is afraid of.

'We still have a chance to secure Pathfinder,' Jonathan says, 'but time is scarce.'

Robert calls upon Jonathan to speak.

Step by step, he details the plans in the same way as in the last three meetings with Paddy. But this time, the advisor is nodding in a way that indicates a more positive outlook.

'So the plan remains to pay a ransom to the rebels for Pathfinder?'

He nods; that is the plan. Paddy grimaces, and Jonathan knows why: over recent months they have spent hours sitting on this sofa trying to make Paddy understand that they must negotiate with Ahrar al-Sham if they want to get to Pathfinder.

'They're terrorists,' Paddy mutters.

'Jihadists, actually,' he says.

'And an enemy doesn't have to become your friend to be useful,' Robert interrupts. 'Paddy, we've already discussed this. We're buying information that is for sale. We need this man.'

Paddy sulks.

'Give me one good reason for buying a taxi driver off some terrorists for one million pounds.'

'Paddy,' he says, 'you know what it takes to win. We need names, addresses. Precision. Hercules is the operation that can give us all that.'

'Are you certain of Pathfinder's identity?'

'It's the right man,' says Robert.

'Why not let the Americans take him and buy the information from them?'

'Paddy, please.' Robert is now struggling to remain calm, and his voice trembles with suppressed rage. 'The Americans? Do you really want to advise our government to get into bed with that bloody clown of a hotelier to create stability in the Middle East?'

Paddy hates being spoken to so brusquely, and Robert's tone is too harsh. Worst case, Paddy might say no simply because he feels offended.

They wait while Paddy rubs his forehead. It seems as if he is close to making a decision about the operation.

'But is the leak definitely under control?' Paddy says, shaking his head and seeming once again hesitant. 'The Minister must have plausible reasons for being able to deny all knowledge of the kind of operation that has been conducted at the House.'

Jonathan can feel small droplets of sweat sliding down the small of his back and abdomen.

This is the man who always starts by saying no, only to – reluctantly perhaps – change his answer to maybe. A cautious strategist, and a furious defender of his Minister.

Paddy's voice rises to a whining crescendo: 'The Swedes are aware of the House and our work in Syria. So will I be reading about this in the *Guardian*, like I did last time?'

No, he thinks, don't bring that up again. They all remember how their joint European counter-terrorism initiative, launched by the Home Office five years ago, had gone. A young Swedish diplomat torpedoed the entire venture, and it all ended up in the papers.

Then something unexpected happens. Robert leans forward to Paddy and whispers into his ear. Jonathan sees the change in the advisor's expression. It becomes calmer, his eyes widen.

'I understand,' he says quietly, once Robert leans back.

Whatever his friend has said, it seems to have worked, because when Robert softly asks whether they should discuss the operation, Paddy nods wordlessly, as if still in shock over what he has just been told.

'So the leak is . . . under control.'

An anxious look of resistance passes across the Bouncer's tired face.

'Okay,' he says.

It takes a second for them to realise that the Minister of Defence's closest advisor has just given them his approval. He will speak to the Minister this evening, he adds wearily.

Robert grins broadly, as if they have never been anything but the best of friends.

'No more issues, mind,' says Paddy, raising a finger.

When they leave Paddy, he is standing by the window in his office looking out. They hurry along the corridors and down the stairs, as if worried that the advisor might catch up with them and say he has changed his mind.

'What did you whisper to him?'

'That the traitor killed himself last week,' says Robert, flashing a smile at him. 'Don't worry, Jon. Everything will be fine.'

If anyone without clearance asks her what she does for a living, then her first line of defence is to reply that she works for a company in Brussels. If anyone pursues a further interest, then she says she develops computer systems; and if, in spite of that, someone wants to know more, she starts talking about databases until she has extinguished all curiosity.

She is used to diverting other people's interest with concepts such as structured information management, bulk data, the programming of system procedures, and other such soporific terms; she knows how to get people to stop caring. In the unlikely event that anyone were to look up the company, they would encounter the second line of defence: a website describing a dynamic and global information technology business. The third line of defence is an infrequently manned reception desk on the eleventh floor of an office block a few streets away from Rue de la Loi, where the curious visitor will be handed leaflets referring them to the website. Amusingly enough, the shield works. Very few suspect those who lie about everything, and do so with a smile.

As usual, Fredrik drops her off not far from the office. He cannot be permitted to know the exact address, which he understands. She asks whether they will see each other this evening. He shakes his head. Unfortunately he has a work meeting.

She kisses him hastily. Then she gets out of the car and they part ways. Fredrik knows what her job is – she doesn't lie to him, but exercises restraint with the truth. He doesn't know where her office is, and this is as close as he is allowed to get to the part of her life that belongs to the Security Service.

The team are already there. She passes two technicians who bid her good morning with hearty politeness, which puts her in a good mood. She has an indisputable impact on the room: her presence generates a swell of attentive faces.

They trust her. All their work is driven by a deep whirlwind of loyalty and trust, with her at its centre. It is a draining and vaguely erotic experience.

The Section for Special Intelligence is such a secret part of the Swedish intelligence world that it does not appear in any regulatory documents and is known to no one except the handful of people back home in Stockholm who need to know. Joining the Section is to make a covenant, promising absolute silence and fidelity.

Out in the corridor she helps herself to an apple from a bowl next to the printer. Today she is due to have a conference call with Stockholm. She needs to speak to Mikael, but first she goes to the mail room to empty her locked pigeonhole. She has received around ten reports about Syria and Islamic State, the kind of thing that now arrives on a daily basis, as well as an analysis of Russian military priorities and two reports about changes in the White House following the unlikely election a week earlier. She glances through the papers while wandering back to her office and dedicates some time to the analysis of American politics and what it might mean for the world. A new War on Terror, perhaps. New alliances in the Middle East and a heightened risk of tension between Shias and Sunnis. An easily annoyed, sociopathic liar as President of the United States makes all developments the more unpredictable. She chews the apple thoughtfully. The acidic juice makes her teeth feel pleasantly dry.

Mikael looks up from his screen with a brief good morning when she enters his office. She sits down in his visitor armchair and squints at the screen. What is he writing? Something about IT security.

While she waits, she has time to notice that his office is surprisingly cluttered; there are books and folders all over the place, in addition to various bicycle paraphernalia. A saddle. A sophisticated pump for thin racing tyres. He really ought to tidy his office, she thinks to herself. But she trusts his judgement; his mind is as ordered as his office is messy.

'Will you be done soon?' she says jokingly.

Mikael is fit; the clear lines of his back are visible through his shirt. It would be a problem if he were beautiful. But he is neither good-looking nor flirty, and has always maintained a stolid focus on his work. It's restful; it makes for a clean and clear relationship.

A final flurry of tapping sees him finish. He brings up the British news.

She looks at the dead man's face.

'It's no suicide, Mikael.'

Mikael nods slowly; he doesn't believe for a second that the man has taken his own life, even if the British police haven't found any signs of resistance or a struggle. For a spy, death doesn't come as a bullet in the back of the neck but as two smiling colleagues. He had presumably let his murderers in, of his own volition, because they were his colleagues. They might very well have had a beer together, as friends, before they inter-rogated him and killed him.

'We have eyes upon us,' he says.

Naturally, they will have got the man to tell all. Anyone facing their impending death always does. Mikael says that they need to assume that the Brits know who he contacted. There is a risk that they are now monitoring the Section. What they need to do now is obtain a clearer picture of the situation to assess the threat.

Mikael spins in his office chair.

'What do you think about targeted surveillance of the Brits' office?'

It is tempting. They need to know what the British are saying . . .

She sighs. Perhaps they could tap Jonathan Green's mobile. They have his mobile number. But she would rather not. It's so risky. They're talking about bugging MI6, and she feels as if they're moving onto an increasingly thin crust of earth that might give way beneath them at any moment. If they are dis-covered, a sinkhole will open up; the Section would be unable to survive a catastrophe of that kind.

'We'll have to see what Stockholm thinks.'

Over the last few weeks, she has felt deep down that it would have been easier if the leak hadn't happened. Or if the Brit hadn't come to them, if she had said no, if someone else had been lumbered with knowledge of the House and the British silent war against Islamic State. She had never asked for that kind of responsibility.

She gets up. There is a report on Syria lying on Mikael's desk, the same one as in her pigeonhole. A British product, an analysis of the battles in Aleppo that have intensified in recent weeks. Perhaps it is an analysis based on what has been said during interrogations of some of the Brits' so-called clients? The thought makes her downhearted. They are so dependent on the British.

As she wanders out into the corridor, she reflects that her office, and the entire Swedish intelligence service, is floating on a surface of turbid, bloody water. The British are close partners, and their knowledge of the Middle East is priceless, but this House sullies everything. Apart from her and Mikael, only management in Stockholm is aware of it – of that she is certain. She cannot be left on her own in this matter; she needs to know what they think.

Down in a sandwich bar by the Luxembourg station her spirits are lifted as she finds herself in the midst of the usual pushing, chatty mass of office workers thronging to order their lunch. She pushes her way past a young man wearing a suit, with a well-groomed beard, who laughs in surprise and calls out in French, 'You must be very hungry, *madame*!' He is joking. 'Make way,' he says. 'Hungry woman coming through.'

This flirtatious exchange makes her happy. He's a handsome man, and she reflects that if a man like that were to actually make a proper pass at her, she'd be tempted to give in. She would resist, of course; she's no schoolgirl. But still.

She catches sight of Mikael on the pavement. She raises her hand, but he doesn't see her because he's talking on the phone. He looks concerned. She thinks he may be burning out; she has noticed that he often stays late in the evening, long after everyone else has gone home, and she knows that he has recently separated, because he has taken to mentioning that he has the kids this week, as only one with shared parenting responsibilities would. Then he spots her and stiffens.

'What is it?' she asks when she reaches him.

At first he seems unwilling to say, hesitating and opening his mouth as if contemplating lying to her, before changing his mind in a split second.

'It's Gustav,' he explains.

Gustav Kempell, Head of Counter-Espionage back at Stockholm HQ. She looks at Mikael in astonishment, and then at the mobile he is holding out. Would she like to speak to him?

Gustav's dry, friendly voice is so familiar. He was her mentor when she started at the Security Service, and has always been a supporter. She doesn't trust many people – Gustav is one of the few that she never doubts – but right now she wonders what is going on. His voice is remarkably flighty when he speaks.

'*Hello, Bente,*' he says. '*How are you?*'

Well, he had needed to have a word with Mikael. She can hear him making an effort to try and make the fact that he is speaking to her deputy, rather than her, sound unremarkable. So what are they talking about? But she doesn't ask; that's not how it's done, it's an unspoken rule. Instead, she asks whether he'll be joining the conference call.

'*I'll try,*' he says evasively. '*Speak soon.*'

She hands the phone back to Mikael.

On the way back to the office, she asks Mikael what Gustav wanted. There's an issue with the IT system and Stockholm wants to run some tests, he explains, and she can see he is hiding his face in the sandwich he is devouring.

She surveys the conference room and its wide, oval-shaped table. The black conference phone is resting in the middle of the polished table like a minimalist space probe. It is from here that the voice of Roland Hamrén, Deputy Head of the Security

Service, is emerging. The volume is a little too high and is breaking up in the treble.

As soon as she hears Roland Hamrén's voice she senses a restless and mutinous anger.

She detests the man. Hamrén is the kind of man who is fundamentally unwilling to acknowledge that women can be more competent than men, and who always believes, regardless of how little space a woman takes up, that she is taking up too much space and asking for too much. Hamrén always manages to find different reasons to question her, in particular. She has always disliked him, but the hatred had arisen from an occasion five years ago when he had been Head of Counter-Terrorism and had forced her to cast suspicion on a civil servant in the Ministry of Justice in order to avoid a crisis with MI6. It had been a dirty game, and Hamrén had made her play along. She had only just become Section Head and could offer no resistance. Hamrén had bowed down before Jonathan Green and forced her to do the same. He had taken away her pride: the pride in doing the right thing. Since then, their relationship has been a case of cut-and-dried hostility, and the fact that he became Deputy Head of the whole Security Service three years ago has only made things worse, if that were possible.

'*We've looked at your British contacts in more detail,*' he says in an edgy, irritated tone of voice.

'I understand,' she says.

'*Your way of handling it is worrying.*' The information she has obtained about the location referred to by the British as 'the House', and British operational procedures in northern Syria, is interesting. But the haphazard way that the information has been obtained is unfortunate.

'I understand,' she repeats, relieved that he is not in the room and can't see her clenching her jaw or Mikael rolling his eyes.

It is a strange sensation to sit and talk to the small black device, as if in worship of it. But that is how it is – she can hear it in Hamrén's voice. A big dose of obedience is expected.

'*The Brits are our partners*,' Hamrén continues. His voice crackles. '*Valued friends.*'

He speaks for a long time about how the knowledge of such powerful British secrets will harm relations with the Brits. The annoyed tone escalates and the sound breaks up. The very fact that they are in possession of unauthorised information about MI6 will harm the relationship.

'*Do you understand?*'

'I understand.'

She draws a large square in her notepad. She takes care to get the lines straight, but she presses too hard and the square contorts into a rhombus.

'*The mere suspicion that you are in possession of unauthorised information is a big problem*,' she hears Hamrén say. What she has done may result in damage, he says angrily. '*An irreparable loss of trust*,' are the words that crackle out of the speaker.

She turns silently towards Mikael and casts her arms out as they listen to Hamrén's mechanical way of quickly and irritably coughing up words. Even if she defers to him completely, he won't be satisfied, she reflects as he continues to talk about the consequences that the leak may have on the relationship.

She opens her mouth to reply, but all that emerges is an audible pause; there is no space for her voice. '*You shouldn't have accepted that British contact*,' says Hamrén. '*That's not what we do to our friends.*'

It is apparent that he won't be letting her speak. She really ought to strike back – she shouldn't let him talk to her in this dismissive manner, as if she were an intern who had made a mistake – but she knows that if she protests, it will only make things worse. So she sits quietly, or answers briefly in the affirmative. She had hoped Gustav would join them so that they could discuss the situation. Indignation floods through her. It is just as well she doesn't get the opportunity to speak; she would only have screamed at the small black device.

'*The material you have received is of such an explosive nature that it might topple a British government,*' he says. '*You must realise that?*'

'Yes,' she replies. She realises that.

She can't help herself as she adds:

'It was the Brit who contacted us—'

'*You should have turned him away,*' Hamrén says, cutting her off.

She battles to slow her pulse. The way he is talking to her – as if were some snotty-nosed brat – is intolerable. She is familiar with the procedures, and considered him of interest, she quickly adds.

She knows where this is going. Hamrén sees that there is a risk of damage to the relationship with the Brits, and needs to be able to sacrifice her, should the need arise. It's not fair, she thinks. She didn't ask for the documents, and she can't stand him treating her as if she had ruined everything. She was just doing her job.

'That man came to us because he thought the information would end up in the right hands,' she says.

'*It was a mistake.*'

That's enough, she thinks, leaning over the table and speaking loudly and angrily:

'Regardless of the relationship, we need to deal with what we now know about the House,' she says. They all know what it is.

The black device emits a negative silence.

'We accept a lot of British information about Syria and the Middle East,' she says. 'But if that intelligence is coming from methods like that, it changes everything. It's illegitimate and we can't rely on it. The very fact that we're using it is a breach of several conventions . . .'

'*We are aware of that particular issue.*'

But she doesn't allow the interruption. It is surprising, she says, finally managing to adopt a tone befitting her role, that they are discussing the leak as if all that mattered was protecting the relationship with the British. They all know what is meant by 'specific procedures'. What bearing does this have on the information they receive from the British if it is being beaten out of their sources?

She slumps back into her chair. She has said what she has to say.

The hum of silence comes out of the speakers.

'*Let it go, Bente.*'

She says nothing. Perhaps he is right. Maybe she should let it go.

'*You should have checked in about your contact with this B54 before you met him. You should have anticipated the risks.*'

She silently drives a biro into the palm of her hand until the pain makes her calm down.

'So what do we do now?'

'*You do nothing.*'

Nothing, she snorts, looking out of the window in her office. She is alone. It is a tough situation, because if she does nothing, then the British will set the rules of the game and determine her future. But if she takes action, she will be going against Stockholm. Refusing orders, sabotage – Hamrén would see it as a golden opportunity to sack her. 'The bastard,' she mutters to herself. Hamrén would sacrifice her without hesitation; at least he is a clear enemy. And the Brits? She has no idea what Jonathan Green is up to, but knows that, beneath the placid surface, he is a dangerous person.

There is a knock on the door. She runs a hand over her face, as if to adjust her expression.

A young technician opens the door. He holds out a box.

'What's that?'

'Your new mobile phone,' he says.

When she doesn't bat an eyelid, he says in a more formal tone that it is the phone she ordered.

'I didn't order a new mobile.'

The technician looks at her in confusion.

'But there was an order . . .'

He falls silent and appears to be trying to resolve the misunderstanding that must have occurred. He is certain there was an order, he mutters.

She is suddenly wide awake. 'Oh, that one,' she says, as if remembering what it is all about. She takes the box from him and smiles.

'I had completely forgotten.'

The technician smiles in relief and skips back to his eager, service-oriented tone. 'No worries,' he says. Would she like him to deal with her old phone?

With a smile she hands over her mobile.

She has only just sat back down again when her new phone buzzes. A new message: *Call me.*

She wanders past the throbbing machinery of the roadworks, cuts through the traffic jam that has formed on Rue de la Loi, and then ambles through the backstreets towards the old quarter behind the vaulted glass façade of the Berlaymont building. She needs a coffee and some air. What does Gustav want? Once she is in the older, higher part of the city, she pulls out the new phone.

Gustav Kempell picks up with a warm and steady voice: '*Hello, Bente.*'

He would like to see her. Can she come by this evening?

She is so surprised she comes to a halt. To Stockholm?

No, he's in The Hague, engaged in certain discussions, and could meet her somewhere in her neck of the woods, he replies cryptically. Might that work? It is apparent that he doesn't want to go into detail on the phone. She is happy to meet him. She feels glad of the opportunity, because she needs him, someone to trust.

'*Just you, and no one else,*' he says. '*Tell no one.*'

That afternoon, Bente drives to the sea. Once on the motorway, she calls Fredrik, but all she gets is his bright answerphone greeting. He's probably in a meeting, she thinks to herself as she types a brief message: *Away tonight. Can you take care of the boys? xxx*. Without really knowing why, she then changes the sign-off to a more restrained *x*, which somehow feels more appropriate.

The sky is covered in pink clouds as she crosses the Dutch border. An hour later, she reaches the seaside resort of Noordwijk. The satnav guides her smoothly through the cornfields and houses, round empty roundabouts and along avenues where the wind rustles the trees.

Then suddenly she can smell seaweed and salt.

Gustav has chosen a modest apartment hotel close to the beach. She wanders along the balcony until she reaches a narrow orange door.

Gustav opens it; he is wearing a cardigan and shirt. He looks reserved, but when he opens the door slightly she notes the vigilant glance he casts over her shoulder before letting her in. He tells her he's glad she came.

The apartment he has rented is a basic two-room affair with beach views. He nods towards the dark windows. Can she hear?

The sea is a whispered roar.

He has procured dinner. There are takeaway cartons in the kitchen containing two portions of beef, potato gratin and sauce that he bought in the small restaurant on the ground floor.

Gustav wants to know how things are going for her in Brussels, how life is. She answers vaguely, as one does when unsure of the intentions behind a question. Sitting with him in a small holiday apartment and eating dinner is bizarrely familiar, and she feels tense from trying to discern what exactly it is he wants. They make small talk, and once they have finished eating they settle on the sofa with cups of coffee.

'What's your mobile number, again?' he says, as if in passing.

She doesn't understand the question; he has her number. He smiles at her with a friendly, inscrutable expression, as if the question were completely ordinary.

He slowly stirs his cup of coffee while watching her with his bright eyes.

'Where was your phone on Friday evening?' he continues.

On Friday evening she was at the Swedish embassy reception. And her mobile ...

'I don't know.'

'You don't know?'

'It was at home,' she says. She had the mobile at home, and then on the way to the Hotel Metropole she realised she didn't have it with her ...

She falls silent.

'Is there a problem with my mobile?'

Gustav tilts his head as if to say 'Yes and no.'

'Essentially, it's you that's the problem, Bente.'

At first she thinks he's joking. Her?

Then it's as if Gustav has finally reached what he has been

avoiding saying all along. The strained warmth gives way, and he becomes serious.

'At 20.50 on the dot last Friday evening your mobile was subject to an attack,' he says. 'A virus. Malware made its way through the mobile and spread on to our servers in Stockholm. Do you understand what I'm saying, Bente?'

She nods, and feels the shock slowly penetrating through her. Has someone got hold of it?

'Have you had any break-ins lately?'

'No,' she replies, thinking that he knows very well that she would report something like that to Stockholm.

The tempo of the questions subtly increases. A quick shift has seen an ordinary conversation transform into an interrogation. Gustav wants to know where she keeps her mobile. How does she look after it? She replies. Does she take it with her? Does she have it locked away when she is at home? He observes her, unmoving, while she answers. Has Fredrik borrowed her mobile?

Then she remembers.

'It was in his coat pocket.'

She hadn't been able to find her mobile on Friday, she says, before correcting herself – because the memories are now coming back rapidly in a whirlwind of fragments, and she remembers the embassy, and the exhilarating sense of freedom, now lost, and she wonders whether she will ever feel it again. She remembers how they arrived at the reception, and how it occurred to her that she didn't have her mobile with her, she says, but that Fredrik said he had his. And then at the weekend, after she had asked Fredrik if he had seen her mobile, she found it in his jacket pocket.

'When?' says Gustav. 'When did you find it?'

'On Saturday morning.'

Gustav is looking at her as if to devour the slightest shift in her expression. She answers promptly and candidly; she's got nothing to hide.

When did she last see the phone before it went missing? She describes how she left the phone to charge on Friday morning at home on the hall table. *What time? Be precise: eight o'clock, half past eight, nine?* Around nine, she had been working from home. So she must have forgotten it when she went into the Section at lunchtime. She had forgotten it? Gustav asks. So when did she remember it again? He listens, hums and haws. Oh, she wasn't that concerned about it. 'Okay, you looked for it. And then you remembered it again at reception?'

Gustav wants her to describe the reception desk. She notices that he is looking for any circumstances in which the phone could have disappeared. Was there anyone about on Friday evening who could have taken it?

She wishes he would drop his expressionless face and just talk to *her*; they know each other. But he maintains a cool distance, his tone neutral and impersonal. With each question, he methodically dissects the course of events, every detail cut out by his sharp attention. They keep going back to the same sequence; she says the same thing at least ten times, as a splitting headache takes hold of her.

'Why did Fredrik have your mobile in his coat pocket?'

She shakes her head; she doesn't know. She was with him all evening. Or almost, she thinks, but for some reason she is reluctant to tell Gustav that they lost each other for a while, or rather that he found some colleagues and forgot her. It's just one of those silly things, and she doesn't want to talk about it.

'Do you remember who you spoke to during the evening?'

She is afraid now, because his cold tone demonstrates how far apart they are. She was with Fredrik and his colleague, she says, they were drinking wine . . .

Then it occurs to her that she caught sight of Jonathan Green. But there is nothing to tell; just a brief glimpse, nothing more. Her thoughts buzz while she describes the evening, which at the time had seemed so promising but is now falling apart into mute, lifeless particles.

'Who else did you meet?' he asks.

She didn't meet anyone else.

His furrowed face contorts into an angry grimace. There is something about the way the tendons in his neck tense that disturbs her.

'Please, Bente,' he asks with sincerity.

'But what is it you want me to say?' she exclaims.

He silently motions her to follow him, and she puts on her coat.

They walk quietly down the stairs and across the promenade. The wind takes hold of their hair and clothes, gusting with ferocious force as they walk across the dunes.

Then they reach the beach. They walk, bent forward, towards the sea. As if crouching against the wind, the houses loom behind them, watching them from their darkened windows. Out here in the wind no one else can hear them.

'Stockholm doesn't trust you.' He shakes his head. 'You've made a mess of things. Your mobile is under surveillance. Do you understand?'

The roar of the sea grows with the breakers before sputtering and waning. Gustav looks unhappy and tired.

'You have enemies. This leak has made a lot of people angry.

And the fact that your mobile's been infiltrated has made people in Stockholm wonder whether you can be trusted.'

She says she understands, but, just there and then, it is impossible to comprehend what he is saying. Her professional life is flashing before her eyes. She has been exposed, her mobile attacked.

'You trust me, surely?' she says.

The idea that he might not in fact be on her side is too painful to contemplate. She can't stand the idea that the man who has been her mentor, that the person who knows her best of all in the industry, is now looking at her with such suspicion.

'You can trust me,' she shouts.

It is as if he barely hears her, as if even the wind were against her and wants to drown her out. His expression doesn't change. Yet it is as if something then softens in him. He nods, like he's made up his mind.

She follows him along the beach, feeling as if she were sinking into the sand with each step she takes. He says nothing, walks quietly ahead of her. Occasionally he stops and looks inland.

Finally, Gustav veers towards the dunes. They sit down, out of the wind.

'Are you sure you don't know what happened to your mobile?'

'*Yes*. I promise.'

She truly has no idea what happened, she realises, and that makes her afraid.

So she has become a problem. She can picture Roland Hamrén in a meeting back in Stockholm preparing the text to say that the Section has reached the end of its useful life, how Bente Jensen has taken unacceptable risks, and now this issue with the mobile phone ... How easy it is for suspicion to poison everything.

As if reading her thoughts, Gustav says that they are examining the procedures, and her mobile in particular. She and her family will also be undergoing checks. He shouldn't tell her that, but he is in charge and responsible for the checks . . .

'Thank you.'

'Don't let me down.'

The sea sprawls, dark and jagged. The waves heave with glowing white crests of foam before crashing onto the beach.

They walk back towards the apartment. Walking along the beach, she can see Gustav's eyes, and she feels some bitter relief in the fact that even he looks heavy-hearted. She doesn't know much about Gustav's life. The fact is, she has never thought about him as a person with a private life, but now, as he stands there in his fleece jacket, his thin hair tossed about by the wind, it is as if he has, just for a moment, become an elderly relative.

'Bente,' he says. 'You should be aware that this might grow. And if it gets out of hand, I won't be able to defend you.'

She looks along the desolate promenade with the strong feeling that everything she has fought for over the years has been in vain, all the work, all the toil. She knows how they think in Stockholm: a mistake like this with her mobile is unforgivable; a mark against you like that doesn't just go away.

They briefly say their goodbyes. He promises to be in touch. Her last glimpse of Gustav is of him standing between the feeble circles of the illuminated promenade, watching her leave.

On the way home, she unhappily recollects their conversation, and the more she thinks, the more she wonders why he was so frank. She anxiously tries to remember how he posed his questions, and becomes more uncertain by the minute. Would he really take a risk like that and tell her about Stockholm's suspicions without approval from further up? The more she thinks about it, the harder she finds it not to succumb to the idea that his honesty is just a new and refined technique for persuading her to admit guilt. But what is it that she's supposed to have done? She fantasises that the car doors won't open, and that she will find herself trapped in this cell, rushing forward forever more.

The next day, everything feels a bit more manageable. Of course she was careless with her mobile, she thinks, and that bothers and worries her, but over breakfast she feels sure she'll be able to demonstrate what happened. Roland Hamrén won't defeat her. Dear God, she isn't a threat – she's a *resource*. And Gustav is on her side; she can't comprehend that she could ever have thought otherwise. The biggest mistake she could make now would be to lose faith in the only person who wants to help her.

She makes up her mind to talk to Fredrik about the mobile. And the pearl earring.

She will ask him exactly when he found the phone, just as Gustav asked her, the same questions and the same method. But not yet.

It is only now she notices that Rasmus has been whining loudly that his device needs charging, and before she is able to ask him to calm down, he waves the device around and hits the cafetière, spilling the contents all over the kitchen table and onto Daniel's hand. When she reaches the office it feels like a breath of fresh air.

Just after lunch, her mobile rings. She is startled, unaccustomed to the new ringtone.

'*Is that Madame Jensen?*' says a male voice lightly in French.

She doesn't understand – who is she talking to? She doesn't want to speak French; that bloody language fits so poorly in her mouth, and she is in the middle of discussing with Mikael how they might find out more about the Brits, even though Stockholm told them to do nothing.

'*Your son Rasmus's teacher*,' the light voice clarifies, and she recognises it. Something has happened, he explains. It would be good if she could come and collect her son. He sounds serious in a way that immediately makes her worried. No, he doesn't want to say more on the phone, it would be better if she came to school as quickly as possible. They are waiting in the head's office, he explains in a subdued tone.

The school playground is deserted, but still vibrates with the sound of shrill cries and nimble bodies. She arrives just after breaktime and the children have disappeared into the large building.

She had hoped to avoid these calls. This school was meant to be a fresh start for Rasmus, for them all. Here he would no longer be the troublemaker, the freak, that all the other parents talked about as someone they wanted to protect their children from. But then they had begun: the teacher's concerned calls, and at the end of the most recent school year she had seen the other parents' reserved expressions. *There's that boy's mother*. She told herself for a long time that it was just an adjustment, that it was difficult to change schools and join a class as a new pupil. She should have known better.

She hurries up the wide stairs and into an empty atrium. Her footsteps strike the stone floor, and echo between the rows of lockers. She passes doors through which voices are audible, like muffled mumbling choirs.

There is something about schools that makes her feel like a little girl, as if these closed doors and cold corridors, with their faint odour of bleach and dust, awaken an uneasy respect in her and at the same time an intractable desire to strike back, refuse, revolt.

Behind a door with a frosted glass window is the staff corridor. Outside the head's office she finds Rasmus sitting on a chair by the wall.

He looks up with a sullen expression and says, 'Hi, Mum,' before looking back down at his mobile. She crouches in front of him. He has a bruise next to his left eye.

'Rasmus,' she says. 'What's happened?'

But her boy remains silent and stares at his mobile with morose obstinacy, as if he could shut her and every other living being away, through sheer willpower.

When he does that, she never knows what to do. It is a sense of powerlessness that is so intense that she wants to scream at him. Although what she really wants to do is scream at everyone at this school, this stiff institution, with all its requirements that he can't handle. Here we go again, she thinks to herself. She wishes she could simply tell him to stop fighting, stop shouting, stop being so different. Doesn't he understand that he is ruining his life, ruining everything? She straightens herself.

The door opens. A broad-shouldered man in an oversized jacket leans out.

'Madame Jensen? Good. Come in.'

He shakes her hand with surprising force. She recognises the head. They spoke when Rasmus changed schools, but since then she has only seen him from a distance at end-of-year assemblies.

'Come in, come in,' the head repeats. And then – in an unexpectedly harsh tone – to Rasmus: 'You stay there.'

As soon as she enters the office, she realises that this is something else, a new and more serious phase in their relationship.

The class teacher is already there, it is apparent they have prepared for the meeting thoroughly. The head nods at a Windsor chair, then sits down. She knows how it works; she was called to similar meetings at Rasmus's last school. It is a lonely feeling to be surrounded by people who doubt her ability as a parent.

The head closes the door.

'So,' he says. 'Yves, why don't you tell us what happened.'

Rasmus has been in a fight, he says, looking at the head, who nods. Then he hesitates, and appears to consider how to explain it.

She waits. She plays the role of a mother in a drama that she senses has already been written, and knows her task right now is to wait and listen.

It began when he heard shouting in the corridor, explains the teacher. When he went to check what was happening, three boys rushed past, chased by Rasmus. He managed to stop her son, who was very agitated. He was shouting and crying, it was hard to get through to him. But eventually he managed to get Rasmus to explain that the boys had been teasing him.

He clears his throat.

Rasmus was often alone at breaktimes. He often hung out on the football pitch. He had a ball he would dribble, shoot at goal, or just sit there with. On this particular morning, Rasmus had been on the football pitch as usual when three classmates had turned up. They began quarrelling. The classmates were making fun of him, according to Rasmus. They called him names. And they took his ball. He chased them. They let him catch up, only to wrestle him down, playfully. They held Rasmus down and took his shoes. Rasmus had chased them into the school in his stockinged feet. That was when the teacher had spotted them.

'Those trainers mean a lot to him,' she says quietly.

Rasmus loves his football trainers. It had become a tradition that Fredrik would take Rasmus to a sports store and let him pick out trainers and other kit. It was an endearing ritual between father and son. Whenever Rasmus grew out of his trainers or they were worn out, he would always get a new pair straight away – whichever ones he wanted. Fredrik enjoyed being with his boy and giving him that, and she explains this. The men nod approvingly. Rasmus got a new pair of trainers from his father two weeks ago, she explains.

They found the shoes round the back of the school building, the teacher continues. He had also rounded up the boys who had taken them, and forced all three of them to apologise to Rasmus. Then he had thought the matter was settled. But at lunchtime, the conflict had continued. The teacher wasn't sure exactly what had happened, but two girls said they had seen Rasmus hit one of the boys who had stolen his shoes with a stick. They had fetched a teacher who then stopped Rasmus.

A dejected silence lies between them. The head sighs.

'Naturally, the boy is in shock,' says the head. 'He'll need four stitches.'

They look at her lingeringly. She understands that they are expecting some sort of acknowledgement of guilt, and a desire for penance. *Your son*, say their expressions, *what's wrong with him?* But she isn't willing to say that her son is abnormal; never. She loves him more than they ever will.

She looks them in the eye and says she is sorry for what has happened.

'I'll talk to him.'

She senses immediately that it isn't enough, not even close. They want an apology that moves her. But she has no plans to be teary, she won't play along in their charade of crime and punishment.

'The boy's parents are going to report the matter to the police,' the head explains. 'This is a challenging situation for the whole school.'

So her son is guilty. What about his mirthful torturers? Saying nothing, she looks at the head, and the teacher, and reflects that they understand nothing at all about Rasmus. Why can't they see his pain and loneliness? He loves his trainers. He was defending them.

The head nods as if he has reached a conclusion.

'It's not certain that Rasmus can remain here,' he says, quickly adding that he understands this must be difficult to hear. But is it not surely for the best that they cut to the chase?

The class teacher nods in agreement. Given that conflicts can also occur after school, he says, when pupils are on their way home, he would prefer that Rasmus is picked up after school.

She nods.

On the way home, Rasmus sits with his back to her, looking silently out of the passenger-door window. He is withdrawn in a way that gives her the peculiar sensation that he has virtually left his body. She looks at his trainers; they are muddy.

'Have they teased you before?'

Rasmus says nothing.

There's no point. He won't answer now, she knows that. She notices how he withdraws deep inside himself. She usually thinks that it is as if he has discovered a gap in reality through which he squeezes and disappears. Left behind is his body, immovable and impregnable.

Jonathan runs calmly through Pimlico. A grey dawn sky arches above the city. He zig-zags between early-rising Londoners on their way to work.

Hercules is finally coming to life. He is breathing more easily, in a way he hasn't been able to since the leak. Waiting at a red light, he ends up in a group of around ten strangers and reflects that he is protecting these people through his work. Through Hercules, he will help to make his city and the entire United Kingdom safer. It's wonderful to be in London, he belongs in the city. Frances is here, his future is here.

When he reaches the riverside, he continues up onto Vauxhall Bridge. On the other side of the river looms MI6's headquarters. In the early morning light, the sandy-yellow, fortress-like building looks unreal. There is a peculiar irony in Her Majesty's most secret activities being housed in a building that mostly resembles a large and ugly cinema.

His life is so closely linked to Vauxhall Cross, he thinks to himself. This place governs his life and his dreams, the boundaries for his ambitions being drawn up in its offices. Every sentence he has formulated down the years in his reports is archived in its subterranean vaults. All the details of agents he has recruited, all the operations he has executed, all the secrets he has uncovered, are now stored within its walls where they will remain forever.

He turns and bounces down the stairs with light steps onto the riverside path.

He hears steps behind him and looks over his shoulder. He can see Robert. He shouts good morning and waits for him. Then they continue along the river past Battersea Park.

Robert is soon gasping. Jonathan is overcome by the temptation to tease his friend, and raises the tempo, enjoying Robert's strained puffing and panting. Simply to mark that he is not exerting himself anywhere near as much, he says between breaths that he has got up to speed on the rebels. It seems completely appropriate to use their agent, Vermeer, as an intermediary in their initial contact.

Robert groans. They have always been in tough and honest competition with each other. Robert would only get annoyed if Jonathan ran slowly, out of kindness. After three miles he further ups the pace, and notices that his friend can't keep up. He pulls away, rushing forth alone along the river for a few minutes, and all he can hear is his own sharp breathing. Rays of sunshine cut across the roofs of buildings, as if providing a victory greeting to him alone.

He slows down. After a long while, Robert catches up with him and stops dead, his face bright red.

Jonathan laughs.

'How are you doing, Robert?'

He moves a little on the spot to avoid getting stiff. There and then, he is stronger than his friend, more alive, less dying. He pats Robert sportingly on the shoulder. Then he stands with his legs wide apart and stretches.

'It's good that you don't want to use the House,' he says. 'I think we can carry out the operation just as well without it.'

Robert grimaces.

'Of course we're going to use the House,' he says, breathing hard.

Jonathan pauses in his exercises.

'That's not what you told Paddy.'

'What we say and what we do are two different things. Isn't that right, old boy?'

Robert breathes out, and wanders about.

Are they lying to the Ministry? His earlier sense of calm is erased.

'Robert, I think we ought to be completely honest with Paddy.'

His friend looks at him with a sombre expression.

'Is that what you think?'

He senses how something in him becomes still. Robert wipes his mouth.

'You like coming to London, don't you?'

The horrible realisation sinks through him like a lead weight. Oh no, he thinks. He doesn't want this to happen, but he can tell from his friend that he has not misunderstood what Robert is saying.

He looks down at the ground.

'I'm sorry, Robert.'

'No you're not, you shit.'

The morning feels at once grey and enclosed. Robert glares at him in silence. This wasn't how he wanted their cooperation to be. He cares about Robert, as a friend; he doesn't want to lose the only friend and rival that he respects. Now the thing he has imagined so many times is happening.

'I should have told you.'

'I've known for a long time.' Robert looks at him measuredly. 'Yes, Jonathan. You underestimate me.'

'But . . . how long have you known?'

Robert shrugs his shoulders.

'A year.'

'A *year*?'

All the times he has been in London, in meetings about the operation, Robert has known all along . . . How is that possible? They have been so careful, he shouldn't have known, but there is no doubt that Robert knows as he stands there with his arms crossed, watching him as if curious about his reaction. His friend's calm frightens him. Because if Robert has known everything for a year, then there is a reason he is telling him right now.

'You have betrayed me, Jonathan Green.'

The way Robert uses his full name makes him shudder. Now it is the Head of MI6's Middle East Department speaking. His friend takes a step towards him and stands there with his massive body looking down at him, in the way he imagines the crusaders once looked down upon their enemies.

'Why do you do this?' says Robert. 'You don't have many friends. Yet you piss on your chips like this.'

'Robert, I . . .'

He falls silent. The man standing there is no longer a friend but his master. Robert has got him exactly where he wants him, in a place where he can both control him and guarantee his loyalty. He feels himself involuntarily kowtowing.

'What do I have to do, Robert?'

'Fetch Pathfinder for me and take him to the House.'

'Robert, I don't want to use the House.'

Few people physically intimidate him, but when Robert leans forward and calmly repeats that he is to take Pathfinder to the House and use those methods necessary, he truly believes this man could harm him, punching him until his fists were bloody.

He won't be able to say no to Robert for a long time to come. This man has waited patiently, still, like a predator, in order to cut into his deceitful flesh at the right moment. Now he is part of Robert's metabolism.

There is a particular kind of despair when one realises one has made a mistake that will change one's life forever. This hopelessness is washing through him.

'Now let's run,' says Robert.

They continue in silence.

Back in the hotel room, he gets into the shower and lets the hot water pour over his head. He wishes he had never met Robert, but that is exactly what it is – wishful thinking. Because he would never have wanted not to have Frances. With Frances he has experienced something he thought he would never experience again: deep desire. Was it so wrong to pursue that desire? So long as Robert didn't know, there was no harm done; it could scarcely be called betrayal.

Frances must have told him, he thinks furiously.

But it doesn't matter. What is happening now has its own predetermined logic. Robert has been violated and is thirsty for revenge, and so he must placate his friend, he thinks as he rubs himself down with a flannel. The best way to deal with Robert is to let him exercise his power. He is ready to degrade himself if it means he can regain control of his life. He has no other choice, either; at least, not yet.

But the House, he thinks. Of course, he can bring Pathfinder in, and question the man. But not using Robert's methods – never.

But he is lying to himself, because Robert's methods were once his own, too. He doesn't want to think about it, but the thought forces itself upon him. When they opened the House, he was just as convinced as Robert.

The shame is like a clammy nausea. He doesn't want to remember.

He regrets that they created the House, regrets what happened there, regrets it so deeply that he thinks he should be absolved of guilt. Over the years, he slowly changed his story until he was almost convinced that he hadn't been a part of what happened there. Almost. Because, as the water rushes over him in the narrow shower cubicle, he remembers the House as it was.

It was his idea. He and Robert had been working in Damascus when the planes hit the twin towers in New York and transformed them into vertical mass graves. That very day he and Robert had been summoned to London, and in a heaving conference room they had become soldiers in the global War on Terror.

Their task, together with the Americans, was to work out how to hold and interrogate a certain type of captive flown in from Afghanistan and other war zones. Captives who couldn't be held in ordinary jails, they said. He remembers how he found a house on the outskirts of the Turkish city of Antakya. The building was in a perfect location, secluded and only half an hour from Hatay Airport, which handled some military aircraft. An hour's flight away was Incirlik Air Base, a hub for every military transport plane heading into and out of the region. He had found the House.

To begin with, clients streamed in. Nameless, numbered. The cells were built at breakneck speed. Then the interviews began. Robert was responsible for interrogation.

He remembered the interrogations. He had been present at some of them. He has told no one, but he was there. Initially, they were calm and effective conversations.

He remembers the hectic list-making. As the person responsible for administration, he was constantly occupied by all the lists of clients that needed to be signed in or signed out and transported onwards. The captives came from all walks of life: battle-hardened mujahideen and young shepherds, street vendors and agitated academics demanding their rights. They spoke Arabic, Pashto, Urdu, and broken English. All of them were, in different ways, involved in global terrorism.

He remembers the way they screamed at night. Grown men crying as if they were children. Then during the day too. It was beyond unpleasant. But how could he have stopped it? It wasn't a decision for him to make. It was London and Washington who set the boundaries. He talked to Robert about it; he protested, he believes he wrote to London and asked them to change the procedures, he is almost certain of it. Yet he cannot escape the aching sensation of guilt. He hates it. If he could, he would cut the guilt out of his body like an alien tumour. He is a good person.

He sinks to the bottom of the shower. Water pours over him.

Did he hit them? He can't remember. Well, he does remember: he hit them, but not often. With a rubber hose. He embraced the rage just like Robert, just like everyone else. They were filled with the same decisive anger; it was somehow wonderful. It was hard to explain to anyone on the outside. It was another world, an intense existence. He remembers the way Robert handled clients with such brutal elation, as if he had found in the House a home for his true self. Personally, he has changed; he will never be able to do the same thing again.

But perhaps something good came out of it all, he thinks. He wants to be able to think so. Because they had justice on their side. They were tasked with doing difficult work but for a good cause. What point is there in regret? It's better to forget.

The House was closed for several years, but Robert has now opened it back up again. But this time he won't do as Robert asks. This will be on his terms. He will conduct a civilised and professional interview with Pathfinder, and nothing more will be necessary. Once Pathfinder has told them everything, London will see Jonathan as the one who opened up an entire new front against Islamic State. He will extract the truth from Pathfinder. He *must* make the man talk of his own accord. And it will happen, he reassures himself, because the prisoner will understand he is at a disadvantage, and that the only thing that can save him is telling the truth.

The phone rings and rings. He can imagine a hundred reasons why Frances isn't taking his call and he can't bear any of them. He has to talk to her now, immediately; he doesn't care if she has a life beyond him. Robert has known for a year. A *year*.

Her voicemail greeting cuts in and he hears her voice, which with sardonic warmth asks him to send a text message instead, and it is as if the despair rises within him like a murmuration of birds. He can't stand being alone with this, he doesn't know what to do. Helplessly, he leaves an overly short message: 'Please call me.'

It is evening by the time he manages to get hold of her. They agree to meet in Soho. The mild autumn has lingered on into November and there are still guests sitting huddled under blankets in the restaurant's outdoor area. It could just be a normal encounter, him and her in the hubbub, surrounded by the happy buzz of other guests. But the very fact that everyone else seems so carefree makes him feel more downcast than ever. He buys them a glass of wine each at the bar.

'Why didn't you say anything?'

He looks at her sideways and notes that she looks like she is waiting for someone. Perhaps it is a glimpse of the future, he thinks bitterly. Sooner or later she will be here in her favourite restaurant in Soho waiting for a new man. He can't stand the thought. He carefully stretches out his hand and touches her fingers.

'You could have told me.'

She pulls her fingers away in irritation.

'Frances, please. A *year*.'

'What do you think, Jonathan? Robert isn't an easy man to live with.'

He nods. He understands that, naturally, but ...

She sips her wine and he watches her lips touching the fine glass. She is so beautiful. She is lonely, like him. He wants to frame it like that: at least they share unhappiness, now that they can no longer share anything else.

'Does it have to end?'

She looks at him as if he were being childish.

For those three years he has always thought that she wanted him more than Robert – that if it came down to a final decision, she would choose him. He has enjoyed the thought.

Frances looks at him over her glass as if he were miles away.

'We've had a good run of it,' she says. 'We had our moment.'

She could say 'Let's get married!' to frighten him. Joking, and then laughing at his worried expression before turning serious, perhaps it could be a joke she was serious about. He was happy when she said, 'Come here, kiss me.' He was happy with her, he could feel depths opening within him, emotions he had thought he didn't have. She made him into something other than the person he suspected he was – a hollow man. Somewhere, he hoped that Frances would one day say she wanted to leave

Robert, and perhaps, he now realises, she was waiting for him to say the same thing about Kate.

'It doesn't have to end,' he says quickly. 'If Robert just . . .'

Frances makes a tired gesture.

'Stop it, Jonathan.'

She has known everything is over for a year. She has known it would end like this and borne that burden alone. It is a form of love.

'How did he find out about us, Frances?'

So she explains how Robert discovered them. It was at the end of last summer, and they were in the house in Tuscany, as usual. In the evenings they sat on the terrace as the heat dissipated, and one evening Robert began talking about him. That Jonathan was such a good friend, she explains. Then Robert asked her what she thought of the breakfast at a hotel in Pimlico. He was hosting some visitors and needed a good hotel, he said. But she understood what he meant, because it was the hotel Jonathan usually stayed at in London, the same hotel he was staying in this time. Frances replied that she had no idea what the breakfast was like. Robert had gone and fetched her mobile phone and said that perhaps she wanted to ask Jonathan, that he was bound to know. Robert was toying with her, he knew exactly what was going on. She didn't know how he had found out, but he knew – after all, he was an important figure in MI6. They talked for a while; it was as if it were an interrogation. He was completely calm but she knew that if she provoked him he would smash her to pieces. He made her promise. '*Not a word*,' Robert demanded. And the way he had said it scared her. Then they had travelled home to London.

'I saw you that week,' he says.

So ever since then. They had spent a night together at the

hotel. He had been longing for her, and was angry and jealous because she had spent three weeks in Italy with Robert without replying to his messages. But when he saw her again he felt calm. He remembers her joking that they should each separate from Robert and Kate. And when he asked her whether she was serious, she laughed and became strangely sad.

'He threatened me, Jonathan,' she says angrily, her eyes filling with tears.

'I understand, Frances.'

'He's a bastard.'

And as if relieved to have finally said something true, she sighs deeply.

'I need to sort this out with Robert,' he says.

She looks at him with contempt.

'Robert,' she says, spitting out the word. 'Robert? What do you mean, sort out? Between men? Is that what this is about?'

What can he say? Yes and no. He is dependent on Robert. He works in a system he has to comply with, and Robert is his oldest friend and cannot become his worst enemy. He can't tell her about Hercules, about the leak – he would like to explain everything so that she could understand, but it is impossible.

'I need to deal with him.'

'You deal with Robert.'

Of course she is wounded. It is as if he can no longer say anything without it coming out wrong. He loves her, but she would only sneer if he said that now. Doesn't she grasp that this is also about his work? He has to try and mollify Robert. So far as he can tell, he has no choice.

Frances downs the last of her wine.

'We had a good run,' she says. 'We really did.'

111

Their home is bathed in evening sunshine. Bente finds Rasmus round the back on the lawn. He is standing dithering with a ball, staring down at his foot which is flicking the ball up in small movements. It looks easy. Ball and foot are drawn together like magnets. The ball falls down and the foot makes a quick, whipping movement to bounce the ball back up again. She stands quietly watching. The boy is skilled. Football is a limited element of existence, but he has mastered it entirely. He is calm and precise. If only he could handle other things in life with the same elegant ease.

'Rasmus, why don't you tell me about what happened today?'

The ball bounces against his foot. It flies up into the air at a slight angle; he follows it with his body and turns away from her. She waits – she doesn't want to provoke him – then asks him to talk to her.

'Why?' he mutters.

Rasmus is the most secretive member of their family. Perhaps she will never truly know who he is. Sometimes it is as if she were in mourning for him, as if he had disappeared – or rather, that inside Rasmus were another boy, trapped, whom she hopes will one day emerge. They are fantasies and daydreams about what he would be like if he wasn't the person he is. She rarely permits herself to think in those terms because it makes her sorrowful, and exhaustion creeps out of that sorrow. There is only one Rasmus.

The ball bounces up, higher this time.

She can't help herself. She quickly stretches out her foot making an interception, kicking the ball away and following in a rapid movement, rushing past him across the lawn. This is a whim and there is a risk that he will get angry – it's his ball after all – but she can't bear standing there watching the bloody football bouncing up and down for all eternity.

Rasmus shouts, and throws himself after her, but she manages to make a dummy move past him. He is quick and strong, and he reaches her. His hard body crashes into her with surprising force as he tries to get through to retrieve the ball. It has been a long time since she felt him that close to her. She laughs and kicks the ball away. It bounces down the garden and he rushes after it. But she isn't planning on giving up; it is as if even the game were to be taken seriously. She runs after him, and has almost caught up when he turns, already controlling the ball. She manages to catch a glimpse of him in a way she rarely does: his whole face is radiating concentration. He loves this, she manages to think to herself. She crouches instinctively when he takes aim and with a lashing, commanding movement fires a rocket of a shot towards her.

The ball hits her arm. It hurts. She slips and falls onto the grass.

He laughs. She is lying on her back and can feel the anger swelling up inside her. She is about to bellow at him that he's not allowed to do that, but there is something comical about her lying on the grass, an old mum, and something about the way the boy is laughing. She hasn't heard him laugh like that for a long time, so happy and liberated. This is her life, she thinks as she lies on the moist grass, and she begins to laugh, too, and suddenly she loves him again and knows that it is a long time since she felt like that. Tears form in her eyes and well up. The boy's face is glowing.

They sit next to each other on the grass at the bottom of the garden.

'What happened at school?' she asks him.

'They took my trainers,' he says.

And he ran after them. He hates them. He hates them because they're always messing with him, he says, and she feels the worry plummet through her. What does he mean, messing with him? He looks dejectedly at the lawn and says nothing.

He is lonely. She knows that now. She can imagine him in the playground, and how difficult it is for him to make headway in the crowd, she can see him alone on the football pitch with his ball, doing his monotonous movements, in his own world. She wishes she could put her arm around him and protect him from everything, climb into his isolation and tell him he isn't alone, but she knows she doesn't have that power. She can't help him when he furiously chases the people who say things to him and torment him, and that hurts her. In that moment, she also hates the boys, hates his school, and his teacher who won't help him.

She strokes his back to make sure he isn't subsumed by his rage; she wants him to be calm and tell her more. He was given his trainers by Dad, he says, lost in his memories. Dad gave them to him. He got them for being good, he says. 'Good and clever,' he says with a hiss.

She strokes his back.

'Why the hell did they need to take my trainers?' he exclaims.

The intensity of emotion is rising rapidly, and she interrupts and says in a calm voice that it was very stupid.

His face crumples. He sobs. She carefully puts an arm around his shoulders and feels him leaning towards her, seeking support. Dad gave him the trainers as a present, he eventually says. Even though he already had new trainers, he got given these ones. But he isn't allowed to say anything else.

She isn't sure she has understood properly, but tells him she understands and reassures him that he can tell her everything. He looks at her suspiciously. 'Yes,' she says, 'anything he tells Dad he can tell her.' She won't say anything, she promises.

So he explains. She sits stock-still next to him and listens.

He came home early one day. He was at school, but after lunch he didn't want to go to his lesson. He doesn't know why, he just didn't want to be in the corridor with all the others when the bell went. So he stayed on the football pitch and then he walked home. When he got home there was no one in. Daniel was still at school, and she and Dad were at work. But then he heard that there was someone in the house. There was someone who seemed to be coughing, as far as he could tell. He took a knife and hid in the living room.

Bente hardly dares to breathe, fearing that the very slightest movement, the smallest sound, might distract him and make him stop talking.

He sat there for quite a long time, he explains. Then Dad came downstairs. He was naked. There was a girl following him. He saw them stand on the stairs and kiss, and it was disgusting. He didn't know who she was and he didn't understand why Dad was with her. He could tell that they were having sex. They were at it for a long time. Then they caught sight of him and the girl screamed and disappeared, and Dad looked weird, as if he didn't

115

recognise him. Then he went into his room and started playing games on his iPad, because he didn't want to see them like that, he just wanted the girl to disappear. 'Whore' is the word he uses to describe her. 'She was probably some stupid whore.' He heard them talking to each other and they sounded angry, they argued, and after a while the house fell quiet and he felt better. Then Dad came and knocked on the door and wanted to talk to him. Dad said the girl had gone and explained that she was just a friend. But he looked strange and sounded strange, hoarse. 'Like this,' says Ramus, impersonating his father: '*Ah, ah.*' It was as if he had lost his voice. He didn't want to talk to Dad, he didn't want him in his room after he had been with that whore, he just wanted to know that she was gone. And Dad promised she was gone. He asked him who she was, and he said it wasn't anyone important, that it was him and Daniel that mattered. You're the most important people in the world, he said. Then Dad told him that the two of them now had a secret. Something no one else knew. And he asked whether he could keep that secret. If he was grown-up enough to not tell anyone about their secret. And he said he was. He remembers that Fredrik smelled different when he hugged him; he smelled sweet. Then they went and bought new football trainers – Dad let him pick any pair. 'I chose these ones,' he says pointing at his feet. He sighs.

'I haven't told anyone,' he says.

'But you could have told me? I'm your mother.'

He simply shakes his head. Why would that be a relevant reason?

Then he gets worried and asks her not to say anything. She has to promise not to say that he told her. She promises, and looks at the house, and wonders how it can remain standing in the evening sunlight, how it can look so sound when everything is rotten. 'I promised Dad,' he says again, as if now realising that he has said too much.

'Rasmus,' she says. 'You can tell me everything.'

But this merely makes him shake his head even more, because that's not how a promise to keep a secret works – if he isn't allowed to tell a secret to anyone else, then he isn't allowed to tell it to her, either.

'You're right,' she says, and he calms down.

The logic is heart-rendingly clear, she thinks to herself. It could cut an entire family in two.

Rasmus knows everything about trust. He is completely dependent on that trust enduring. She understands him, he uses exactly the same reasoning as her colleagues do in secrecy assessments.

She is in no hurry to go inside; better to sit on the grass with her son for a little while longer, because then there is no going back.

An enemy. That's how she has to regard Fredrik. In war, there is only one victory that is decisive – the final one. Now she knows what awaits her: a battlefield.

Her body is curiously heavy when she walks across the lawn and back into the house. Everything around her looks different and she sits down at the kitchen table as if numb. But the silence in the kitchen is too dense, and she gets up and starts to sort the larder before emptying the dishwasher and putting cups and glasses, plates and cutlery, in their rightful places.

All this will disappear, she thinks. Everything they have built together will come crumbling down. She's holding two wine glasses that should be in the cabinet above the kitchen counter, but she is tempted to crush them against the beautiful marble. Yet what is the point of shattering them? They're just glasses, and the damage has already been done.

He is with another woman. The thought is like a sharp kick to her stomach, and it winds her. What happens now? Her body becomes denser and more compact. She gasps for air. It is as if the room were closing in on her. *He is sleeping with someone else.* All the late work meetings and trips to Copenhagen ... Why didn't she spot it? Her heart pounds.

She can't stand still. It is like her body, in blind anxiety, is looking for a way out, and is driving her in and out of the other rooms in the house.

Rasmus comes in from the garden. She doesn't want him to see her like this, and she hurries upstairs. She feels the smooth painted surface of the banister against her hand, and shuts her eyes.

'Are you okay, Mum?'

Rasmus is standing at the bottom of the stairs and looking at her in concern.

It is as if her son is rescuing her. She smiles and says there is nothing to worry about.

'Dad should bloody well apologise,' he says as he passes her on the stairs. And it occurs to her that it must have been here that he was standing with the woman when Rasmus interrupted them.

She locks herself in the bathroom and sinks down onto the edge of the bathtub. It's all so hopeless, she needs to gather her thoughts in peace. In a few hours he will come home, and by then she needs to know what to do.

What has happened to my family? she thinks. A deep sense of despair runs through her, and slowly sets into a mess of hate that is as heavy as concrete. She could kill him. How *dare* he do this to her and the boys? She is calmer now.

Part of her is already thinking about tactics. She can hold him accountable, ask him, and then confront him with what Rasmus told her, but he will probably deny everything and claim that Rasmus was mistaken, that everything is a misunderstanding, that the boy is lying. Because if he were so inconsiderate as to buy the boy's silence, he will be prepared to defend every inch of his lie. What a shit! How could he do that to his children? Because she believes Rasmus; the boy doesn't lie, and he wasn't mistaken. But that isn't enough, she needs to tie Fredrik down with facts. Dissect his lies with the knife of truth.

She makes lasagne, and they eat at the kitchen table. She doesn't want the boys to notice anything, but they look at her quizzically as she talks about how fun it would be to see a film together.

The fourth chair is empty. Usually this would be nothing out of the ordinary, but it is as if she can't stand to see it like that.

'What's up, Mum?' says Daniel.

Rasmus gets up and leaves the table without a word. She lets him go. Daniel stays where he is and looks down at his plate of lasagne. They keep eating. The food is ungainly and difficult to chew. The mince and white sauce fill her mouth and disgust her.

'It's nothing to worry about,' she says.

She wishes she could say the words to overcome the silence she has accustomed them to. She just wants them to be happy. For them to live their lives with confidence. She reaches for Daniel's hands and caresses them, as if saying grace. The boy stiffens and slowly withdraws his hands as if they have been burnt.

After putting things away in the kitchen, she stands aimlessly looking out of the window. She should have been more vigilant; it is incomprehensible that he has been able to deceive her like this. But she has trusted him, and she has loved him. She barely remembers who she was before she met him. A whole life together, and now this. She drinks wine alone in the kitchen and watches bad TV. The boys come downstairs and say goodnight, none of them mentioning Fredrik at all, but she can sense their dogged worry.

It is almost midnight. Then she hears him at the front door. There is a faint 'Hello' from the hallway. She has been in the study, going over his social media again, raging, stubborn, and she gets up. Suddenly she doesn't know how she will manage to go down to meet him. No, she can't do it. She stands there, with blood rushing through her head, and pulls herself together to step forward, to go down the stairs and into the abyss.

Fredrik is standing in the kitchen drinking a glass of water.

'Rasmus was in a fight at school today,' she says.

He turns around and looks at her, worried. In the clear light of the kitchen he is transformed and has become a stranger. She has the uncanny feeling that he is someone completely different.

She explains what the teacher saw. Fredrik stands by the kitchen counter and listens with a serious expression. She notices that he prefers to look out of the window rather than looking her in the eye. 'Dear God,' he sighs. 'Yes, that's serious.' She has to fight to contain the impulse to wag her finger and say: '*You* did this. You have made Rasmus feel this bad.'

It occurs to her that Fredrik may have forced him to lie before. Perhaps Rasmus is actually a totally normal boy who shouts because he is being crushed by all the secrets.

'I'll talk to him,' he says.

'I've already talked to him. He has quite enough on his conscience.'

You can't be allowed to frighten the boy into yet more silence, she thinks. What a shit! How can he be so coolly calculating? It surprises her.

Does he suspect that Rasmus has told her? But if he is worried that he has been discovered, he is hiding it well. 'We have to hope he doesn't become more withdrawn,' he says with his back to her, and she has the strange feeling that his face is contorting, that he might turn to face her at any moment and smile scornfully.

The blue light bathes Fredrik's impassive face as he scrolls restlessly through his feed with a finger on his mobile. She pretends to read a book – it is a taxing charade. Then, finally, he puts away his phone.

She waits.

When she is sure that he is sleeping, she quietly sits up in bed. She can't help bending down to smell him, but he smells of his usual shampoo. Then she carefully puts her bare feet on the floor, and shuffles around the bed, taking care not to step on the points where the floor creaks.

His mobile is lying on the bedside table, her fingers find it in the darkness.

Standing in her study, she opens the safe and pulls out a leather case. She works quickly, opening the case on the desk, pulling out a USB and inserting a cable. Her fingers are deft. USB to cable, cable to phone. She has done it many times before, but never to her own husband. The mobile vibrates softly to confirm the code has been installed.

She waits for it to take hold – it should only take a minute or so. All is quiet.

That is how easy it is to cross a line. She has promised herself never to do this, but 'never' is a word for amateurs and those newly in love. Given the situation, targeted surveillance seems a reasonable measure. She doesn't want this, but Fredrik has forced her hand.

In the early days, he had always been curious. He often asked about counter-terrorism, bugging, and how to carry out surveillance. Was she a spy? Was she chasing Russians? She had laughed and, because of secrecy, all she would offer in reply was a smile and teasing kisses. Over time, he came to understand the depth of her silence. He realised that her work was not only a job, but a life that he would never share with her.

It is ready.

She is tempted to wake him up and show him how it works; he would have found it interesting. It is a strange idea to involve Fredrik in the surveillance of himself: a tickling rivulet between laughter and tears.

She sits in the dark in the study. She can see him on the screen as a stationary point on the map – or rather, his phone – fixed with precise coordinates south of Brussels. She really ought to wait to search his phone until she is in the office, a safe environment, but she can't wait.

She wants to go through all his messages and emails and find out exactly what happened, yet she hesitates, her mouth dry. She barely dares to look at the screen because she knows that once she finds the evidence for his infidelity the pain will be unbearable.

She hastily flicks through some messages and emails and soon finds a thread about meeting up for coffee. From someone called Chloë, a week ago. A few days earlier there is a brief and slightly flirtatious exchange with someone called Amanda about having lunch together. *Are you coming out with us?* asks someone called Alice three weeks earlier. Someone called Heloise asks one Thursday whether he is already at the restaurant. They send meeting times and addresses, links and files. She glances at the date and thinks back, trying to remember what he said at breakfast, what he was like when he came home. She reads the names and memorises them all. Alice. Catherine. Heloise. Marie, Chloë, Amanda. These women clearly know him, and she has no idea who they are. Judging by their tone, they are competent and intelligent women. Many of them seem to be colleagues as well as friends. Perhaps he's sleeping with all of them. She must consider them all as threats.

Naturally, he is in contact with a string of men: Jacques, Patrice, Thomas, Jean, Martin, Timothy, Mats. Some of the names are familiar and she wonders how much they know about what Fredrik is up to. Perhaps there is a silent agreement amongst them to keep her out of the loop; the thought is so humiliating that she is obliged to push it to one side.

It is as if she has glimpsed a completely new dimension of his life, populated by people she didn't know existed. Why does she know so little about her own husband? Even his tone is different. He is factual, briskly professional. Sometimes, in an occasional guarded joke, she is reminded of the Fredrik she fell in love with long ago and whom she thought she knew. Who is he, who is this enemy?

They are in a hurry the next morning. The rush provides a good cover. She makes coffee and talks to the boys and sets her gaze everywhere except on Fredrik.

On the way out to the car he says he is going to Copenhagen and will be gone for the night. She can see on her mobile that he has indeed entered several trips to Copenhagen in their shared calendar. What a bitter parody! The calendar usually gives her a pleasant feeling that their lives are in harmony; she wonders which of all his meetings and trips are actually real. A pulsing spot of pain is growing across the top of her head.

All four of them are in the car together, as a family, a habit that might stop at any moment. She watches Rasmus lumber towards the school playground and thinks sadly that all she wants is to catch up with him and hug him and tell him it will be okay.

After dropping off the boys, she and Fredrik head for the city centre. She bites her cheek, bringing tears to her eyes, because all she wants to do is scream, 'You shit! How could you?' But however exquisite that battle might be, she would lose it.

She drives through the city in silence while a light drizzle falls onto the windscreen. She even manages to be normal enough to say, 'Have a good time in Copenhagen, see you tomorrow.' She watches him hurry to the main entrance of the glass skyscraper in northern Brussels where he works, where Chloë and all the others are waiting for him.

Sitting in her office, she contemplates the nebula of thin lines on her screen. More than three hundred names joined together in a dense cosmos of phone calls and emails. Slowly, she twists and turns Fredrik's network and clicks on names and numbers.

Metadata refers to the impersonal, precise details of where, when, how long, and which phone numbers a mobile has been in contact with. Interpersonal communication as a mathematical model, free from emotions and always accurate. Metadata usually puts her in a good mood. She usually enjoys opening up a mobile and examining the vibrant life within. But this is different, because the surveillance she is directing at him also covers her and the boys. There they are: Bente, Daniel and Rasmus Jensen, reduced to nodes in his network.

She can see that he calls Mats for as many minutes as he calls her, and that hurts. He sends fewer messages to Daniel than to Chloë and Elisabeth. These are facts; she can't avoid these truths, but they are painful.

'Have you got a minute?'

Mikael sticks his head round the door. She quickly minimises what she is working on and turns in her chair.

He wants to discuss the leak. What should they do? Stockholm told them to do nothing, but during the morning they have been able to trace calls between Jonathan Green and the British Head of Middle East operations in London, Robert Davenport. Metadata, naturally. They know that Green is in London and certain sources state that an operation called Hercules has been given the go-ahead ...

Mikael falls silent.

She understands. The Brits are pushing on with the operation that the leak was warning them about. The one involving the House.

'Are we still contributing to British reconnaissance in Syria?'

'We're not, but Stockholm is. The National Defence Radio Establishment is providing London with some Russian military communications from across northern Syria.'

'So what do you think?'

They ought to keep an eye on Hercules, says Mikael, adding drily that they should probably inform Stockholm if it transpires that Sweden is contributing to an operation involving torture. He sighs. 'No one is altogether sure what the Brits are up to,' he says.

He is right, but she doesn't have the energy to deal with his reasoning right now, although he doesn't notice this. She hums and haws as he talks about analysing British intentions. Perhaps he ought to try speaking with Stockholm anyway. He could give it a try, at deputy level, he suggests.

'No,' she says briskly. 'I'll handle any contact like that.'

She sighs and thinks about what Gustav said to her. Stockholm will be carrying out a check on her family. Perhaps it has already begun; she wonders what they can see if that is the case. A family in crisis, presumably.

'Are you okay?'

She smiles quickly to counteract the resolute expression that is making Mikael look so puzzled. She is just tired, she explains. There's a lot going on with the kids.

'If there's too much on your plate just let me know.'

He smiles at her, and perhaps he is being considerate, but she can't help hearing a certain degree of calculation in his gentle tone. She knows he wants to be Head. And why should he make contact with Stockholm? she thinks – that's her responsibility. Perhaps he senses an opportunity to make himself more visible to the bosses in Stockholm. Perhaps he is hoping for close dialogue with Roland Hamrén or another chief in Stockholm who can offer him a leg up in his career. She needs him out of the office, he is too forward.

'Perhaps we could talk about this in a while?'

The question makes him start.

Then, finally, she is once again alone.

After working for a few hours on Fredrik's email, she doesn't know what to think. She has combed through them, using the usual analysis programs, but the result is not at all what she expected. Not a single email, not a single line has enabled her to discern an affair. There are no keywords hinting at anything more than flirting, no obvious sexual allusions and no patterns in how he maintains contact with the women to suggest that any of them are anything more than friends and colleagues.

She is certain that Rasmus wasn't lying to her. She knows her son: he saw Fredrik with another woman.

She dials an internal number.

'Anne, could you come in.'

A woman with a dark pageboy haircut appears shortly afterwards and closes the door behind her. Anne is one of the new recruits, a sharp young expert specialising in the analysis of mobile traffic. 'Here,' she says to her, handing over a note with Fredrik's number. Could she speak to a technician and do a thorough examination of this mobile?

Anne glances at the note.

'Make sure you get everything.'

The woman nods.

'What are we looking for?'

'Intimate relationships.'

Throughout the morning, she manages to retain control over her finely calibrated facial muscles. She chairs a meeting discussing next year's budget. She gives no hint of what is going on. But then it is as if she were struck down by grief. She can't do it any more; she gets up and reaches for her coat.

It is a relief to get home; she practically collapses onto the sofa. Just for a while, she thinks as she closes her eyes.

It is raining.

But she has been woken by a different sound. Voices, from one of the rooms.

She has just managed to sit up when the basement door flies

open. A girl with short dark hair bounds barefoot into the hall. She is half naked, wearing only a bra and pants.

She stares at the giggling, dishevelled creature reaching out a hand and shouting down the stairs. A moment later Daniel appears, his upper torso bare. They kiss each other ravenously.

She doesn't know where to look, it is too intimate. He is already a young man with another woman, she feels embarrassed to see him like that.

They don't notice her at first. Then it is as if her body were broadcasting its presence and makes them look up. The girl lets out a shrill cry and huddles up with her arms over her chest, while Daniel merely stares at her in amazement.

'You're home.'

'Yes, I'm home.'

The girl's face is burning red and she looks like she wants to become invisible. She is familiar – is it one of Petra's daughters? Daniel has slept with her – she can't stop the thought.

'This is Julia,' says Daniel flatly. 'My girlfriend. Julia, my mother.'

'Hello, Julia.'

The girl mumbles a hello.

'Why didn't you tell me?'

'I don't know. Do I have to?'

He glowers sulkily at her. The abrupt tone is so unlike her beautiful, guitar-playing Daniel. It hurts her; she has a right to know who is coming and going in their home.

They stand silently before her, embarrassed but still defiant.

'Julia would like her earring back.'

At first she doesn't understand. The one in the car?

Daniel nods. Yes, the pearl earring.

'Have you been in our car?'

He doesn't answer. But she can tell she has guessed correctly, because the girl becomes slightly redder and sighs anxiously.

'You drove it.'

'Yes, but only round the block.'

'Are you out of your mind?' she roars. 'You don't have a driving licence. You could have run someone over – *in a bloody Security Service car, you brat*,' but she doesn't add the final bit.

'But nothing happened.'

She has no intention of even gracing such an idiotic statement with a response. Without saying a word, she gets up and fetches the pearl earring from where she left it in the bathroom cabinet. So it was nothing more than that, she thinks to herself. She can hear them whispering to each other, but when she returns they immediately stop and gaze at her downheartedly. 'Here,' she says, handing the jewellery to the girl.

Daniel is sulking in the basement after she called him an idiot for driving her car without permission. As for her, she is wandering around the ground floor and is angry. What is happening? Daniel takes his girlfriend on a bloody joyride in the Section's car and Fredrik is sleeping around and lying to her – no fucking way is he in Copenhagen today, she thinks to herself. She wishes the pearl earring had belonged to the other woman and that she had found it a couple of weeks ago so that Rasmus could have avoided having to be the bearer of his father's rotten lies. She is tempted to line up Fredrik and Daniel and hold an interrogation that lasts until every untruth has been dissected.

And where is Rasmus? He ought to be back from school. Perhaps he is at a friend's house?

'Do you know where Rasmus is?' she shouts into the basement, only to be met with injured silence.

Is it only her who wants a family? It feels like they are against her. Perhaps Fredrik and the boys have quietly agreed to leave their small community and leave her as the only one under the illusion that they belong together – it wouldn't surprise her.

She calls Rasmus but his phone is off.

They can all go to hell, she thinks to herself.

The rain has eased off as she walks to the car. She decides to go for a drive – just out to the fields, perhaps she'll take a walk. She glides through the suburban streets and on to Waterloo. She knows there was something she was meant to remember, but she has no idea what. It is only when she has parked the car and started walking, and reached the middle of the fields, that it hits her. She stops and emits a loud shout.

The school playground is deserted. Large puddles have emerged from the asphalt as she hurries towards the school. It closed more than two hours ago; perhaps he's taken the train home with one of his classmates.

But there, sitting on a bench, is Rasmus.

'Darling, I'm sorry,' she says. 'I forgot.'

He doesn't return the embrace and looks at her dejectedly.

'Sorry,' she repeats, as the terrible mother she is. She completely forgot the new routine she had agreed with the teacher.

'Why didn't you call?'

He despondently shrugs his shoulders. 'Mobile died.'

She can't bear that he has been sitting here alone for several hours waiting and that it is her fault. He could have gone round to one of his friends', she says, putting an arm around him.

Then he looks at her and seethes: 'So it's my fault?' The teacher said he wasn't allowed to go home with the others and he promised. She promised to pick him up.

The rain patters onto her head as she walks behind him towards the car, the shame dripping down her.

She opens her eyes.

The evening was subdued, none of them had the energy to talk properly to the others. She had a bath and fell asleep due to gloomy exhaustion. But now she is wide awake.

An idea has taken hold of her and will no longer fit into her dream, so it wakes her. She quickly gets up and puts on her dressing gown.

The night air is chilly and raw after the rain. She hurries down to the car, standing there glittering with rain.

The ice-cold surfaces inside the car make her shiver. Sitting in the front seat she turns on the satnav. She has to click around for a bit until she finds the log. Here are the last fifty journeys made by the car, neatly listed with coordinates and time stamps. Why didn't she think of this sooner? The information was there all along, literally under her nose. The car records all movements, every metre, with exact time stamps. Every route is tracked using GPS and inscribed as a blood-red line on a map. The metadata of daily life.

She quickly finds Daniel's little outing, down the street and over to the square, around the houses and back again.

Fredrik's trips are also here.

She slowly goes through the car's latest routes. She feels calm and focused now. She can see the journey to and from the supermarket on Saturday neatly recorded, and is struck by the fact that she used exactly the same route both the Saturday before and the Saturday before that. She can see their morning drives to school and work. In the last week they have made twenty-five trips in the car. She thinks they often do things carelessly and without planning, but this shows their lives to be more regular and predictable. They move through their daily lives with few deviations.

But now she is searching for deviations.

When she reaches last Wednesday she finds one. Just before five in the afternoon, the car drove from Fredrik's office north of Brussels to a location in the city centre. The journey took just under half an hour. Then the car was parked there for more than three hours. It then departed from that location at twenty to nine in the evening and came home.

Fredrik had the car that day. She remembers him complaining the week before about how much he had on his plate at work, yet he left the office early. And he didn't drive home but went somewhere in central Brussels, near Grote Markt.

Perhaps they have friends who live there, she posits. Or maybe it was a client meeting. But what kind of client? It's so miserable, so dirty, she already knows what this is. She pulls a pen out of the glovebox and writes down the coordinates and times on the palm of her hand.

She continues to go through the log, her fingers trembling.

The Friday before, the day Rasmus said he saw Fredrik with another woman, she finds yet another deviation. Fredrik drove them to school and then to the place in Brussels where he usually drops her off. But instead of continuing north to the financial district, he then turned around and drove home. She scrolls on through the log: the same thing the most recent Friday.

And that evening they went to the embassy reception.

The windscreen has steamed up, like a compassionate shield. She turns off the satnav and tries to control a dull rage.

She gets out of the car. It is still dark. There is a thick blanket of cloud above the house, but beyond it she can perceive a paler blue tone shimmering in the air, the hint of a new day. She can't change what has happened, it is the future she must be victorious over. She pulls her dressing gown tight around her; the chilly morning air is making her thoughts take a more distinctive form.

In the warmth of the hallway she stops when she catches sight of her coat hanging beside Fredrik's. He is lying to her, and he is also lying about the mobile. She is *certain* that she didn't put her phone in his coat pocket.

On Wednesday, Fredrik left the office early. But she remembers clearly how he complained that he had to work late that day. Instead, in the early afternoon he drove to the city centre. Sitting at the kitchen table with her mobile, she looks up the coordinates for that location.

A hotel.

Lies, as well as the art of discovering them, are something she is the master of. She can feel the contours of deceit.

Jonathan's mobile rings twice before falling silent. He knows the signal; he has been waiting for it. He quickly packs and a little while later he steps out into the hotel's underground car park. A car rapidly flashes its headlights.

He gathers his thoughts, everything in him focusing on what awaits him. There is a freedom in getting to work: the avoidance of private life with all its emotions and difficult relationships, becoming instead part of an organisation.

The two men in the front seats greet him without introducing themselves. They are handlers, logisticians.

They drive him north through London in a long unbroken silence before hurrying him into a ground-floor flat in Lambeth, near the Imperial War Museum. The flat is big and dark, and exudes dust and worn elegance. No one lives here. He thinks it must be part of the estate of an old, eccentric woman who lived alone for her final decades.

Once inside the flat, the handlers relax. They lumber around checking everything works – heating, water – and they put some food in the fridge. He knows the procedure and gives them his mobile and watches them take out the SIM card and battery and put everything in a bag before handing him a new phone. It is clean and encrypted, says one of the handlers. And probably bugged, he reflects to himself. The other one explains the usual rules of conduct and he listens politely – he knows them, but the rule is that they must always be said. Don't leave the flat, don't call outsiders, in an emergency just call the number saved on the mobile.

The pipes are whistling. Around him there is a normal working day taking place. He taps the pipes gently. 'Be careful,' says one of the handlers. 'And please stay away from the windows,' says the other. 'Don't make a racket. Rest instead.' He says that he knows all of this, but they merely nod. He will receive more information shortly.

'Grandma will be here soon,' says one of them.

Then they leave. He sinks into a shabby dark plush armchair.

A little while later a woman in a suit arrives. They exchange greetings; she is Grandma – the coordinator. She looks at him curiously, as if assessing whether he seems ready.

He knows the procedures, but he is still nervous because he is unpractised. Daily life at the embassy has left him untrained.

Grandma places a garment carrier over the back of a chair. It is time.

He changes in the adjacent room. It feels like shedding his skin. It is a form of liberation – right now he doesn't want to be himself. Checked shirt, brown chinos, burgundy tie and tweed jacket. He examines himself in the mirror on the wall. There he sees a man with short reddish-brown hair and a pale, nondescript face.

He tries a smile. No, he thinks, too broad – he looks like a salesman. He smiles again. This time it is better, the face has a softer, milder expression.

He could very well be an academic. An ordinary man with an ordinary life. He takes a step closer and sees a chilly severity in the gaze. It is too tense, too vigilant. He closes his eyes. Then he opens them again and looks at himself as if he were a man who sees the best in everyone. Who wants the best. Who listens. The face has to be open, he has to make Vermeer feel safe. Is this a man radiating assurance? Warmth?

His eyes are softer now, the features more receptive.

One might see him as a caring person. A therapist, perhaps. That's good.

Grandma gets up from a chair and looks him over with a frown. 'Stand still,' she says. He stands in the centre of the room and lets her look at him, as if he were a mannequin. She evaluates him with a practised eye, loosening his tie slightly, putting two pens in the breast pocket of his jacket and then nodding.

'Smile,' she says.

He smiles.

The coordinator doesn't reciprocate but gives it her objective consideration. Then she puts a laptop on the dark dining table. 'Read this,' she tells him. It is as if they are staging a theatrical performance, and the screen sets out his role. He is part of an illusion, a secret production for which everyone and no one in particular is the audience. She waits while he reads the instructions.

'Do you know what to do in an emergency?'

He nods. During an operation, even the ordinary urban environment must be considered enemy territory. He is no longer Jonathan Green, but a man seeking medical care, a man who will introduce himself as George if asked and will show fake ID before disappearing, shedding his skin and dissolving in a string of controlled retreats. He has a layer of identity concealing a second layer of identity that conceals the Jonathan Green he actually is, and inside Jonathan Green are things he has never

136

told anyone. No one truly knows who he is. No one will ever get to know him deep down; not even he really knows who he is, where his emotions are rooted.

Grandma asks him a question.

He focuses on her.

She looks at him sceptically, holding out a car key. Is he okay? He smiles. How long have they been standing there? He's fine, he says, taking the key. Just fine. And somehow he means it, because he feels nothing: he is someone else now. They are ready.

Be prepared, says the voice on the phone. Pick-up will take place shortly. He waits. In his inactivity he tries to avoid thinking about Robert, Frances and everything that is part of his own life.

Instead, he thinks about Vermeer. Ever since he recruited the young student in Damascus twelve years ago, Vermeer has worked for them. Being an agent for MI6 is a real secret – the kind you take to the grave. Extremely few people will ever be aware of Vermeer's secret life, it is as if it has barely existed. He will age inside his secrecy, and when he dies, an archive of secrets never told will disappear with him.

He remembers Damascus and the daily game of cat and mouse with Assad's Moscow-trained security services. It had been an excellent training ground. The threat on the streets and in the echoing corridors of the Syrian state was constant.

Hours pass. He drinks water from the tap in the kitchen and wonders whether to call Frances, but suffocates the insane impulse at the last moment.

Then, finally, a text message: *Taxi outside*.

And outside the main door there is a polished black cab waiting.

He allows himself to be driven towards the city centre in

silence. What happens next has been predetermined down to the last detail and he is still fascinated by how smoothly the practicalities run. An intricate plan has been built around him and there is a satisfaction to being at its centre.

He leans back.

Will Vermeer distrust him? It has been more than ten years since they met.

His thoughts move quickly and clearly as he plans, trying to predict unexpected twists. Traffic is heavy. He is worried they will be late, but the traffic begins to move more freely.

The taxi stops outside Harrods and he pays as if it were a real taxi, because everything is a cover now – even the smallest details should conceal what is actually happening. Then he gets out into the crowds rushing by.

Inside the department store he saunters through the different sections, matching the tempo of the people around him. He notes a man wearing a practical windcheater moving in his vicinity, then a woman in a pale cashmere coat. There are intelligence services who would be interested in his meeting. If he is spotted he has to abort. He stops in the concession for a conservative menswear brand and looks over his shoulder: the woman walks past.

Two well-turned-out men smile and welcome him with a nod – in their eyes he is a prospective customer. He strolls through the concession looking at the jackets. No, he's just browsing, he says before leaving and moving on. No one seems to be following him. He changes floor and goes into the concession for an Italian brand, chooses a shirt and tries it on in one of the cubicles. When he comes out he sees nothing that concerns him. A tailored light-blue shirt – he buys it and does a lap of the floor to be sure that the signal has got through. One bag means all clear, two bags means abort.

He takes the lift down to the car park and emerges into the symmetrical darkness.

He drives east. The traffic is clear as he keeps an eye on the cars in his mirrors. There is potential meaning in everything: a green car with two passengers. A motorbike thirty metres behind him. A van in the outside lane with tinted windows. Coincidences, patterns. For those unable to interpret courses of events, there is nothing to see. A professional opponent can melt into the masses, disappear chameleon-like into the flickering events.

He pulls off the main road.

Just a few minutes left now. He parks, and walks languidly up the stairs and into the entrance of the hospital. He is on time. At reception he asks for directions to the Ear, Nose and Throat clinic and at that moment is just one of the many visitors, clad in a reality clinging to him like a second skin, intensely real in the way that only a carefully planned manipulation can be.

Corridors. A lift.

Up, out.

Empty dayrooms, sunshine penetrating through walls of frosted glass.

Around him are doors into patients' rooms, staff rooms, shadowy beds with still bodies. Two nurses in blue uniforms pass by talking to each other and ignoring him. A doctor steps out and they almost collide, smiling briefly at each other as a form of polite reflex. He glides through their world, sailing calmly towards his target.

The waiting room is lit in such a way that every particle is illuminated. Opposite him is a woman in a thin down coat. She is reading a gossip magazine. He is in position.

He is early and has time to pop to the toilet. There he is, in the mirror above the basin: a middle-aged man with calm, honourable facial features. All he can see is impenetrable ordinariness. Good. He returns to the waiting room.

'Simmons?'

For a fraction of a second he is out of character, he is just Jonathan, sitting in a waiting room. Then he reacts and becomes George Simmons with a slight smile. The nurse shows him into a consulting room. Before she disappears through a white door, she tells him to unbutton his shirt.

Alone in the room, he takes off his jacket and button-by-button exposes his pale, freckly torso. Then he sits down on a chrome metal stool and waits. Like a patient, just as it should be.

The first time he met the man to whom they assigned the code name Vermeer had been in Damascus. They had been tipped off about him by their networks. The man they met in a luxury hotel was a young Syrian studying medicine. A thin and slightly old-fashioned, upright young man, completely inexperienced, one of the many idealists dreaming of a free Syria. But they had tested him. Jonathan can remember the chilly winter Friday after prayers when they had flown him to a doctors' conference in Dubai and given him his first assignment. Over the years he had been able to use his position as a doctor in the Syrian army to pass them useful information. When he had become the personal physician for a number of generals, he became a golden calf for MI6. They gave him the code name Vermeer because the intelligence he provided them with was so clear and precise, filled with distinct details. As the years had passed he had given them insight into the health and medication of the Syrian elite, their most intimate secrets. Then, when the war had come, he had joined the opposition with his brother. Then he had fled.

It has been more than a decade but Jonathan still immediately recognises the doctor who enters through the door. The same gangly build, the same well-groomed beard. He is the same, but the lines around his mouth are sharper. He has the seriousness of a grown man, but there is also something haggard about him. The war claims victims even amongst those who successfully escape.

'It's been a long time,' says Vermeer, standing in the doorway with a cautious smile.

They shake hands. They always refer to him as Vermeer, and it is strange to see him here in a British hospital with a name badge on his white coat showing his real surname, Malki.

Jonathan cares about all the agents he recruits, but this man has always brought about a particular sense of attachment in him. There is something about Vermeer's mild manners that makes him want to protect him, take care of him. He admires Vermeer for his precision – how he got his code name – but his agent has no idea that he holds a special place in the hearts of Vauxhall Cross, which is for the best as it would only make him nervous.

In the Damascus years he would lie awake at night worrying about Vermeer ahead of assignments. When his agent was scared, it was up to him to calm him down. He was Vermeer's protector, charged with providing clean phones, changing addresses and leading the Syrian security services astray. He would love to reminisce, but there isn't time.

Vermeer gets out his stethoscope and leans forward, putting the cool membrane against Jonathan's ribcage.

'Malki, we need you.'

The doctor calmly moves the stethoscope to a new point on his chest. He is listening.

'We need to establish contact with your brother's friends.'

He meets Vermeer's gaze. The dark eyes are close.

'Nothing more than that. Just contact.'

Vermeer moves the stethoscope.

'I have nothing to do with them.'

He notices that the man is afraid. Afraid that the phantom before him will suck him into a war that will ruin everything he has laboriously built up, forcing him back to what he left behind. He is Dr Malki – he doesn't want to be Vermeer again.

'You have to,' he says in the same calm voice he used to use with Vermeer. 'All we need is contact with Ahrar al-Sham, immediately.'

'But they'll know . . .'

Worry shines in his eyes, his pupils trembling from the force. Vermeer shakes his head.

He has to get through to him, avoid him withdrawing. In a flash he puts a hand on the back of his agent's neck in a protective and dominant gesture. He feels the man tense before relaxing and letting himself be steered.

'You are one of my best agents,' he says quietly. 'I have come here because our government needs you. Just do it and then carry on with your life as normal.'

'I can't.'

'Remember, we can influence who is considered appropriate to provide specialist medical care in this country.'

He lets go of him. Vermeer straightens himself. It is so sad to have to resort to blackmail, but if he is choosing between this doctor's future and the security of the country, then the choice is easy.

'They'll know I'm working for you.'

'No,' he says with a smile. 'Suspect, perhaps. But nothing more.'

Then he explains that later this evening the police will come to his home. They will interview him, his wife and his eldest son. He sees Vermeer's eyes widen in protest but merely raises his hand to calm and finish his point. The visit from the police is part of a national counter-terrorism initiative. The police will make a string of arrests across England and will also take him to the station, before releasing him later tonight. There is no need to worry, there are no suspicions or charges against him or his family.

'That's your cover.'

Vermeer glowers at him, but he understands.

No one expects Dr Malki, brother of a Syrian Islamist, to be one of MI6's most skilled agents. By strengthening his identity as a Muslim being discriminated against, he is absolved of all suspicion.

This is something he teaches his agents: use the truths of life as cover. Don't make things up if you don't have to, because all fabrications are fragile. Better to play on people's expectations and prejudices. Make the enemy think you are harmless, or even a friend. Then they will be ignorant of your true intentions.

He whispers the message Vermeer is to give the rebels, word for word. 'The British Government sends its greetings to the leaders of the Ahrar al-Sham coalition. One million pounds sterling for the man from Raqqa they are holding captive.' He whispers the prisoner's name. Then a phone number.

'Can you remember that?'

Vermeer gives a tired nod.

Someone knocks on the door.

'I'm busy,' he shouts angrily, once again becoming Dr Malki.

The nurse's voice is muffled by the door as she says sorry. The red light outside the door indicating the room is occupied is illuminated but the door is unlocked. Someone might come in by mistake.

143

Vermeer glares at him, the stethoscope useless in his hands. The slightly yielding expression previously on his face has been surprisingly quickly replaced by a tough vigilance that reminds him that this man, despite his doctor's coat and timid manner, is an experienced resource.

He gets up. He would have preferred to leave him as a friend, but it can't be helped.

Back in the flat after the meeting with Vermeer, he paces around the room, waiting. He is part of an operation now and must be protected from all forms of surveillance, he *knows* that, but he doesn't want to be kept like this: it feels as though someone were shovelling soil on top of him; the flat is suffocating him. He roots through the kitchen cupboards. He is lucky and finds an open bottle of whisky and pours himself a dram.

He phones Grandma and asks for permission to take a walk. She issues a flat refusal. She will be in touch when he is needed, she says hanging up. *When he is needed.* As if he were a circus animal being kept in anticipation of the next number.

It is a truly horrid feeling knowing that Robert wants to do him harm and he tries to handle it by drinking another whisky. It is Robert's coolness that frightens him – he didn't get angry. If Robert had shouted and punched him he would have felt calm. If only he could sit down and talk to Robert, he thinks. After all, they are friends. If only Frances would give him a little time to deal with Robert, they could solve all of this together.

Darkness falls. He is sitting in the armchair drinking the last of the whisky.

He decides to ignore the fact that his phone is bugged. He calls Frances.

It rings. Just as he is about to accept with disappointment that she won't answer, she picks up.

'Hello,' he exclaims. 'Are you at home?'

He regrets it instantly, it's a stupid question and he doesn't want to know.

Yes, she is at home, she says quietly. He can hear her walking through rooms, perhaps she steps aside into the bedroom; he imagines her there. It is strange how familiar her voice is – that soft, lingering tone.

'I didn't have anything much to say.'

Somewhere in the room behind her is Robert, he can hear the faint sound of music on the stereo. He can picture exactly what it looks like, how beautiful she is, how distant yet close she is.

'Jonathan,' she says. 'It's not appropriate for you to call.'

'I understand.'

So formal. When had their relationship ever been appropriate? But his words can no longer spellbind her, he has nothing that impresses her. He wants to say that he loves her, but it is too late – it would do no more than awaken mild irritation in her. He realises that he shouldn't have called, but he doesn't want to accept that this is over – not like this.

'I won't bother you again.'

She doesn't reply. Dear God, he really has lost her. Perhaps they were never a couple but only really two individual people who needed each other. But she meant something to him, she reminded him of something he had lost in himself. He closes his eyes and can imagine her face close to his, like when they made love in the darkness.

'Frances?'

'I have to hang up now.'

'Can we speak later?'

'Of course,' she says without meaning it.

He bids her a good evening and hangs up.

Have a good evening! What is this meaningless drivel? He should have said something she could take away with her, he should have said: 'I love you. I don't know whether I can bear never seeing you again.' Words like that had always felt like clichés and embarrassed him, but he should have said them. 'Why are you staying with Robert? Was I nothing more than a distraction for you? A diversion? A counterweight to him?'

That's it, he thinks, as if forced to minimise the import of what has just happened. He can picture her putting the phone down and going back to Robert. Perhaps Robert asks who it was and she lies, saying it was a friend inviting her to lunch tomorrow, and order is restored.

He needs to get out.

He twitches the heavy curtains and looks down into the deserted, dark, rain-soaked street. He can't see a guard – there is no one sitting in any of the cars. He puts on his coat and wonders which way is best before remembering that the kitchen has a door opening onto a small back garden.

The fresh air is wonderful. He moves quickly over the wet grass and finds a narrow gate in the brick wall. But there is a code lock. He swears quietly, afraid that it is all for nothing, but he isn't planning to give up now – he takes a few steps back, takes a run and throws himself up, clawing at the ivy climbing the wall, and heaves himself up with a celebratory and boylike sense of freedom. Then he swings down on the other side.

He is in the small lane behind the large, well-to-do houses, and soon he is walking through the streets near Paddington. Standing on that desolate residential street he is free, but he is immediately unsure of what to do with his freedom. Free from what? He doesn't know how to extract himself from the slow car crash that is his life at present. But he pushes all the gloomy thoughts to one side and focuses on a simpler and more achievable goal – getting drunk.

He walks along a few streets. Wasn't there a pub near Warwick Avenue? He has a vague memory of a picturesque side street where he and Kate once had a drink – back when he had looked forward to having a drink with her. But it is as if the pub has been swallowed by the ground – perhaps it has closed down, like so many other things.

The streets filled with dark, leafy trees and tall white stone façades stretch away from him in all directions. He can't risk a taxi, so he walks. After a while he reaches the main thoroughfares and wanders along feeling like an idiot. If only he could find a pub. All he wants is a beer, but it is as if the city itself is against him.

It is so unfair that Robert hates him; wouldn't it be beautiful if Robert just let Frances go so they could all be happy? It is a fantasy and he wishes it was true. Lost in his thoughts, he walks towards Paddington and jumps when someone right beside him says his surname – not his real name but the false one being used for the operation.

'Bradswaithe!'

He looks up and has no time to react before the handlers are standing in front of him. One of them takes hold of his arm.

'Let go of me!' he hisses, before realising how absurd the situation is and calming down. 'Yes, yes,' he mutters, getting into the backseat of their car.

The other handler passes him his mobile.

'Grandma wants you to call her.'

Where the hell did you go? says the coordinator when he gets through.

'No more bloody nonsense like that,' she adds. If he needs exercise he should do a few laps of the garden.

He apologises.

Stay sharp, she interrupts. Vermeer has been in touch. A representative of Ahrar al-Sham is willing to make contact with them shortly, so they need a suitable meeting place.

Give me three options, she says, *and get back to me.*

At night he is back in the House. He walks down the stairs. His fingers search the rough wall. He has to go a long way down – it is as deep as a well. The basement chill fills the darkness. This is somewhere you perish. He still has to go all the way to the bottom because he knows that is where it all begins. Yet he just wants to walk away from it and up to the light. He is scared. He reaches the final steps, and then he is lying on the floor, his face pressed against the stone floor, and someone says to him: 'Take hold of the arms. Hold him down.' His legs kick, searching for footing. He writhes; they can't hold him down because then he won't know what's going to happen. An arm strikes him in the dark. He defends himself, and the arm flounders like a disgusting worm in the darkness. He has to stop it. The arm gesticulates and waves in the air, then he grabs hold of the wrist. 'I have it,' he shouts. He holds on so tightly his fingers go numb. 'Hold him down,' someone shouts. 'Let go of me,' he screams, trying to get loose. He runs, rushing up the stairs; it is all so hopeless. The stairs are steep, he struggles to make progress. There is no mercy. He knows that if he stops he will be lost. Then he stops. He should leave, but he can't. He slowly starts going down the stairs again and wakes up panting and knows he can't get out, that it won't end. The ruby-red numbers at his bedside show it is just after five in the morning. The room is silent.

It is early but the young analyst Anne is already waiting on a chair outside Bente's office. When she spots her boss, the young woman gets up. It almost looks like she is going to offer a salute. With a subdued good morning she follows Bente into her office.

Overnight, they have succeeded in breaking into the encrypted parts of the target's phone, she explains once the door is closed. Fredrik Jensen – the target, she corrects herself with an embarrassed grimace – uses a messaging app called Signal.

Bente is familiar with Signal. Many criminals and members of terrorist networks use the service since its encryption is so powerful.

'I understand. Show me.'

Anne sits next to her at the computer and opens a program that provides a view of Fredrik's phone. She is serious in a way that only young people can be, unused to working directly with her boss and therefore unnecessarily formal. 'Do you want me to show you?' she says, and Bente waves impatiently. 'Yes, yes, show me now.' She scrolls down the never-ending thread of messages on the screen.

Darling, Fredrik has written to the woman.

A little further down he refers to her as *my kitten*. The other party in the thread is a woman calling herself Jane Smith. The woman caresses him with words. *You're beautiful*, she says. *Handsome*.

It is beyond doubt what she has in front of her. His deceit is sorted into neat chronological order; there are more than five hundred messages. She forces herself to read on; perhaps because she needs to see the honest, pure filth, so that she could later say there was no turning back. This is the end of the relationship she thought was a constant, the love between her and Fredrik that she had believed was only between them. One heart, sent at 9.56.

Darling, I miss you.

'Is it all from his mobile?'

'Yes. And only from Signal. They only communicate using that service . . .'

The analyst looks anxious. This is naturally a strange situation for her. They are talking about her boss's husband as the subject of surveillance.

'Start from the beginning.'

The very first message is three weeks old. It is from the woman, Jane: *I would like to see you again.*

She tries to pretend that she is working, that this is just another mobile phone they have infiltrated. She wants to remain professional, but the words – the damned words – eat into her with their awful silkiness and sexual charge. She can't contain herself. She hadn't expected him to be so uninhibited in his deceit, as if nothing else were at stake.

I want you.

See you tomorrow? Heart.

She excuses herself, half choking, and just makes it to the toilet. She had yoghurt with fruit and a cup of tea for breakfast and now it sprays out of her in a brown mess. Afterwards she rinses her mouth, washes her face and listens attentively for any sounds in the corridor outside, thinking that this must be what it is like to be betrayed. Should she cry? She isn't sure. It doesn't feel like she is in her body; it feels foreign, as rigid as a piece of wood.

She has seen him disappear into his thoughts and believed that he was just thinking about work or was distracted, but perhaps he was daydreaming about this woman. He must have compared her with the other woman, it occurs to her, and seen deficiencies.

Anne is sitting facing the door, as pale as if she had just been informed of an unexpected death. She hands Bente a glass of water, and it is such an unexpectedly considerate gesture that she feels a large sob catch in her throat. The water is ice cold. It is the best glass of water she has had for a long time.

'I'm so sorry,' Anne says in low voice.

They slowly scroll through the thread.

They quietly continue reading: they have agreed to meet one evening three weeks ago, at the end of October. Perhaps Fredrik already has the address, because it isn't here, just *Come round to mine*. Heart. Checking the date may be a form of self-torture, but she has to, and quickly compares it to the family calendar on her mobile. Yes, there it is: *Fredrik, Copenhagen*.

All these trips to Copenhagen.

'Go to the beginning,' she requests. Then they read. The most recent messages are from the day before. From Fredrik, sent just after nine. That means it was just after he had dropped her off in the morning.

Can't wait for Sunday. Heart.

She has given Rasmus a lift to a friend's house, where he is going to watch football, and when she returns and comes in through the front door, she can hear that Fredrik is at home. She can hear him rattling around the kitchen. Her pulse increases, because she realises that it is going to happen now. She slowly takes off her shoes and coat.

Fredrik has taken the dish filled with lasagne from the fridge and is in the process of cutting out a large, sticky piece when she enters into the room, and it hardens her resolve because there is something devastatingly bitter about seeing him standing there helping himself to food that she has cooked and that he is taking for granted he can eat. She has to make an effort not to go up to him and strike him down with one blow from her fists.

'Hello,' he says.

She leans against a kitchen counter.

'I know what you're up to.'

He turns around in surprise and asks what she means.

'Rasmus told me the day before yesterday,' she says, feeling breathless from agitation. He told me about the trainers.

And now he understands what she means. The hand holding the knife cutting the lasagne stops and his face softens with fear, his eyes widen, startled fear shining from his pale face. But it is as if a more conscious part of him immediately takes up the baton, as if he hopes to avoid this threat clearly approaching him and he says: 'What?' As if he were puzzled, concerned and innocent; but that time is past the moment she sees him like that.

'You know what I mean.'

He shrugs his shoulders as if he doesn't understand, as if it is once again she who is the excessively suspicious, hysterical woman, and if she had a hammer and nails she would nail him onto his sanctimonious cross; he just manages to emit a snort, and the tiny patronising exhalation is what blows away any remaining love for him; a little breeze is all it takes, she doesn't even have time to think before her arm is in the air and the palm of her hand strikes his face in a violent slap.

He looks at her, dumbfounded. Then his rage also wells forth and he sputters: 'What the hell?'

Finally she isn't alone in her anger; it is an unfortunate union. Hit me then, she thinks. She wouldn't hesitate to hit back, again, harder – she is fitter than him. She feels a dark and overwhelming urge to hurt him, a desire to pull the kitchen knife out of the lasagne and stab him fast and hard in his soft, deceitful flesh.

'Jane Smith,' she says. 'Is that her name?'

Then it is as if something completely snaps in her. 'How could you do this to me?' she screams. 'How could you force Rasmus to keep quiet, how could you do something so awful to your own son! You're abusing my child,' she shouts, hitting him straight in the chest.

And it is as if this blow brings him to life: he shoves her to one side and stands there doggedly, listening quietly. 'Who is she? Who is the woman who was here? How long has it been going on?' She fires off the questions in rapid volleys. But she notices how he is paralysed and disappears off into the inaccessible niches where she can't reach him. Say something, she thinks in despair. She hates him, but she wants him to say something, to explain, to confess, to beg for forgiveness – after all, they have a life together.

Through the intoxication of her fury, which is wonderful and alluring in its simple unrestrained power, the desperate realisation emerges that this is not a battle she will win by crushing him. Because this is her life, too. Making a tremendous effort, she stops herself.

They glare at each other.

The headache is swelling: like a sharpened point, the pain emerges from her skull and brings tears to her eyes.

'Do you know what the worst thing is?' she says. 'The worst thing isn't that you're seeing someone else, but that you're lying about it.'

Of course that isn't true. But she can't bear him standing there looking wounded. The words seem to have set something within him in motion, because he tilts his head to one side, looks at her with an expression that is both sad and scornful, and says:

'No, the worst thing is that you never trust me.'

He is right, she thinks to herself. She doesn't trust him, she will never trust him again. Now he is trying to push her off balance and blame her for his deceit, it is just another line of defence; she knows his slimy tactics. They reach rock bottom, a silence to which they have rarely sunk previously, where there is nothing between them but rage.

'Do you love her?'

They are horrible words, but they jolt him exactly as she hopes. She has always been colder than him, and even now, part of her is retaining her composure and constantly trying to position itself advantageously. He shakes his head, as if unwilling to tolerate more.

'Are you going to interrogate me again?' he says maliciously.

'I want to know what happened.'

He says nothing.

'Rasmus told me what he saw,' she says after a while. 'And I believe him. He's your son. How could you use your son like that? Haven't you noticed the state he's in?'

Now she is pushing on a pressure point, she throws herself at it with all her might, and notes he is reacting because he loves the boys to the bottom of his heart. He rubs his face, as if taking protection behind the palm of his hand, and stares. It happens startlingly quickly, but she manages to understand everything; she's trained to read things like that.

'It wasn't meant to happen,' he says angrily, because he doesn't want to be a bad father. 'I didn't know what to do.'

'You had a choice,' she says. 'You could have taken responsibility, but you chose to blackmail your own son.'

'I didn't blackmail him.'

'You forced him to be silent.'

To that he has no answer.

And then it is as if Fredrik realises he has lost, that there is no point in fighting. He starts crying.

She has seen him cry so many times over the years they have been together, and these tears are the ones he usually uses to make himself vulnerable and to cast himself as the wronged party. She doesn't feel sorry for him. She tells him to stop. Stop feeling sorry for yourself. But he continues crying. Perhaps these tears are real, perhaps he sees what he has done, what he is losing. And suddenly she is upset too. What has happened to us? she thinks.

They sit at the kitchen table. Fredrik stares at its white, shiny surface with a numbed expression.

He met her through work, he explains. It just happened. He organised an open workshop and during the break she came up to him and started talking. She remembers him mentioning a workshop around three weeks ago. She is called Jane Smith. And what happened then? They met. Where did they meet? She is leading an interrogation now, but he doesn't notice. He says they met at her home. And in a hotel.

'And here too,' she points out.

He nods, ashamed. Yes, here too.

Then she asks him what she has been thinking all along. Was it her she met at the Swedish reception at the Hotel Metropole?

He nods.

For a short while she can't maintain her resilient façade and looks away. She was right.

Now she remembers something else she had completely forgotten: when they were invited, Fredrik had suggested he could go alone. She didn't like receptions like that, he had said. It was true. But she wanted to go, and was surprised that he had said that, and, she had to admit, she was suspicious. Why hadn't she listened to that suspicion? He seemed pleased that she wanted to come with him.

Have they fought and struggled just to reach this point? Then she realises they are at the beginning of a drawn-out parting, and that makes her sad.

'I trusted you,' she says.

It is odd to talk about him in the past tense, but how could she do otherwise?

He says nothing.

'You're the only person I've trusted,' she says.

What happens next nobody knows. They are standing at the precipice of a future where every word uttered will be of enormous consequence; she can sense it clearly. The question she cannot bring herself to say floats between them: *Why* did he do this? And it is as if he hears it; they have been together for so many years that he still understands what she is saying when she is silent.

'I feel lonely with you, Bente,' he says. 'You're distant, you aren't with me. You only care about me when it suits your needs.'

'That's not true.'

He nods. It's true.

'You always want things your way.'

'What do you mean?' she says.

'Your work, everything. You're always most important.'

'You've always been allowed to do as you please,' she bursts out.

She realises straight away that she has revealed herself. Yes, she wants to be in control. Perhaps she wants that too much. Even when she relinquishes it, it is still her who makes the decision to make an exception.

He says:

'I don't know what there is left between us any longer.'

'So you go and sleep around.'

'I'm not sleeping around.'

'What the fuck do you call this, then? We live together, we have children together and you fall for the first bit of skirt to show you a little attention.'

'She's good to me,' he barks.

'So now you're irresistibly in love?'

'She wants me – unlike you.'

The words cut into her, because he means them. And he says that Jane is good to him in a way that no one has been for years, while she is shut off and self-absorbed and a neurotic control freak. She looks at him quietly. He is teary-eyed and she thinks: Oh, *now* it's coming, his customary attack, where, through tears, he becomes the vulnerable, wounded one and then he accuses her of being insensitive and inconsiderate, and trying to twist everything to *what it is really about*, his catalogue of her defects, how she doesn't understand who he is, what he needs, how they should develop together, how she is stopping him from being the person he is, all these passive-aggressive clichés. She is so sick of him. At the same time, part of her can't help but be impressed by his natural gift for emotional manipulation of this kind. As expected, he starts talking about her need for control and hisses:

'Dear God, you can't even deal with the tins in the larder not being ordered the way you like them!'

This wasn't what she wanted to talk about. *She wants me*: those words gnaw at her insides, undermining her desire to fight. There is a small fragment of truth in what he is saying, because she wants to be in control, she cares about her work and perhaps she gets too absorbed with it at times. But she also shows compassion, love, she has always trusted him. She loves him and the boys, he can't deny that. No, she thinks. He mustn't be allowed to twist everything to being about her. The deceit is his, not hers.

As she lies on the sofa bed in the study, it is as if all is lost for a second time. It is getting light. Now, close to sleep, a heavy sense of despair awakens in her. Over the years, she has thought about what she would do if Fredrik was unfaithful. To handle the shock, to be ready and able to act quickly. But now she feels paralysed, all she can do is stare into the darkness. She feels ashamed and stupid; how can she have missed this? She has been made fun of. She had thought she was the most important thing to Fredrik, when in reality she had been utterly worthless in his eyes.

She remembers when she meant everything to him. She remembers when he came home with her the first time to her new, tiny flat. She remembers him sitting under a hand basin in the maternity ward crying with relief when Daniel was born,

after the doctors had almost had to make an emergency inter-
vention. She thinks of all the times they have slept together;
she let him come in her just a few days ago. Did that mean
nothing to him?

While the room gets lighter, she unravels all the memories like
an old piece of fabric. She picks unhappily at the small things,
the words she remembers, and tests their durability – it is as if
there is a lie growing inside all the memories.

Perhaps Jane is just one of many. Perhaps there is a Chloë
before her, an Amanda, an Elisabeth. If he wasn't in Copenhagen, was he ever at the office over the last few years when
he said he was working late?

She tries to distinguish which memories can still be saved. But
even the future that she has only managed to think about as a
hope is now being torn apart. They won't grow old together,
won't see their boys and be reminded of them as children. They
won't age together, continuing to support each other down the
years in spite of everything.

She sees the woman in front of her at the reception, close to
Fredrik. She sees him lean forward towards the woman's ear
to be better heard, and how she strokes the hair behind her ear
and exposes her throat in a sensual movement, and perhaps it
is to receive a kiss. He must have kissed her there, she thinks.
The pictures flood her mind, they are transformed and displaced.
She sees Fredrik put his arm around the woman's waist, sees
them kissing in an intense embrace, naked in the hall, in bed,
in a hotel. She tries to push them away, but they won't stop.

It is as if the gravel paths are frozen in a forgotten era. The air is chilly and fresh. Jonathan pants as he runs down the slope; he is running for all he is worth. The anger is pulsing through him like black oil.

He has been sitting in that blasted flat waiting for almost twenty-four hours. No one has been in touch with him since they picked him up the evening after his meeting with Vermeer. But he knows they have him under observation. He has wanted to call Frances, but he doesn't want Vauxhall Cross to listen in on another attempt to move her, and perhaps she won't even pick up. He understands that he needs to be clean, but he hates being cooped up and he detests the thought that his confinement has almost certainly given Robert pleasure.

The two handlers arrived early, without warning. They came to collect him like a dog that needed taking for a walk. When they dropped him off in the car park by Kenwood House he got out of the car without a word and ran until his lungs smarted.

He loves being on Hampstead Heath early in the morning. When he lived in London, he and Robert used to come here to run. But this morning he is not part of the colossal calm that hangs above the grass. He is vigilant and turns at every sound.

He crosses a waterlogged patch of grass and reaches the woods. He is alone.

Oaks and beech trees tower over him, forming a muffled, green-glowing cavern. His effort increases by the minute and crumbles his thoughts to pieces until all that is left is a mumbling stream inside his head before even that falls silent.

He normally likes to push himself when running, and has to remind himself to maintain a calmer tempo. Yet after a while he attains the same feeling he usually does, that his worries are shrinking as if he were replacing them with a pleasant sense of emptiness with every mile he runs. Alert and focused, he runs towards the centre of the park.

He can see the pond. He ups his pace and reaches the far end at exactly the right time. Catching his breath, he steps from foot to foot on the gravel path.

There, another runner.

A man of about thirty, wearing black running tights and a thin anorak. Short, blond hair. No, he thinks, this is wrong.

The runner approaches the same way he did, using the path along the edge of the pond.

Typical – the entire park is deserted and yet he still can't be left in peace. Now the annoying question arises as to whether he should let the other runner pass and do another lap, and be forced to have him in front of him the whole way, or whether he should disappear before the other runner arrives and then return. Because this is the meeting place. On the hour, every hour, until ten o'clock this morning was the agreement.

The other runner is now a hundred metres away. He squints.

Perhaps it is how the man is looking at him as he gets closer, perhaps it is his thin, ruddy beard. He doesn't know, but he tries. When the man is fifty metres from him he begins running again, and goes round the end of the pond at a steady pace.

Behind him he hears the rhythmic steps of the other man.

He turns off onto a narrow path crossing a patch of grass. His legs respond with pleasure on the uphill; he is strong, but holds back to make sure he doesn't lose the other man. When he reaches the summit and ducks into the trees, he notices that the man is still there, fifty paces behind him.

The man is following.

He is surprised. He has to admit that he had expected a messenger for Ahrar al-Sham to be someone of Arabic appearance, not a sandy-haired white man who might as well be a younger version of himself.

Agitation and slight fear make it difficult not to run quicker. He heads into the trees in a wooded area and chooses a new path, moving forward through the gentle interplay of grey light and shadows.

It is like a silent game between him and the other man. A quick glance at his watch tells him he is running each kilometre at a steady four-and-a-half minutes. The joy of rushing forward through the chilly morning makes him smile.

He can hear the other man's steps getting closer.

Then they are side by side. The messenger is younger but bigger than he seemed from a distance. The man could easily push him over. They silently run alongside each other through the trees. The unspoken violence is ever present; he knows he must be careful.

The thought that the rebels may have an entirely different plan in mind for him passes through him with peculiar clarity. They might abduct him or simply kill him, courses of events over which he has no control. Vauxhall Cross is tracking his fitness watch via GPS and knows where he is, but it will still take a while for anyone to get here if the man turns violent. If he is kidnapped, they wouldn't be able to stop that either. All they would find would be a fitness watch in the woods.

He sees the messenger make a rapid movement with his right hand and thinks: knife. The man's hand rises in a slow movement. Trees pass between them, ferns brush his calves; he is intensely alert and ready for battle. An object . . . not a knife, but he can't tell what it is.

'Take it,' the man pants.

He holds out his hand.

The object drops onto the palm of his hand. A mobile.

Without a word, the messenger ducks away and disappears rapidly into the trees.

Jonathan continues alone through the rustling woods and emerges onto a sloping meadow. He stops, leans forward and groans loudly. His lungs want more air than he can manage to breathe in.

He examines the phone. A simple pay-as-you-go with a scratched case. Used and anonymous.

The sudden ringtone is loud and shrill. It is as if the artificial sound disturbs the woods: the birds fall silent.

When he puts the mobile to his ear, he hears a man with a calm, nasal voice say:

'*Listen carefully.*'

London accent. Not the same man who gave him the phone, this voice is lighter. The man says a series of numbers. He listens, trying to remember the series. Then he holds his breath and tries to perceive the details: the intonation of the voice, and in the background the tiny noises of the environment. A faint hum. Traffic. Cars passing.

'Repeat that.'

The man repeats the number series. Two figures, period, six figures. Then minus. Two figures, period, six figures. He closes his eyes and lets the coordinates form a pattern that he can remember.

'*Understood?*'

He says yes.

'*Every morning for the next three days. We'll be waiting for you.*'

The call ends.

He repeats the number series out loud to himself. Then he turns around.

After a kilometre or so he reaches a road running through the park. A man in a loden coat with a Labrador on a lead dodges anxiously out of the way when he explodes out of the bushes.

'Do you have a pen?' he gasps.

The man merely shakes his head in confusion.

A pen, he has to find one.

He runs along the park road and onto a well-kept avenue. He finds a corner shop close to Gospel Oak station and asks for pen and paper. The surprised-looking woman in a pink cardigan behind the counter looks at him in amusement. She gestures at the newspapers. He swears silently and pulls a fiver out of the pocket of his running tights and picks up a copy of *The Times*. The woman hands him a pencil that she sharply points out is only a loan.

The figures are close to falling out of order. He closes his eyes, calming his heart rate. Then he writes them down, one after the other, in the margin.

The handlers are waiting outside in a car.

Back in the flat, he sits with his mobile in his hand. He has entered the coordinates and already checked several times that they are correct. The location that the figures refer to on the map is nowhere near the Turkish border. What's going on? he thinks to himself in dismay. The meeting point isn't near the Turkish border, it is tens of kilometres inside Syria in northern Idlib. Deep in the war zone. He is overcome by lassitude as the realisation hits him that if there is one place on earth where he will probably die, this is it.

Bente examines her appearance in the vanity mirror and kisses a tissue. Cherry-coloured lipstick, foundation and a light application of mascara. Perhaps that is the deepest form of loneliness: spending an entire sleepless night lying alone because Fredrik is unfaithful, and then hiding the fatigue with make-up.

On the main road she calls Anne, who has already been in touch this morning. The number used by Jane is connected to an address in Ixelles, the analyst explains. Jane is an alias. Her real name is Heather Ashford.

She vaguely recognises the name, but doesn't know where she has seen it. She has plenty of time, and the address is only a kilometre or so from the office. She'll get there before the slut leaves for work, she thinks to herself. A little surprise.

She plays Eric Clapton at top volume while rolling towards her target. It calms her. She only listens to Clapton when she is alone in the car; no one else in the family likes the music. Heather Ashford, she thinks: sounds like a stripper. She knows exactly what she is going to say to that woman. She is going to make her realise that the gates of hell will open wide for her if she continues seeing Fredrik. To give herself strength, she sings along to the words of 'Cocaine', loudly and not altogether clearly.

But her positive fighting mood deflates when she ends up in all the roadworks going on in the city centre. Sitting in an incomprehensibly static queue of traffic on Chaussée de Wavre, she realises there is a risk she will be late.

She pulls the car up onto the pavement and parks it sloppily at a jaunty angle, gets out and begins to jog towards the address. She doesn't want to be sweaty or out of breath – she wants to meet her opponent in a calm and dignified manner, but nevertheless she is running.

It is an idyllic street with small borders of flowers and generously proportioned main doors. A neighbourhood for the bourgeois city dweller. It is half past eight when she presses the buzzer.

No one answers. She swears silently; perhaps the woman has already left for work. She had hoped to hear the woman confess and to enjoy frightening her, but standing outside the door she tells herself that this will have to be a different kind of visit. She buzzes a number of other apartments and someone eventually makes the mistake of letting her in. She sneaks in and ambles up the echoing staircase.

The door is of the classic kind – tall French double doors – found in all turn-of-the-century buildings. She presses the doorbell and hears an angry noise from within. She waits but hears no steps on the other side of the door, rings the bell again and waits another minute. No one is home.

The door is old but the lock is eye-catchingly new. She looks up at the ceiling but can't see any surveillance – no cameras or sensors.

She gets out her pick gun.

It is risky and illegal, but it doesn't matter now. If she can't meet her enemy, then she at least wants to know how she lives.

The picklock slips into the lock, discerning the patterns of the cylinder and creating the right notches and teeth. Then, with a heavy clicking sound, the lock releases. The door opens when she tries the handle. She quickly steps inside and closes the door behind her.

A long, dark hall. She listens for noise from inside the rooms. No alarm, no camera.

It occurs to her that Heather might be sleeping.

'Hello?' she calls out.

No, the flat is empty. The hall opens out onto two large rooms.

She passes through a galley kitchen. The fridge is empty apart from a bottle of wine and a jar of olives.

The bathroom is also clean and tidy – there are a multitude of small bottles and soaps. In a little basket next to the sleek cast-iron bath tub are two bottles of shampoo and shower gel that distinguish themselves from the others. She recognises them – they have the same products at home. It's the brand Fredrik likes.

Naturally, he has known what would give him away. He has been careful not to take the woman's scent away with him, instead showering after their liaisons and using the same shampoo and shower gel as he would at home. She has to sit down for a moment. A headache is bursting through her forehead.

She goes into the living room, where there is a large sofa, partly wilted flowers in a vase, lots of books. So this is the kind of woman he wants, she thinks – a reading Heather. She tries to imagine who she is. A lover who reads Tolstoy; how wonderful. She looks around for photographs, pictures that might give her more information, but there is nothing like that – just ugly photography and watercolours. There are also no folders containing papers, bills, anything that might say more about the person living here. She pulls the drawers of a bureau open, searches the shelves in the living room, but finds nothing that tells her more about her enemy.

Two tall windows face the street. It is a beautiful view. How exciting it must have been for Fredrik to come here to visit a young woman with good taste living in a period apartment. Like in a film. A fantasy.

A wide bed sits in state in the bedroom. It is so perfectly made – the covers are stretched and folded. Pale, colour-coordinated pillows are positioned at the head. Cool tones characterise everything in the room. There are some fashion magazines and a vase of immortelles. Like in a hotel. Or a place of refuge. She doesn't want to think about what has happened here, but she can't avoid the thought because it gives her a dark and forceful energy.

Next to the bed is a candelabra. It has been used – a solidified dribble of wax is still on the brass. She can imagine the soft glow of the candlelight on the bed and walls, Fredrik walking naked across the broad floorboards, and she feels the fury vibrate within her.

Candles to fuck by.

She is blinded with rage. She grabs hold of the candelabra and slings it across the room with all her strength.

Even as it leaves her hand, she realises her mistake. It was a violent impulse – she couldn't stop it – but of course she hadn't stopped to think. She sees the candelabra travelling across the bed like a peculiar trident and, even before it hits the wardrobe on the far wall, she has already come to regret it bitterly. The candelabra strikes the wood with an impact that makes the tall piece of furniture wobble and bounce before settling back on the floor.

She is there in a flash, but it is too late. She swears loudly. There is a clear gash in the wardrobe door – two or three centimetres – next to the handle. The smooth white surface has cracked, exposing the wood. The candelabra is in one piece, but the candle has broken off and one arm is slightly bent. The floor is covered in flakes and crumbs, and there is an ugly scratch on the parquet.

For a while she stands there completely perplexed by the damage and her own stupidity. This will be visible, she thinks with a loud groan. She quickly goes into the kitchen and finds a dustpan and brush. Then she crawls around by the bed and sweeps up the pieces of wax, down to the tiniest flake of their romantic light, until the floor is completely clean. She rubs the mark on the floor for a while with her jacket and is relieved to find that it disappears.

The candelabra is made of brass. Having to stand there trying to bend back one of its arms is difficult, and very degrading – her face reddens from exertion. Finally, it looks like it did before.

But what should she do about the wardrobe? Perhaps she can leave it, she thinks, perhaps the woman fucking her husband doesn't take much notice of what her wardrobe doors look like. To be on the safe side, she carefully opens the wardrobe to check that nothing inside has been disturbed.

As if as an afterthought, a suitcase tips onto the floor. A bundle of papers slides out.

It is as if she had unleashed a sequence of small accidents. Trembling, she puts the empty suitcase back in the place she thinks it was before and quickly gathers together the sheets of paper. Letters. She stops, because she recognises the pale blue logo on each page.

It is the emblem of the British Embassy.

Jonathan's new passport is lying on the dark dining table, along with a driving licence and ID card proving he works for the aid agency Syrian Assistance.

George Bradswaithe, aid worker, tasked with bringing humanitarian assistance to those in need in northern Syria. A British citizen, born in the same year as he was, in the same part of London.

He has played the role of good Samaritan before. Aid worker is his showpiece – he could give a lecture on humanitarian aid.

It's a good cover. People generally think the best of aid workers.

It surprises him sometimes how willingly other people believe him. To him it is strange to simply trust what people say, or what a document says, what is visible in pictures. How do you know it is true? His first instinct is not to trust others. When colleagues gave their names, he knew that they rarely gave their real names. He had met so many people who said they worked as journalists, doctors, researchers, and knew that they actually performed a completely different role. Just like him. Everyone has a hidden life.

He is going to travel from Brussels. If anyone wants to know, he will say he has been participating in a human rights course.

But for that, he needs a certificate, he thinks – a document proving it. He roots through the papers. He is fretful; the slightest uncertainty disturbs his mood. Then he finds a thin piece of paper stuck to another. An attendance certificate from a fictional conference. Good.

He thumbs through the passport and reminds himself to memorise the dates of the stamps. A lie lives its own life, and in order for it to survive, it must become its own truth. He must be able to provide a cohesive explanation, down to the finest details. He must be able to explain the lies as if they were vivid memories. Then words harden into shields, and stories become ramparts providing protection. Then everyone will believe him.

One after the other, he picks up the documents and checks the details to make sure they agree. Careful planning has gone into these documents, but he wonders how much protection they will offer in reality. A false identity is useful if the Turkish border police arrest him. But in Syria it is worthless. There he is just another vulnerable body. What's more, he is a British body, valued highly in the Syrian kidnapping market.

He examines the plane tickets. A sense of worried expectation buzzes inside him. Arriving in Antakya just after one o'clock tomorrow.

He has been kept in quarantine for more than forty-eight hours, but now it is time. He sits in front of the TV waiting for the video conference to begin. He can still say no, he thinks. Theoretically, he is quite free to open his mouth and say no. But what use is freedom of choice if every consequence is catastrophic? He has betrayed Robert, and is bound to a future he cannot control, let alone predict, but the alternative of going against Robert is worse.

In front of him is the document *OPLAN version 1.6*. Why version 1.6? he thinks to himself nervously. He helped to write the first draft of this operational plan. Someone has apparently revised it. He dips in and out, wondering how many lethal misjudgements have been made it in.

He detests Robert at that moment. He hates the dead analyst who stole the documents, and he hates the Swedes and everyone else ruining things for him – hates them with such intensity that his entire body is tense.

The screen comes on. He looks at the time.

'*Can you hear me?*'

'Yes, I can hear you.'

Grandma is visible on the screen now. 'Stand by,' she says harshly.

Behind her is an empty conference room with a large table and office chairs filling the view. It is only a few miles away, but it might as well have been on the other side of the planet. The coordinator adjusts her glasses and aims a remote control at a point beyond his field of vision.

'Say something.'

'I don't know what to say.'

She looks up with a smirk. 'Thank you.' She asks whether the picture is okay. He says it is a little out of focus. Something happens: the picture changes, gets sharper.

She asks him to stay there, the meeting will begin shortly. Then she leaves through a door and disappears from view.

He waits in front of the screen with headphones over his ears. A buzz fills the headphones, like a myriad of voices. He is part of a machine, a node in the network centring on Vauxhall Cross. He leafs through the ring-bound plan, anxiously shuffling his documents.

Now something is happening in the empty conference room on the screen. Robert and two men from Counter-Terrorism come through the door. Then Grandma, the operational coordinator, and behind her two men that he knows are Syria experts. Then a cluster of IS experts. Even the most secretive organisations are brimming with people.

They turn their faces to him.

He will be met in Antakya when he lands, the coordinator explains. A local agent will be waiting for him, all he has to do is walk into the arrivals hall. A photo of a young man with a round face and fluffy moustache appears on screen. His name is Hakan. He looks young, he thinks; perhaps a little too young.

They go over the journey into Syria.

A photo taken by a drone fills the screen. His route from Antakya runs like a red line across the Syrian hills and mountains to a point on the plains. The exact time he will cross the Syrian border has not yet been determined.

'Why not?' he asks.

One of the analysts explains that it depends on the Turkish border guards. At the moment, the area where they are going to cross the border is sparsely patrolled. On average, four patrols per day pass that point. But the Turks make regular changes to their routines. The coordinator quickly adds that Hakan will have the latest information.

'The rebels will meet you here.'

He sees a cursor move across the yellow-brown surface. The picture zooms in – it is like falling vertically at a very great speed. He sees a house surrounded by a wall and a road leading to the building. The house is in a field at the foot of the hills. Perhaps it is an old holiday villa in northern Idlib.

The picture vanishes and he can once again see the conference room.

'I had hoped to meet the rebels at the border,' he says.

'You got the coordinates,' says Robert. 'The rebels are in charge.'

Then they review the team. Four men will be with him throughout. They will provide him with protection and facilitate the infiltration. Once he has Pathfinder, he should call the number saved on his mobile, and the money will be deposited into the account provided by the rebels.

The final details are checked. One of the men checks that he has received all the documents and that the air ticket has been issued in the right name.

'Have you got any questions?' asks Grandma.

I don't want to do it. He could say it. The moment in which it is still possible to say it is upon him. But how could he stop things now?

He shakes his head. 'No questions.'

The coordinator nods and wishes him luck. The others agree. 'Yes, good luck.' Which means: 'We don't know what happens next. You're on your own. You might die.' That's what he hears.

'Robert,' he says. 'Can I have a word with you?'

Robert waits while the others leave the room.

'We said I was going to collect Pathfinder in Antakya. In Turkey. Not that I would be going to *Syria*.'

'That's true. But we also didn't say that you were going to fuck my wife,' says Robert.

The screen goes black.

Anne looks at the letter. It is without a doubt the British Embassy's emblem. Bente sees that she is thinking the same thing as her. This is what every nightmare in the intelligence business centres on. Infiltration.

Anne sits beside her and says that the apartment is owned by a British foundation, but Bente is barely listening.

She opens the list of diplomats. They use it to record all foreign diplomats and EU civil servants, and an army of neat faces is now scrolling up the screen. There is Jonathan Green staring at her with his remarkably cold blue eyes. *Trade Attaché.* Underneath is the Section's own comment: *MI6 Station Chief, Brussels.*

She looks up Heather Ashford. Her fingers are trembling.

A woman with dark hair and a barely visible, neutral smile. That's her, the woman she saw with Fredrik at the Hotel Metropole. *Assistant, Trade Delegation.*

A deep sense of futility pushes her into her office chair. They have been defeated.

The woman reports directly to Jonathan Green. She probably isn't even called Heather Ashford.

She gets up and goes to the window. Her gaze is drawn across the city and its grey sky, the pigeons wheeling above the park hunting for scraps. Fredrik is only of interest to the Brits as her husband, as an easy way to get into their home. It isn't even a relationship, just an infiltration aimed at her.

The safe. They are looking for the documents that B54 gave her; what else would be worth taking a risk like that? They are monitoring her, they know the layout of the house, and they understand that the documents must be there in the safe.

She turns to Anne.

'Not a word about this to anyone. Talk, and you're history. Do you understand?'

Once she is alone, she rests her forehead on the pane of glass and tries to gather her thoughts.

A dry fear is rattling through her. Perhaps this is how it all ends. Over the years she has sometimes suspected she was under surveillance, but now there is no doubt.

With uncanny clarity, she sees what will happen next. A suffocating security check will penetrate her life. They will never trust her again. She looks at her mobile – the new one. Lying there on her desk, it looks like a shiny, unpleasant beetle. Of course it's being bugged by Stockholm.

She knows the procedures for when betrayal, deceit and infiltration are suspected. The organisation will isolate her. She will be discreetly removed from her post and all the people who have been a part of her life.

She has always been good at breaking down big problems into smaller, manageable chunks, but she can't do it right now. This is too big; it is as if her whole life were collapsing under its own weight. How could she believe him when he said he didn't know how her mobile ended up in his coat pocket? How could she have missed that her husband was seeing another woman? How could she have been so blind? She is ashamed, because she has been gullible when two decades of professional suspicion should have taught her to identify treachery of this kind.

Mikael knocks on the door and asks if she wants to come to lunch.

'I'm in the middle of something,' she says. 'You go.'

They'll talk about her, she thinks as she closes the door. It won't be long before the group of people that knows gets bigger, and they'll talk about her. They'll say she betrayed them.

Then she catches sight of the photographs on the desk next to her screen. Fredrik, smiling. It looks like he is taunting her. She puts the photograph into a desk drawer. But then she changes her mind and gets it out again, removes the picture from the frame and tears it up in a wild movement.

Fredrik is standing in the garden waiting for her, just as she asked. 'Hello,' he says flatly. He probably thinks that she doesn't want him in the house because she hates him. It's true, she does hate him, but the real reason is of a more operational nature. She doesn't want to risk anyone else listening to them.

Somehow, she feels sorry for him. A highly professional organisation has exploited him to get to her. If only he could see that he was a victim, an idiot taken advantage of, if he could grasp that degradation and see that she is the only one who will look out for him in all of this. Then, perhaps, she might begin to forgive him.

'Fredrik,' she says, 'I need to tell you something about the woman you've been seeing. She's not called Jane Smith.'

He looks at her, tired and sarcastic. She knows what he is thinking, that this is just one of her paranoid fancies. She pulls out a copy of Heather's photo and holds it out. 'Is that her?' He looks at the photo, his brow creased.

'Yes, that's her.'

'She's called Heather Ashford.'

'I'm sure you know best,' he says.

'She doesn't care one bit for you, Fredrik.'

He glowers at her.

'I realise that it's difficult for you to understand,' he says, 'but there are people who are capable of showing more love than you.'

She reflects that she has to look at the conversation as part of her job. See him as a threat, an enemy, but an enemy she knows well. Because Fredrik is acting on behalf of a foreign power and she has to try and manage this disaster so that it doesn't get worse.

'She told you to take my mobile, didn't she?'

'What are you talking about?'

He looks at her as if she were insane. Oddly enough, he really doesn't seem to understand what she is talking about.

But the agent has been in their home, it must be her who took the mobile, she thinks. Then she remembers the log in the satnav: Fredrik had come home on Friday, the same day as the reception in the evening.

'She was here on Friday, wasn't she?'

When he says nothing, she repeats herself more sharply:

'Wasn't she?'

He nods.

'You brought her here two Fridays in a row.'

It is as if the house were a silent accessory. Everything is soiled but, purely professionally, things are at least a little clearer. She can picture Heather and Fredrik coming into the hall together that Friday almost two weeks ago. They have sex in the bedroom. Then Rasmus comes home. She flees. She is close to failing in her mission, but manages to persuade Fredrik that they should meet again at his house. The next Friday she is lucky. She finds a mobile and realises who it belongs to. The plan is probably to gain access to a computer, but a mobile phone is a real find. In the evening, at the reception, she puts the mobile in his coat pocket in the cloakroom at the Hotel Metropole.

'She works for MI6, Fredrik.'

He looks at her in astonishment. Then he laughs, loudly and ostentatiously.

Fredrik is obviously convinced that she just wants to ruin everything for him and control him. He will never believe her. It doesn't surprise her but it makes her so angry.

She gets out her phone.

Gustav answers after three rings. *Kempell?*

She is standing opposite Fredrik and looks him in the eyes while she briefly explains to Gustav that she is standing with Fredrik.

'. . . *In your home? Did he say that?*' Yes. On Friday. Gustav falls silent at the other end of the line. He is thinking, possibly testing different ways of handling her calling like this. She says she has the name of the woman and has been able to confirm a connection between her and Jonathan Green.

'*Is he still seeing her?*'

Bente holds the phone slightly away from her face.

'Are you still seeing her?'

Fredrik stares at her.

'The Head of Counter-Espionage would like to know.'

The frown between his eyes dissolves and his expression evens out.

'Yes,' he says. 'I'm still seeing her.'

'*Is he there? Can I speak to him?*'

She hands the phone to Fredrik.

'He wants to speak to you.'

Fredrik takes the phone and holds it to his ear as if he were afraid acid will come out of it. She hears the calm intonation of Gustav's voice as he speaks to Fredrik, who stands there silently staring into space.

'I understand,' he says then.

He looks at her, and she can almost feel his gaze slightly tickling her face: the way she is transformed into someone else in his eyes while Stockholm is speaking to him. Now he believes her; she can see that. The fear is radiating from his eyes.

Afterwards he looks completely empty.

'Oh God,' he says with dry despair.

His world is also falling apart. They are united. But she doesn't feel sorry for him, she feels no unity, just relief that he realises the extent of what he has done, that she no longer has to be the only one who knows and has to carry this burden.

'Bente, I didn't know ...'

'How could you?'

'I was just lonely.'

He was lonely? She doesn't know what to say.

He stares at her, but not at her as the woman he has betrayed, but as a representative of the agency that she is the embodiment of in his eyes, with all its power – its power to crush him. His face is drawn into a startled, humiliated grimace. Perhaps he finally realises how deceived he has been.

A little while later Gustav calls. They are coming down to Brussels, he says. Him and a team.

'*We need to get hold of the agent,*' he says. '*Fredrik will be our bait. Talk to him.*'

They sit on the veranda. A lingering rain patters onto the grass. It occurs to her that it is Friday evening. Just a week ago she was on the way up the stairs at the Hotel Metropole with the man she loved, blissfully ignorant. He has destroyed that love.

She explains what will happen now. He is going to help them make contact with Heather.

He nods lamely.

'You are to stay in touch,' she says.

He looks down at the ground and says nothing. She is giving the orders now. Continue the relationship. Don't do anything to make her suspicious. He should behave as he usually does towards Heather. Otherwise she may realise she has been exposed. Stockholm wants to question her, she explains. But the Brits mustn't smell a rat, otherwise they will send her back to England and she will vanish. Does he understand?

Fredrik nods, anxious and submissive.

'Have you arranged to see each other again?'

'Yes, the day after tomorrow.'

'When?'

'Three o'clock.'

'So you'll see her. Sunday at three o'clock.'

Fredrik glares at her with timid fascination. It strikes her that he has never seen her like this before, as a professional, as Head of the Section. She is talking to him like an employee. Funny that at the moment they are furthest apart they are working together for the first time.

'I don't know if I can do it.'

'Do what you usually do,' she says. 'Use your charm.'

It feels so good not to be the only one feeling terrible – there is comfort in his suffering. Perhaps even a certain degree of revenge. Yes, she thinks, looking at him sitting on the garden chair and anxiously clasping his hands. Of course revenge alleviates the pain – anyone who claims otherwise has never been betrayed.

Rolling fields, dry yellow and filled with root vegetables, pass by the car window. The piercing sunlight causes him to screw up his eyes. It is like travelling into a memory. He can see the mountains now. The van rattles, reminding him of the zinc coffins in which dead soldiers are repatriated.

The fact that he and Kate have been here is an unreal feeling. When they lived in Damascus, they would take the car up through Syria in the summers and visit Palmyra, Aleppo and even sometimes over the border to visit the city they are now approaching: Antakya. That was how he found the House.

The noise makes it difficult to talk and Hakan is sitting quietly in the front at the wheel. He seems reliable, calm and thorough – a typical fixer. They leave the main road at a large crossroads and join another road heading across this flat landscape, straight as an arrow. They pass warehouses and low rows of houses, which didn't use to be here. Then he recognises where they are. He sees the typical mansard roof and the square shape of the house in the middle of the fields.

After all these years he is standing outside the House again. The heavy door is just as he remembers. Hakan carries his bag inside before saying that he will return later this evening, then disappearing into the white heat of the blazing sunshine.

He stands in the cool darkness of the hall. The slightly sweet smell of scented cleaning fluid makes him stop and close his eyes. He has spent so long trying to persuade himself that he bears no guilt. But now it is as if that voice within him had fallen silent.

He used to stand in the hall, there in the corner, or out in the yard, and see everything through the doorway. Why don't you help? Robert used to wonder. As if it were just a sofa. Then he became accustomed. Yes, he got stuck in like everyone else.

He reaches out with his left hand and fumbles; there is the handrail. Touching the familiar, cold cast iron sends what feels like an electric shock through his arm, and he reels backwards. 'Hold the rail so that you don't fall,' Robert used to remind him. 'In case they struggle.' Robert was helpful when it came to things like that. Easy-going, merry almost. He remembers the details now. The ties around the wrists. The clients had to lie down, face to the ground, bodies one metre apart in rows.

He helped to take them down into the basement. It was heavy work – some were compliant, while others offered resistance. When he said he didn't want to do it, he was tasked with preparing for interrogations instead. Ensuring that everything they needed was to hand.

He finds the light switch. A bare light bulb illuminates the walls. There is the basement door. The same worn, verdigris-green door as before. It absorbed all sounds; almost all of them.

At the time they were using the House, he was convinced – he *knew* – that they were doing the right thing. They crossed a line of blood and piss, but he never thought it would take him years before he found his way back across that line.

He pushes the door open. The handle is welded straight to

the metal door; he feels the familiar, grating surface on the palm of his hand. He peers into the darkness. There are the stairs.

The darkness in the hall is interrupted. He jumps and quickly closes the basement door.

'Welcome, sir.'

He nods.

'May I take your bag, sir?'

'I can look after it,' he mutters.

But the soldier bends forward and picks up the bag.

Leaving the dark hall, they enter a flagged courtyard. He squints in the harsh daylight. It is strange to find everything the same. The large flagstones in the yard, roughcast white façades and windows with dark frames facing onto the square courtyard. He follows the soldier up the wooden steps to the upper floor.

They have given him the biggest room. The only furnishings are a bed, a cupboard and a desk, just as before. Everything is the same.

'Thank you,' he says to the soldier. 'Leave the bag there.'

He looks down onto the courtyard. It is as if they were all bewitched, he thinks. What happened in the House was separated from the rest of the world. As if they were adhering to a different form of gravity that ignored all other laws. The bodies had no inherent value, only the information that they contained, the truth to be found within them; only that. They were to peel the truth from each body. The grimness was necessary. He became someone else – or that is how he wants to remember it.

He hears voices downstairs. Someone laughs.

He steps into the courtyard and shades his eyes with his hand. Under the overhanging roof at the other end of the yard are four men sitting and smoking. When they notice him they get up, as if taken by surprise, and step forward to greet him. The only one to give his name is a wiry, tall man with arms like grained dark wood.

'Sergeant Pepper.'

Is he joking? He nods at the sergeant and decides to play along and gives his own cover name: George Bradswaithe.

The other soldiers approach and greet him politely.

Supplement is the dry designation for men like these. Supplements to people like himself. The terms have changed over the years, but they have always had the same dry, administrative tone that catches the attention of politicians and parliamentary committees: supplements, increments, extra resources, E-5.

They peer at him with curiosity. To them, he is one of the strange grey eminences that appear, nameless, from the depths of a secret machinery.

He notices that he has interrupted something. They are waiting for him to leave and he wanders off to the archway and towards the basement.

He carefully opens the door and goes down the stairs.

The narrow staircase; he remembers it, remembers every step. Then he reaches the large room with a vaulted ceiling, just as he remembers. There is the passageway leading to the cells.

The air is cool. A chill that would slowly penetrate the body and make clients' teeth chatter.

'Close the door,' they would shout. 'Give me the towels. Put him there.' They were knowledgeable and experienced, Robert and the others. He used to go out into the yard when he couldn't deal with it. He remembers the broiling heat and the dull sensation of participating in violence so gratuitous that it was hidden from the entire world.

In the years since, he has felt the dark gravitation of the

House. He has never left it. Over the years, he has got used to the guilt, its weight. Yet he still feels dizzy standing there.

He is lying on the bed in his room. The evening light is cast in wide strips onto the floor. He is warm, and the sweat clings to him. He tries to think through the plan, everything he has read, everything they discussed at the last meeting, but he is too upset, and notices how he quickly begins to mix things up. The fear is a pungent and acidic odour present in his sweat. The difference between life and death is found in the details.

It is impossible to stop the thought: that his familiar body, with its pale skin and reddish hair, liver spots on his back and freckles on his arms, lying there on the bed, will also become his corpse. A dead weight handled carelessly by strange hands, shipped home in a zinc coffin and kept in cold storage, before being buried, rotting and crumbling.

Or not, he says to himself in an attempt to stave off anxiety. Perhaps he will soon be back in London, the victor. Pathfinder will lead them to the heart of IS, and they will use all their might to remove Hydra's heads. Vauxhall Cross will see that he has dealt responsibly with the leak in Brussels. He knows that the leaked documents haven't been sent on from the Jensen family computer or their mobiles. The surveillance of them in recent weeks has captured all traffic – there are no gaps. He is thorough, he is putting things right. He can picture Heather finding the external drive in the Jensen family home and eliminating the documents. Perhaps it has already been done; the thought makes him calm.

Before they leave, he checks his equipment. He changes clothes and chooses carefully what to take. His hands are shaking. He wants to pray, but to whom?

Down in the kitchen the soldiers are sitting around the large table. They are cleaning their weapons and listening attentively to the sergeant, who seems to be instructing them but falls silent when he appears.

'Ah, here you are,' he says.

The men continue to quietly handle the parts of their weapons lying on the table. They work with experience, deftly cleaning and oiling. Then they eat dinner. The soldiers talk quietly with each other, glancing sideways at him at the end of the table. He understands their reservations; he is a stranger to them.

After the meal, while the soldiers stow their kit in the car, he stays in his room. He can hear them shouting to each other in the courtyard. The sun has set when they leave for the border. Cool night air rushes through the open car windows. The soldiers are silent, absorbed in thought. Hakan drives without saying a word.

As they approach the border, traffic gets heavier. They are close to a town. There are people moving along the verge in the darkness, appearing like dazzled animals in the beam of the car headlights.

He has been here in the past, before the war. Back then, the town had been a place for large trucks and lively markets, with small stands along the sides of the roads. It is different now. People wander across the road holding plastic carrier bags, silent and resolute. The bombings have increased in recent weeks and the shadows moving along the verges are those who have managed to escape. The war is so close that he can hear it as a single dull rumble beyond the mountains. A Turkish military jeep passes by; a little later, an ambulance rushes past in the opposite direction.

They roll on through the fields. Ahead of them, he perceives the dark silhouette of the mountain tops.

The village is a dreary collection of houses, separated by potholed roads, tangled patches of waste ground and enclosures containing solitary goats. Not a person is to be seen. The village appears to be deserted, as if the inhabitants had withdrawn in the face of impending danger. But there is life: the dogs are barking like mad.

Their guide turns out to be not one person but two. Two slight boys are standing in the courtyard of one of the houses on the outskirts of the village. They aren't more than teenagers, he thinks to himself anxiously when he realises that they are to take them across the mountains. But the soldiers appear calm; the sergeant offers them cigarettes. Hakan interprets when the sergeant talks to the boys. Then he comes up to Jonathan and says he is leaving. Good luck.

One of the soldiers hands him a helmet with night vision and a microphone, an earpiece, a tactical vest with a knife, compass, water bottle and ultraviolet torch neatly slotted into various pockets, all in case they are separated during their hike across the mountains. Jonathan is dressed for war and it makes him agitated. He becomes someone else: wearing the helmet with the night-vision set over one eye, a glittering green landscape opens up around him. The soldiers quickly test the radio frequency amongst themselves; he can hear them clearly in his ear. Then, tied together by technology, they are ready.

The boys bound away rapidly into the field. The soldiers move in a kind of gliding double time. Years of training and battle lie behind the way they take formation. It is different for him. He is worried about losing them from his sight.

A scattered white light is growing above the fields. Weak to begin with, then quickly blindingly strong, which is when the sound of crunching gravel and humming engines becomes audible. He throws himself down into the darkness. The tall dry grass stings his face, surrounding him with a dense and acid smell, warm soil. He pants, spitting grit out of his mouth, and waits. Then the patrol is gone.

The mountain looks closer than it is, and it takes them over an hour before they start climbing. The incline is constantly increasing. Sometimes he has to climb on all fours to get up the rocky slope. His rucksack weighs him down, wanting to pull him out and backwards. If he loses his balance, he will tumble down and be smashed to smithereens on the rocks, so he pushes himself to the ground, pulling himself up and feeling his legs shaking. He manages to stop briefly to drink water, catching his breath as he lies in the grass with his feet resting on a large rock. The soldiers move quickly and deliberately in front of him. Carry on, he thinks. He can't fall behind.

He doesn't know how long the steep climb lasts, but he is completely exhausted when they reach the summit and sink heavily to the ground. The long valley opens up before them.

They have crossed the border.

They follow trails along the side of the mountain and down into the valley. Precipices gape like open shafts. The boys have led the group across the border and now they want to return. They speak briefly to the sergeant, pointing. Then they turn around and head up the slope. For a while, Jonathan is able to glimpse them between the rocks as pale green shapes in the darkness. Then they are gone.

He loses sight of the soldiers. 'Wait,' he says in a low voice, but gets no answer in his earpiece. Then he sees the white dot of an infrared light shining a couple of hundred metres down the trail.

He can't see them. Then he slips, tumbling onto his knees in the grass. Flies swarm towards his face. He gets up, only managing to discern something of the swollen, putrefying mass of flesh lying in the mire. The stench hits him, dense and suffocating. He fumbles and falls to one side with a small cry.

He finds them huddled in a dry irrigation channel. He slides down to them. They say nothing but he knows they are wondering why he has taken so long. One soldier has pulled his jacket over his head to form a small tent and turns on his infrared light to examine the map. The others crouch at the edge of the channel, training their weapons on the surrounding area.

He pulls off his night-vision set and rubs his face. Sweat is making the straps moist and they scratch; in the end, the irritation is all he can think about. In the pitch darkness he can see neither the soldiers nor the ground or sky. The only things perceptible are the smell of dry grass and warm, dusty soil. He can hear the others breathing around him.

'*What are you doing?*' says a voice in his earpiece. He puts the night-vision set back on and there is the sergeant's shimmering green face in front of him like in a strange dream.

They follow the wind, trotting across open ground. He doesn't know the infiltration route in detail, he has to trust the soldiers completely. He can't fall behind again, but his rucksack weighs almost twenty-five kilos and makes him clumsy. The contents are clunking about and he is worried that things will come loose and start making a racket. Everything has to be firmly secured, everything must happen in absolute silence.

The sergeant signals a halt.

The soldiers have raised their weapons and are crouching, fanning out beside a plantation. What can they see? Small figures are running back and forth between the rows of bushy orange trees. He isn't sure at first whether his eyes are deceiving him. They are children. Small children quietly gathering oranges in the middle of the night. They rush back and forth between the rows of trees collecting fruit in a wheelbarrow. There is no playfulness in their movements, they are working quietly and deliberately. It is an uncanny sight because they are not behaving like children but like miniature adults. Perhaps someone has sent them here to find food under cover of darkness; perhaps there is no adult looking after them any longer. He stares at them as they run around in their nocturnal kingdom of the dead.

They jog for an hour until they reach a grove of cypress trees and take a break. He is so tired following the quick march that he simply lies down. The soldiers disappear into the trees.

The plain is visible in the dark. A hammering salvo from an artillery cannon is audible above the valley, followed by two dull explosions.

It is time. The sergeant appears, handing him a pair of binoculars and pointing. He can see individual houses. The terrain is so open – all he can think about is that they must be visible from a great distance. A good sniper would be able to pick them off one at a time. In the early grey dawn he sees a large house surrounded by a wall and a garden, barely five hundred metres away. The building is bigger than he had thought from the drone photo, but he recognises it and nods.

He hears the soldiers speaking in low voices to each other.

'Sergeant, what do we do?' he asks.

Their four blackened faces turn to him in the half-darkness.

'You stay here. We go in and take them out,' says the sergeant in a tone of voice indicating that he is wondering whether this man from MI6 has any idea why they are there. 'And we collect the package.'

'The package?'

He realises they mean Pathfinder.

'We're not taking anyone out.'

The sergeant and the others look at him silently. He is completely dependent on them; without them he will die out here in a field in northern Syria. But they don't trust him. If they are forced to choose, they will leave him behind, he thinks.

'We have our orders, sir,' says the sergeant calmly. 'This is the objective.'

'And I have mine. I've come here to *talk* to the people in there.'

The soldiers look at him mutely.

'You're under my command,' he says.

The sergeant crawls forward. The whites of his eyes shine against the backdrop of the camouflage paint.

'We'll fetch the bastard for you. But how we do that is up to us. You stay here.'

He can't understand what is happening. The plan was to buy the release of the captive. He can tell they are preparing for battle, they will kill him, they don't understand what is at stake. 'Wait,' he whispers, but the sergeant doesn't reply.

'Let's go,' he hears the sergeant say. 'Collection in thirty.'

As if responding to a silent signal, the group rises and rushes across the field.

He can't wait. This is his assignment, he thinks, they're ruining everything. He tears off his rucksack and runs after them as fast as he can.

Exhaustion and fear clarify his thoughts. He is afraid; he is sure the rebels have them in their sights right now. When he reaches a ditch he throws himself down. His legs are shaking, but he has to carry on. In front of him in the dark he can see the soldiers a long way across the field. They have already reached the house.

He hears a quiet shot pierce through the morning tranquillity. Then two rapid bangs – *tak-tak*.

It is as if the entire house comes to life. He can hear screaming. A prolonged salvo destroys the silence with its loud bangs. He throws himself to the ground and, lying on the hard earth, he hears yet more shots.

When he doesn't hear more he lifts his head. Is it over? He gets to his feet and runs until he reaches the wall around the house and clambers over. He doesn't notice at first that he has got caught in the barbed wire coiled around the top of the wall; it catches his combat vest. He tugs, horror-struck, taking the wire and pulling in despair while feeling blood running down his hand. Then he is free and tumbles down on the inside of the wall.

He draws his pistol and runs crouching towards the house, throwing himself against the white roughcast walls of the building. He can see no one and hear no shouting, no voices.

It is as if fear were shutting down parts of him. All he can think about is that he must find Pathfinder before the bloody soldiers kill everyone.

A wide staircase leads up to a veranda that the rebels have converted into a fire trench. Crouching, he creeps up the stairs, slipping; the ground is covered in thousands of shell casings.

Just off the veranda is a large, bare room. He stops and listens. There is nothing there apart from a dirty sofa and some rugs on the floor. Then he sees the body, like a sticky bundle by the wall.

Now he hears steps; someone is running towards him on the other side of the door. He raises his pistol.

The man stares at him in surprise with his mouth wide open. A young man with a chinstrap beard, wearing a T-shirt and tracksuit bottoms. If things had been different, he would have greeted the man courteously and thanked him for seeing him, explaining that he was there on behalf of the British Government.

The man raises his assault rifle.

In that moment he thinks: Him or me, and if I die, that second will never be followed by another. Blood rushes through his body; he just wants to live.

He fires.

*

196

The shot is deafening in the bare room. The man collapses in the doorway. Jonathan's ears are whistling and buzzing and there is a strong smell of gunpowder. He squints; what should he do? Where is Pathfinder? Violent explosions are audible from upstairs, salvos of shots filling the house.

He doesn't have time to react when a strong hand clamps over his mouth. He flounders, instinctively striking out with his arms to defend himself, but the hand presses harder, covering his mouth and nose.

'Shut your face.'

He relaxes.

The sergeant is nothing more than a dark shape close to him. 'In here,' he whispers.

Someone shouts in Arabic: *Don't worry. Keep calm.* It is incomprehensible. Then there is a shot, then another. Someone screams.

The sergeant pulls at his jacket as if he were livestock and shouts: 'Down!'

He presses himself in amongst the sandbags. The impact is like a gentle slap on the back. He collapses and is lying down, and for a long time his body is shut off and heavy like a rock. He gasps for breath.

Then he finds air and the world opens up before him. The sergeant shouts at him: 'Up, up!' He gets up laboriously.

'Two minutes,' the sergeant bellows.

He stumbles forward next to them, the sergeant still holding his jacket as they run out of a dented gate.

'Where is Pathfinder?' he shouts.

But the sergeant isn't listening, merely pointing at the gate that has been blown open.

'Run,' roars the soldier.

A morning mist covers the fields. He rushes onward.

A dull, pulsing sound is approaching and rapidly increasing in intensity until it becomes a throb dominating the world. Then he sees the helicopter, like an enormous, angular bird sweeping across the plain and heading straight for him. He crouches, as if it demands submission as it sweeps out of the sky and kicks up earth and sand in a thudding whirlwind.

There, in the swirling dust, he can see two of the soldiers emerging from the house with someone between them. An emaciated, gangly man.

The night sky is fading. He can see the mountains, they are flying close to the ground. The soldiers are sitting opposite him. They are pumped up, shouting to each other through the noise. Then they fall silent, sitting immovable for the rest of the flight. As dawn breaks they cross the border.

Pathfinder is sitting still, between them in the throbbing space. He is bony thin and silent, glancing occasionally at him and the sergeant who are sitting opposite. It is as if he realises that at this moment in time he has no power whatsoever over his body, and has surrendered to the fact that he is being transported from one place to another. He doesn't make a fuss when the soldiers put a hood over his head after landing and lead him across the blustery apron at Hatay Airport where Hakan is waiting for them with the car.

He is relieved at how compliant Pathfinder is. On the way to Antakya he turns to the man in the backseat and says in Arabic that he has nothing to worry about, they just want to speak to him. That's all. A conversation.

Back at the House, one of the soldiers jumps out and opens the gate. Hakan is nervous and floors it, making the car screech into the courtyard. Once inside, the soldiers calm down. They pull the captive out of the backseat and he silently allows them to lead him to the basement. Jonathan would have preferred not to hold the interrogation in the windowless, messy basement room, but they can't guarantee security if they lock him in one of the rooms in the house, he thinks. If the man cooperates they can always move him later on.

After the long night it feels wonderful to take a quick shower. The steady water rinses the dirt from him – it feels like a long exhalation. Afterwards, he finds a towel from the cupboard in his room and notes how well organised the operation is – there are even new, soft towels. He feels better. He is ready to get to work; yes, he is looking forward to talking to Pathfinder.

Sunday morning arrives grey and chilly. Fredrik makes breakfast, they perform their morning routine, forming the slenderest impression of unity. Fredrik tries to tell a funny story to the boys and they smile cautiously. They have noticed something is wrong. The silence is pushing them apart into different rooms.

Why hasn't Gustav called? she thinks. Fredrik is due to see Heather in less than six hours, and she still doesn't know what the plan is.

She is willing to do anything to get away, and after breakfast she asks Rasmus whether he would like to go to the park for a kickabout. He looks at her quizzically, as if she had gone mad. Then he fetches his football.

'What's wrong with Dad?' he asks once they are in the car.

How can she explain to him what is happening? 'Dad is working together with Swedish Counter-Espionage to bring down an enemy agent. Dad is a bastard.' She's tempted to say as much.

'He's just stressed,' she says.

Everything that is happening is happening in the light of an unavoidable farewell. The boys too are approaching a parting of the ways, although they don't know it. Daniel is spending the night at Julia's again. He has his life, but what will happen to Rasmus? There shouldn't be so much pain in young people's lives, she thinks, looking at him sitting beside her in the passenger seat.

The satnav comes on. She hasn't turned it on.

The car's Bluetooth is connected to a different computer. She turns around in her seat and looks out of the windows and in the mirrors. There are cars around her that have also slowed down for a red light ahead. She stares at the drivers in the other cars, but they all seem wrapped up in their own lives and completely disinterested in her. One of them is hacking into her satnav.

The traffic starts moving.

The park is nearby, but the map on the screen is showing a route to a completely different location three kilometres away. The usual clear, female voice used by the satnav begins speaking to her. *In one hundred metres, turn right.*

She turns. Rasmus looks up. Aren't they on the way to the park? he asks anxiously. She nods and says she just needs to do something else first. He looks sceptically at her; he doesn't believe her. Perhaps that's what the boys will take with them into the wide world, she reflects. The art of keeping quiet and seeing through lies.

She quietly follows the route. The person who entered it into her satnav has been watching her for some time and knows where she is. Rasmus is lost in his impenetrable thoughts as they leave town and continue along the main road.

Remain on this road for two kilometres.

She glances anxiously through the windscreen and in her rear-view mirrors.

Just outside of Nivelles, the satnav tells her to turn right and then announces she has reached her destination.

A car wash?

She drives to a vacant door and waits. The door slowly opens and reveals a dark opening. The man-sized brushes in the car wash stand ready for action, drooping slightly sadly.

Just as she is about to drive in, the back door opens and someone gets into the backseat. She doesn't have her service weapon, she has Rasmus in the car and he cannot come into harm's way. The boy's eyes pop open and he begins to turn around, but she puts a reassuring hand on his shoulder because she can now see who it is.

She drives into the car wash.

Gustav looks out of his window. The brushes close in on the car and start rotating at full force.

'Tell your boy to turn his data off and put his headphones on,' says Gustav calmly.

So he knows that Rasmus usually has headphones, she thinks in surprise, and wonders whether they ever leave anyone in her family alone.

'Who is he?' asks Rasmus in irritation.

'Just a friend. Don't worry. Put on your headphones.'

The lather runs down the windscreen and water thunders against the roof. Rasmus sits next to her, focusing intensely on his phone which he has connected his headphones to – he is scared and that makes her angry, she shouldn't have to put up with this.

'You're under surveillance,' says Gustav. 'I couldn't find a better way to meet you quickly.'

She looks out of the windscreen at the whirling storm passing over the car as he explains that they have been able to confirm everything. Heather Ashford is MI6.

'The Brits have got you under surveillance. They're in your electronics. They're listening to everything.'

She nods; it doesn't surprise her. She doesn't even have the energy to be upset.

Gustav asks her to tell him what she knows about the agent. It is odd to describe the most sordid details of her life while Rasmus is sitting next to her. But it makes it even easier. She briefly outlines what Fredrik told her, about what she found in the satnav and about the apartment in Ixelles. But nothing about the candelabra, because she knows that Gustav would see her in a different light.

Cascades of water rinse the body of the car.

'What are they saying about me in Stockholm?'

All trust in her is gone, Gustav explains. Management have been unhappy with how she has been handling things since she made contact with the British leak without checking with them first.

Yes, she thinks. That was a mistake.

'Now we're aware of the House, but what are we meant to do with that information? There are some things not even spies want to know. You should have talked to me,' says Gustav mournfully.

This is personal for him too. She is his favourite and it makes her sad that he is looking at her as if she were letting him down.

'We're taking over,' he says. 'Fredrik is receiving his instructions at the moment. He will be at the hotel at noon and will see Heather at three o'clock.'

Gustav grimaces self-consciously. He hopes that she understands that they need to question her, about everything, to establish exactly what happened and ascertain what damage there is. It will be a clear warning to London to leave them alone.

'It would have been easier if you hadn't spoken to Fredrik,' he says. 'You could have told us without fighting with him, then we could have kept an eye on MI6 in peace and quiet. Ordinary counter-espionage work. Now the Brits know that you're aware of Fredrik's infidelity.'

She understands his line of thinking, it is a purely tactical assessment. But does he really think she should have kept quiet and let Fredrik keep sleeping with Heather?

'They don't know that I've discovered Heather's real identity. And Fredrik is my husband,' she says, looking angrily at Gustav. 'Do you know what he did to my boy here? Rasmus discovered him and Fredrik forced him not to tell me. Has he told you that?'

Gustav sighs. No, Fredrik hasn't said that.

'I understand that this is hard for you, Bente,' says Gustav, and then it is as if he were embarrassed to say more.

'I want to be there at the hotel.'

'I don't think that would be a good idea.'

'Don't tell me what is a good idea,' she exclaims.

Rasmus lifts one headphone and looks at her, puzzled. 'Is everything okay?' She smiles hastily at him and tells him to put his headphones back on.

Once she is certain that Rasmus can't hear she says to Gustav: 'Fredrik is a wimp. He doesn't think he can do it.'

The car wash door opens. A beam of milk-white daylight appears. She turns on the engine. Without saying a word, Gustav gets out and wanders through the opening. Rasmus looks up and looks at Mum's friend in confusion.

The small boutique hotel is fashionable in an exaggerated and slightly vulgar way. She can't quite stomach that Fredrik chose this particular hotel for their meetings.

She looks around. This being a Sunday afternoon in November, the lobby is sparsely populated – just a few tourists and two businessmen in suits preparing for a meeting. She lingers nearby, listening, waiting. But they are genuine. Their humdrum, porous business talk follows her as she heads for the lift.

On the way up, she thinks about the apartment in Ixelles, and worry simmers within her. The gash, she thinks. She can no longer pretend that Heather won't have noticed it. Naturally she would have noticed something like that, being trained in the same methods as she is.

Of course, if she had known who Heather was she would have behaved differently. Perhaps the agent doesn't live there, she reflects. Perhaps Heather hasn't yet discovered the damage.

Fredrik is sitting on the edge of the bed in the room that counter-espionage have booked. He stares at her uneasily and she sees a pathetic middle-aged man sitting there on the brink of disaster.

Gustav is standing by the window. When she comes in he waves impatiently at her to come and join him.

'You were right,' Gustav whispers. 'He's on the edge.'

She looks over her shoulder. Fredrik is shrunken and pale. No, it won't work.

'Can you talk to him?'

If he leaves, then yes. Gustav gives her a measured look. They'll be waiting in the room next door, he says, disappearing through the door.

Then it is just the two of them. Fredrik has buried his face in his hands, like an ashamed child. There are many things they ought to say to each other, but not now.

She crouches in front of him.

'Fredrik, look at me.'

He looks up. His eyes are red with tears. He looks at her

205

as if all is lost, and she is tempted to yell at him to stop feeling sorry for himself. But, of course, she doesn't say that. It wouldn't help.

'Do you know what we usually say in the Security Service? The individual means nothing, the assignment is everything.'

Now he is listening, wide-eyed, as if hoping for salvation.

'This is my work,' she continues, as if speaking to a child. 'All those times you wondered what it was that I do – well, now you know. You are part of it. That man is my boss. I've worked for him for as long as you and I have known each other,' she says, checking herself to keep her voice gentle. 'And now you work for him too.'

He nods slowly. His face crumples in an ominous sob.

'You've made a big mistake,' she says, putting her hands on his knees. 'But you can make things right.'

He gulps, on the verge of tears.

'I thought she was one of yours.'

One of hers?

He shrugs his shoulders impatiently.

'Yes, one of your colleagues,' he says. 'She said she knew you. That you worked together. I thought . . .'

Then it is as if he hears how silly it sounds and falls silent with a resigned sigh.

The British are good, she thinks. They saw something that was true and used it. A calculated risk: claiming to know his wife. And then they could tempt him with the closeness she could never give him.

He sobs.

'I was curious,' he says quietly. 'I didn't think . . .'

'I understand, Fredrik.'

She strokes his knees.

'Just do it,' she says. 'If you care about me and the boys, then do exactly as my boss says.'

And finally there seems to be a little resolve in him. She gets up and hurries into the corridor and knocks on the next door, calling out that they should get some coffee. Returning, she takes one of the whisky miniatures from the minibar and hands it to Fredrik.

'Drink.'

The tearful fear is gone – he has accepted that he must play his role. He obediently knocks back the spirit. Then she tells him to wash his face with ice-cold water, lots of water, it mustn't be visible that he has been crying.

Robert has sent a compilation of questions that his department needs answers to. Does Pathfinder really have answers to all of these? Are they within him? But there is no use in adopting the man's fear as one's own – he is annoyed that the thought even crossed his mind. The man is a terrorist, he tells himself, or at least a man who cooperates with terrorists. He gets up and goes to the doorway. The courtyard is desolate beneath the scorching grey sky.

He must get the prisoner to focus and regard questioning as a shared effort that leads them both out of this basement, he thinks.

The soldiers fall silent when he comes down the stairs. The man's torso is bare and he is wearing the hood. He is facing the wall with his legs spread wide apart. His body is leaning forward and his hands are resting against the wall, as if he were performing a peculiar balancing act. He can now see that the man isn't even holding his hands against the wall, he is in fact leaning with his fingers stretched out so that only his fingertips brush the coarse cement. Two of the soldiers are sitting on chairs beside the man's body and smoking. When he comes in they stand up and stub out their cigarettes with their boots.

'What the fuck is going on here?'

They look like they've been interrupted.

'We've just been warming him up a little.'

'How long has he been standing like that?'

The soldier shrugs his soldiers.

'Sit him down.'

Together, the soldiers take hold of the man's arms and as soon as they let go, he collapses, his knees giving way as he tumbles to the floor. The soldiers groan at the effort of heaving him up.

'Stand up,' one of them hisses.

The man struggles to get onto his feet.

'Take the hood off him.'

They seat him on the chair and pull the hood off. The man blinks, squinting at him, his lips are dry. It is clear he is dehydrated.

'Give him water,' he says to the soldiers. He has to make an effort not to raise his voice.

Idiots, he thinks. This is really not in line with the procedures for questioning, but he says nothing. The soldiers pull out a bottle and pass it to the man, who struggles to open the twist cap as his fingers are stiff. He finally manages to open the bottle and drinks quietly until it is empty.

He waits while the soldiers go through their procedures with the man. They photograph him with a mobile, pull out an iPad and press his hands against the screen and take his fingerprints. It is obvious that this is a well-worn ritual, and he lets them do it.

He says to the man in Arabic:

'Listen carefully, Khaled, because this is important. I want you to answer my questions truthfully and in as much detail as possible.'

Does the man understand what he is saying? Fear is making him nod at everything. He tells Khaled to calm down.

'I just want to talk with you.'

The man nods.

'Not hurt you.'

The man nods.

'Say your name and where you come from.'

He answers in a low, hoarse voice.

His name is Khaled and he was born and lives in Raqqa. He points out where he lives. So that intelligence is correct. It is also true that the man runs a taxi company, but was recruited to drive Islamic State leaders when they occupied the city. But the man simply stares at him when asked why he collaborates with terrorists.

'I drive a taxi,' he says.

Jonathan asks the man to point out the routes he used to drive, using a map on the screen being held up by the soldiers. The man looks confused. He would drive all sorts of routes around the city, he said. He shows them, but he moves his trembling finger back and forth over around a dozen or so streets, in no particular order. The man says he owned a taxi that was commandeered by the new city administration – the new masters.

'Daesh?'

'Yes, Daesh.'

He has also driven further afield towards the Iraqi border. He points.

'Who did you drive?'

He isn't sure. Lots of people.

'Who was in your car, Khaled? You need to tell me.'

He looks anxiously down at his hands, at the bright-red marks left on his wrists by the ties.

'I can't remember who was in my car,' he says. 'All sorts of people. Sometimes there were members of the morality police, sometimes it would be someone who seemed important – some leader.'

'What were they called?'

'I didn't know them. I didn't want to ask.'

'Try to remember. I think you know.'

He hesitantly says a few names.

'Can you show me where you drove those passengers?'

He gets the screen out again, and once again pulls up the map of Raqqa. Were there addresses he would go to more often than others? he asks. Any houses or neighbourhoods he returned to that he can point out?

The man replies vaguely.

'Here,' says the man. 'Here. Here. And here, I think.'

The man's trembling fingers move irresolutely across the retina screen. If favourably disposed towards him, one might agree there was a pattern discernible from him pointing at the map. He takes notes. They sit like that for over an hour, him asking a question and Khaled pointing. But the man isn't specific enough, he seems to confuse things. Finally, Jonathan decides they should take a break.

He gets up from his chair and tells the soldiers to provide the man with food.

'We'll speak again in a little while, Khaled,' he says. 'Then you can tell me more about your work.'

The man is still sitting on the chair when he returns to the basement. The soldiers are standing around him, even the sergeant is there now. He ignores them. He sits down on the chair opposite the man and leans forward. What is that red mark on his forehead? A swelling. He looks at the soldiers, but they just look bored.

They start again. He asks the man to point out his routes and the man runs his index finger over the screen. Perhaps this will work, he thinks. If Pathfinder just keeps answering his questions, everything will be okay.

He asks a question about one of the most senior leaders in IS. Khaled has said he recognises the name. Now he hesitates, his answer delayed – he is taking too long.

'You need to answer,' he says.

Khaled looks perplexed.

'It's very important that you answer.'

He searches the screen with his finger. Eventually, he stops with his finger on a location on the edge of the map. He doesn't seem certain.

Doesn't he understand what is at stake? Perhaps he just wants to give an answer, any answer; he looks frightened. They will need to verify his answers back home, compare them with other data, and then ask new questions, even more detailed; this is just the beginning.

'Good,' he says encouragingly.

Next question. An address; he asks him to say who lives there. London apparently has vague intelligence to suggest a commander, but needs this confirmed.

'What is he called?'

'I don't know. I think he is a commander.'

He rocks gently back and forth on the chair until one of the soldiers bellows at him to sit still and he stops as if turned to stone.

'Tell us about the commander. What is he called?'

The prisoner looks unhappy, he doesn't know, he doesn't know the man. It continues like this for a few minutes. A name, but he doesn't know who it is. An address, and he hesitates, changing his mind. The soldiers move restlessly around the room. It is like balancing on a narrow, swaying plank of wood above an abyss, but he wants to succeed. If only he can do it his way, he knows he will be able to lead the man through the questions, step by step, and get answers.

He pulls out a series of photos. He points.

'Do you recognise him?'

The prisoner shakes his head.

'And him? Do you recognise him?'

He hesitates. Then shakes his head again.

'You have to answer, Khaled.'

It is as if the soldiers can no longer contain themselves. One them lunges forward, quick and heavy, and delivers a stinging blow with the palm of his hand straight across the prisoner's face.

The force of the blow throws the man sideways in his chair. He tips over. And, as if a new order came into force when the man fell to the floor, the others throw themselves forward. He can't stop their blunt, heavy bodies. Bent over the prisoner they hit his face and head with their hands.

He claws at their broad shoulders, scratching with his hands to get rid of them, his mouth dry with anger. He shouts:

'Stop, stop!'

He senses how the very smallest movement by the man on the floor might unleash fresh desire in the soldiers to hit him. They are exhilarated like children finally released from uncomfortable clothes.

'Get out,' he snaps.

One of them pats him on the shoulder as if it is a rugby match and they have just scored. Then they leave.

He helps the prisoner to get up. The man's nose and mouth are bleeding. He slumps down onto the chair.

'I'm very sorry. That wasn't supposed to happen,' he says.
He passes him a bottle of water.
'I can't keep those soldiers away if you won't talk to me.'
He says nothing.
'Do you understand? I want this to end as much as you do.'

He finds the sergeant on a chair in the sunny courtyard.

'Keep your men away. I'm trying to have a conversation. How do you think that will go if you do this?'

The sergeant gives him a measured look.

'But what results are you obtaining?' he answers with an indolent smile.

'Good results,' he says. 'I would be getting them quicker if I was left to work in peace.'

The sergeant stands up and shrugs his shoulders.

'I'm in charge of questioning. You are under my command,' Jonathan says.

'We don't follow your orders.'

'You will do as I say,' he says.

He can't get through to the soldier. There is nothing in the calm, contemptuous face to indicate any degree of uncertainty. He has never experienced anything like it.

Then the sergeant nods, as if tired of dealing with this irascible bureaucrat.

'Okay,' he says. 'But we don't have much time.'

He certainly agrees with that. He feels at once relieved, because now there is some order. He hasn't lost control, not yet. The work ahead of him will be done by evening – of that he is certain.

He leaves the basement door ajar and feels the fresh air flooding in. The sergeant seems to be keeping up his end of the agreement because no soldiers appear. They talk about the prisoner's work again, about who travelled in his car, from which addresses. Once again, he shows him pictures of IS leaders and asks him for their names and where they live.

Everything that the man says will be turned into coordinates for bombing targets and into intelligence for small teams like Sergeant Pepper and his men. They need to kill Hydra.

As the light from the doorway becomes weaker and deepens, they continue talking, and over time they find the rhythm he had hoped to achieve, with the prisoner eagerly awaiting the next question, aware that this is his salvation.

Evening comes. He gets up and thanks Khaled. They are on the verge of shaking hands, there is a mutual satisfaction over how well this has gone. The questions have been answered. He fetches bread, hummus and more water and then leaves him to eat.

The heat has dissolved into mild coolness. The smell of cigarette smoke wafts in through the open kitchen door while he is sitting at the table writing his report. A few hours later, when he closes the computer, he is satisfied. He is tempted to go and find the sergeant and his men and say, 'What did I tell you?'

She leans forward and watches the screen over Gustav's shoulder. There is the lobby. And there is Fredrik visible at an angle from above through the hotel's CCTV, which they have discreetly hacked into.

Gustav turns to her. Is she sure she wants to stay?

She nods, of course she does.

He probably wants her to leave, she thinks. Perhaps it's a bad conscience that prevents him from simply shooing her out.

She notices that the other men are embarrassed, focusing on the screen to avoid thinking about her, the betrayed woman, standing behind them.

It is three o'clock on the dot.

Fredrik is wandering about, it looks suspicious. Then he looks up to the camera. 'Stop it,' she wants to say to him. 'Pull yourself together.'

He is hidden by a group of guests filling the lobby with their bodies and loud, lively voices. Conference delegates, to judge by the large plastic wallets dangling off colourful lanyards around their necks. Gustav mutters that they should switch cameras. Perhaps they aren't conference delegates at all but actually British intelligence operatives causing a distraction – it is impossible to tell.

They wait.

It happens so quickly that at first she doesn't understand what she is seeing. A short woman, petite, wearing a dark suit appears. Fredrik catches up with her and catches her from behind in a small dancing movement with his hands around her waist. For one merciful, floating moment it is as if she doesn't feel the pain.

They kiss each other.

She wants to look away in an attempt to obliterate what she is seeing, but she can't because it is so horrible and simultaneously deeply fascinating to see her husband kissing another woman.

And now she recognises Heather Ashford.

Fredrik shapes his mouth into a warm smile. He used to smile like that at me, she thinks. Perhaps he isn't playing a role at that moment, perhaps he is smiling at Heather simply because he is pleased to see her, in spite of everything.

Gustav asks her to sit down.

The couple soon appear on another monitor, as seen through the camera in the lift. There they are, standing next to each other while the lift carries them up.

'Now the third camera,' says one of the agents.

They wait.

Something is wrong. They ought to appear in the hotel corridor, but the lift is stopping on the wrong floor. Heather quickly exits the lift and disappears from sight. Fredrik tries to stop her, then the lift doors close.

'Bloody hell!'

Gustav is shouting. The men are already throwing themselves out of the door into the corridor. She is close behind them as they rush towards the lifts. Perhaps it's my fault, she thinks, snarling at her own stupidity and lack of self-control. Or perhaps Fredrik was too obvious; it doesn't matter now.

Fredrik is standing by the lifts like a pale and terrified creature in the soft light of the hotel corridor. He raises his hands
in resignation.

'Where is she?'

Over the course of a few thumping heartbeats she sees the
person she loved. She smells the scent of his fresh aftershave.
She wishes she could just hate him, it would be easier.

'Where is she?' roars one of the men.

'Fourth floor. She knew.'

His face trembles.

'Sorry.'

The metallic slam of a fire door hitting a wall echoes up to
her in the emergency stairwell. She tears down the stairs.

Her enemy is escaping two floors below her.

She knows there is only a minute or two before the woman
disappears and leaves them in uncertainty; they will never know
what really happened. She has to know, she thinks as she rushes
downwards.

Heather is still running, she can hear her rapid paces as she
passes the second and first floors on her way down.

Bente bursts through the door at the bottom. Two operatives
standing on the magenta carpet in the lobby turn to face her, ready
for battle, before recognising her. They shake their heads: not here.

The car park is deserted. She casts her gaze over the expanse
but can't see Heather anywhere, only two operatives from
counter-espionage who are spying out between rows of cars.
'Where is she?' she shouts over the car roofs. They are going to
lose the enemy, Heather is getting away, she cannot accept it.

She spots a movement in the corner of her eye. There, in
a black car ten metres away. Instinctively, she crouches and
hurries closer.

Suddenly, the car reverses at speed out of its space. She thumps the side and manages to glimpse red rear lights and a dark saloon sweep by her. She tumbles to the side. For a moment, she lies on the concrete floor staring at shiny black paint and tyre treads.

She crawls to her feet, groaning with pain. The car rushes through the car park. She runs. A moment later a silver-grey Volvo also sweeps up the exit ramp. She has to catch up, is all she can think, but she can't remember where she parked her own car. She holds up her key. There: two lights flash.

She sees the black car just as it drives into the Cortenbergh tunnel. Traffic is heavy, there is no space to make individual choices. The pain in her hip is pulsing more strongly now. When the two lanes merge on a curve she also catches sight of the silver-grey car, a couple of seconds behind the black one as it reaches the mouth of the tunnel. Heather is in the left-hand lane; she won't choose the exit returning back to the city centre, but probably won't turn off towards Schaerbeek either as it's all too easy to get stuck in suburban streets. Heather is heading out of the city.

Gustav calls. She can see she already has three missed calls from him. She just makes it through the large crossroads before the lights change, undertaking three cars in the inside lane and increasing her speed to the sound of ill-tempered honking behind her. '*Where are you?*' Gustav's voice fills the car. She doesn't reply; she needs to concentrate on the traffic and slipping into the gaps, adjusting her speed, following a rhythm she can't control.

'On the N23, heading for the airport.'

The margins are fine. In the afternoon traffic there are countless souls boxed up in their vehicles and she must be careful.

The swift flow can quickly turn into a stationary armada of hot metal.

She barely makes it when the black car turns off at the roundabout near Zaventem, heading not for the airport but onto the road south and away from Brussels. The silver-grey car has dropped out.

She races along the road heading away from the city. Where is she going? Two hours away is the French border, then Charles de Gaulle Airport, Paris.

Palisades of trees drum past. The high speed transforms reality in an onrushing flicker. She drives using gentle movements and an even speed, ten seconds behind the black car. What should she do if she catches up with Heather? She will hurt her. *Vengeance is mine; I will repay.* She has no other thoughts, she is filled with a sense that everything is happening according to unshakeable laws.

She has to brake sharply when she encounters a lorry inexplicably overtaking another lorry, and she gets stuck behind them. The lorries' dirty containers loom above her like a wall.

She just catches sight of Heather's car turning off.

Gustav calls again: has she made contact? He wants her coordinates and needs her to describe the car. A black saloon, she can remember two letters from the registration. She is on the R0 heading south.

No one is in a greater hurry than an escaping spy. Everything is about being able to act without hesitation, without making mistakes. Something about the resolute way Heather is driving suggests she knows exactly where she is going. The British Embassy and London are presumably working to evacuate their resource, out, away, to safety abroad, where she will disappear without trace under cover of a new identity.

She looks in the rear-view mirror but no one seems to be following her. When she looks forward again the car is gone.

It can't simply have disappeared, she thinks, slowing down, afraid to make the same mistake as the men before.

There. A narrow road.

She brakes hard. A van that has been behind her pulls out into the outside lane and passes her while pressing its horn. She turns into the small gap into the greenery.

A private road with a strip of grass up the middle. No more than a tractor track.

The trees vault over the road. She drives slowly until she reaches a crest. The black car is nowhere to be seen, but it must be here, there was no other way to leave the main road. She turns off the engine.

When she bends down she feels the familiar shape of the pistol-butt under the seat. She pulls out the weapon, puts on the holster and opens the car door.

The woods are silent. Dark shadows, small trees.

After briefly hesitating, she follows her instinct. She gets out of the car and goes into the trees, following the slope down through the brushwood. She stops, listening in the grey light.

She reaches an overgrown ditch and heaves herself out of the tall grass with difficulty. Pain cuts into her hip.

She doesn't spot them before she straightens: two large red-brown stallions standing right in front of her in a paddock. Their heads are watchfully raised, their muscular bodies unmoving. Their eyes are like wet black stones. They are looking at her.

She hates horses, they frighten her. She can't read them, she doesn't understand them.

One of the animals snorts with a dull, panting noise. Perhaps they see her as a threat. She doesn't belong here.

A short distance from the field is a stable. Beyond the paddock is a neat lawn running up to a house. A manor. There are large oaks growing beside the house. The tops of the trees tower above the lawn and house and frame everything in a way that gives her the unreal sensation that she is looking at a postcard.

The horses snort.

There is no one within sight. There is no one visible by the house, in the windows. She pulls out her mobile and sends Gustav a message with her GPS position – it is reassuring that he knows where she is.

She strides up a gravel path, walking slowly towards the house. Her weapon is heavy under her jacket. Her steps crunch loudly in the silence. She is visible, vulnerable.

Someone is taking good care of the stable. The gravel has been raked with great care into straight lines. The green lawn is immaculate.

The horses snort behind her, smacking their lips with disdain.

The front door of the manor opens. A middle-aged man with a sandy shock of hair, wearing chinos, a shirt and moss-green gilet, steps out. He raises his hand in greeting and smiles broadly. Then he comes down the steps and walks towards her.

The man has a fleshy, blotchy red face.

'*Bonjour*,' he calls out. 'Welcome!'

In her state of extreme vigilance, she feels as if everything is in slow motion.

'Hello,' she says, before falling silent.

She glances past the man towards the house and trees, turning her head and looking across the lawns. Heather is nowhere to be seen.

The man in the gilet walks smiling towards her along the gravel path.

'I'm so glad you could make it,' he says.

The man's gilet is open and he reaches into it with his hand for something. She tenses, prepared, but he merely pulls out a pair of sunglasses.

They shake hands. The man has a firm grip, he is stronger than he looks.

'We're going to show you the whole property. But I thought we would start inside.'

He says this calmly and cheerily, but she doesn't perceive him to be calm.

She looks over her shoulder. There are the horses.

The man gently touches her forearm.

'Well done for finding us.'

The man is talkative and says it is difficult to find them from the main road. If coming from the north you can hardly see it, there is a sign but you can only see it from the other direction.

'This is a truly beautiful house,' he says, pointing at the manor. 'Built in the early nineteenth century. We have several interested parties.'

'Who are you?'

The man stops short.

'Me? I'm the estate agent.'

He smiles, and as if setting her on the right track, then says:

'I spoke to your husband the other day. He said you were coming today. To see the house.'

He touches her arm.

'Shall we go inside?'

*

The man politely holds open the door. She enters a hall with square flagstones. A beautiful manor residence from 1825, he says, as if introducing her to an actual living person. Eight bedrooms, all in excellent condition.

She walks quickly through the house, entering a large farm-house kitchen with glittering detailing, before returning to the hall before the man catches up. She casts a glance up a staircase and then goes into the dining room. The man hurries after her. 'Isn't it magnificent?' He smiles. 'Late Empire-style,' he adds.

The rooms are light and peaceful – peaceful in the way that rooms only are when no one has been in them for many years. There are heavy velvet curtains in the windows, and she can perceive the smell of dust and moth-proofer. She turns to the estate agent.

'Can I take photos?'

'Naturally. Take as many as you like.'

She quickly pulls out her mobile and takes photo: the man's face is visible as a reflection in the glass. It isn't completely focused, but is identifiable, like a composite.

'It's marvellous, isn't it? The seller is amenable to including the furnishings too,' he adds. 'Since it's a probate sale . . .'

She hushes him.

The horses neigh. But there was another sound at the same time, far fainter, inside the house. Clicking.

Like steps on floorboards.

She rushes through the dining room and into the living room filled with heavy antique furniture before stopping to listen again.

'Where is she?'

'Who?'

The man looks troubled, he seems to think she is completely incomprehensible.

She manages to glimpse a shift in one of the mirrors hanging on the far wall, something dark moves rapidly through the reflection outside the house. She turns on her heel and runs to a window.

Heather is running across the lawn.

Bente falls headlong against the wall. The man crashes down on top of her, she stares into his contorted face. He reaches for her arms, trying to hold her down, and strikes savagely and hard at her face. She dodges and fumbles at her side. Her fingers close around something heavy. She swings towards his head and the object hits him under the eye. He falls to the side. She strikes him again and it is as if a small twig were being snapped when his nose is broken; the man falls backward, bawling.

A glass ashtray. She discards the bloody glass lump.

She hurries outside and runs across the lawn. The stable, she thinks.

The horses' heavy panting fills the darkness. The warm smell of dry grass, manure and the pungent odour of horse urine. She can hear the animals, their massive bodies moving in the stalls. Perhaps they sense her fear. Then she finds a light switch.

The room is illuminated by a glaring light. A cement passageway with a row of stalls. Beside her, one of the animals is staring at her. A black eye, unblinking and fixed. The oblong head nods.

The two stalls furthest away are empty: the doors are ajar. She imagines breath being held: someone who daren't breathe. She listens.

The pistol is heavy in her hands.

Heather's terrified face gapes at her. Motionless, she stares up at her from the stall where she is sitting, hunched like a child who has lost all hope.

Her thoughts in recent days have been incessantly focused on this woman who has forced her way into their family like an impalpable demon with the power to destroy her life. But the woman sitting there on the dirty stable floor is no threat, she is just a frightened woman whispering: 'Please, don't shoot. Please.'

The cone of subdued light hovers above the wooden table. Jonathan blinks at the light, barely awake. He must have forgotten to switch it off, he thinks to himself. Then he realises his mobile is vibrating.

It is Robert. His voice is strained and angry, and he makes no apology for calling in the middle of the night. '*We have reviewed the report,*' he says. '*It's not possible to verify much of it.*'

Fear pierces him like a long needle. The answers Khaled gave don't match the overall picture, he hears Robert say. '*And what bothers us,*' and now he can hear Robert checking his voice and making an effort not to sound too angry, '*is that a lot of it is total drivel. He's lying to you.*'

He sits up. He can't simply accept that the interrogation was unsuccessful. Which parts can't they verify? he asks while reaching for his clothes. Robert sighs at the other end of the line and wearily rattles off parts of the report.

He knows that Khaled didn't lie, he can tell when someone isn't telling the truth. He tries to explain this to Robert, who merely hums in irritation. He notices that he is defending himself and the man, as if they are bound together and about to sink into dark water together.

'*We don't have time for this,*' says Robert.

'Just let me talk to him.'

'No, *the others will have to take care of him*.'

He knows, they both know, that their conversation is essentially a one-way communication, the result of a series of decisions made in the Ministry of Defence by the powers that be, and that Robert is merely conveying the joint decision. He knows that he can't stand against the enormous power of that kind of bureaucracy, but he doesn't want to – he can't simply let it happen.

It is just after one o'clock. He dresses quickly and hurries through the house and across the yard.

Khaled is lying curled up on the basement floor beneath the harsh light of the fluorescent tube. Jonathan shakes him abruptly.

'What have you done?'

The man squints at him, scared.

'Why didn't you tell me the truth before?'

The man sits up and looks at him, perplexed.

'Your answers don't check out.'

They each sit on a chair. He pulls out the screen and scrolls, showing him a picture of a commander. Khaled gave them a name and an address, but there is no commander called that.

'I think he's called that.'

'You *think*? That's not good enough.'

'I may be wrong. I tried to remember, I promise.'

'Don't you understand what you've done?'

Perhaps the man really has been truthful and told them everything he remembered, but if none of it is true, then what does it matter? The heavy feeling that everything is hopeless makes him slump in his chair. He can't bear the thought of what will happen next, and it is intolerable that he can do nothing to prevent it.

A wild, desperate resistance awakens within him. In spite of it all, he is still the British Government's representative – the soldiers must obey him. We'll sort this, he says to himself, looking at the screen. He scrolls to a section of the report that Robert said they had been unable to verify.

'Tell me what this commander is called and where he lives.'

The man stares at the picture and says the same name as before.

'That's the wrong name.'

'Then I don't know.'

The man spreads his arms out. He says he is willing to do everything he can to help, everything. And then he repeats the same name as before. But that name isn't correct, according to Robert. It is so bloody frustrating that he doesn't know what to do.

'Focus. Try to remember.'

The man sobs.

'Please, help me. I'm just a taxi driver. I didn't know any of them . . .'

He tries to calm the man down – there, there – patting him on the shoulder while his own hands tremble. He shows him a new photograph and asks for a name and address. The man tries to gather his thoughts, but the fear is not helping; he opens and closes his mouth, shakes his head, he doesn't know.

'I can't protect you if you don't answer.'

Then the moment he has been trembling at the thought of arrives. He hears the door open and the soldiers come sauntering down the stairs. He gets up and tells them to wait outside, but they ignore him and direct their attention at the captive. With an enormous effort he quashes his quaking anxiety and repeats himself in a sharp and brusque tone:

'Wait outside.'

They pause; it is as if he has managed to penetrate through their assuredness and stop everything. But then the sergeant regains the upper hand with a scornful snort.

'Move.'

'No, we're not done.'

He stands in the sergeant's way, like a child in the school playground encountering a superior enemy but still not giving way.

When the soldiers step forward and pull the prisoner's clothes off, he knows the man is lost. But he says nothing. He steps to the side, what else is he supposed to do? The prisoner is standing in the middle of the concrete floor, a soft and pale body with bare, shrivelled genitals, and he thinks: If I stay in the room they won't do too much harm to him. His presence will hold them back, he persuades himself. It will act as a reminder that Her Majesty's Government is watching their actions, that they are serving their country, that certain standards are expected.

The soldiers are tired and irritated. One of them walks up to the prisoner and, as if bored, punches him hard in the stomach. He collapses. Another soldier bends down and pulls a noose over his head, attaching it to a drain so that he is soon standing on all fours with his skull close to the concrete floor, anus facing up. Everything occurs wordlessly, like silent theatre. He wants to intervene and turns to the sergeant, but can't form the words.

When the soldiers bring a bucket of water and pour it over the prisoner, he backs up against the wall. Strictly speaking, it is of Khaled's own making, he tells himself while the sergeant pulls out a bundle of towels – the same white ones as in the linen cupboard in the house.

*

The sergeant crouches by the captive's head and explains to him in English that he will give them the names and addresses of everyone who has travelled in his car. One of the soldiers interprets. The man groans. The air stinks, liquid runs along the floor. The soldiers breathe out, sitting on boxes. Jonathan keeps out of the way, furthest away in the room. The man is huddled in a pile and tethered to the drain. The sergeant pushes his side with his foot and makes him stand on all fours again. He holds the small screen under his nose and shows him a photo.

'Who is that?'

The prisoner groans hoarsely.

'What's that?'

The sergeant stretches and shakes his head. Then he walks around the man and gives him a hard kick between the piteously parted legs, right on the balls. The prisoner groans loudly. Then another kick, and another, the body spasming as he vomits into the drain. The soldiers get out their weapons, reinforcement rods, and start hitting the man across his back and legs and the soles of his feet with swift, rhythmic blows anywhere they can reach, gasping with the effort, and through the panting and dull, slapping impacts he hears a monotone roar coming from the man.

He looks away. 'Stop,' he mumbles, but there is no one listening. It can't carry on, he thinks, and perhaps it is because the scream is so terrible that all he wants is for the prisoner to die so he can escape the bawling, he wants to destroy the soldiers so he can avoid seeing their actions. He goes upstairs and hurries into the courtyard, but he isn't quite sure what he is meant to do. He hears the man's subdued cries through the doorway.

No. He has to go back. When he re-enters the room the sergeant is standing there with a wet rag pushing it into the prisoner's mouth until it looks like he is going to push it all the way down his throat.

They hold out the screen.

'Who is he?'

The sergeant pulls out the rag and waits. 'Who?' he repeats and the man pants and looks at him, Jonathan, but what is he supposed to do? The sergeant swears and pushes the rag back into his mouth. The sergeant soaks another towel and swings it around the captive's neck, sitting astride his back and pulling at the towel as if it were a bridle. The man shakes, twisting and turning, and is pushed to the floor under the weight of the sergeant's heavy body. The sergeant pulls the towel with all his might. After a while the body beneath him starts to shake and he lets go.

He is lying on the floor. They pour a bucket of water over him. They nudge the listless body with their boots. With a bizarre form of helpfulness, they carefully assist him into the usual position, slumped on his knees.

The sergeant crouches and holds the screen under the man's face.

'Who is he?'

The man mumbles.

'I can't hear you. Speak up.'

He has to stay in the room. That's the least he can do, he thinks to himself.

The sergeant has stopped for a break. The soldiers are smoking in the yard.

'Give them the right answer,' he whispers in Arabic. 'Please, just do it. You know them,' he says. 'I know you know them.'

The prisoner stares at him groggily – can't he hear what he

232

is saying? Then he appears to panic and starts pulling at the noose, panting, gasping for air.

'I don't know,' he pants, 'I don't know.'

'But you said you did know.'

'I don't remember. Help me, please. Help me.'

He is trying to save the man, that's how he sees it. If only he can get the man to talk to him, to give the real names and places, then he can still save him – what does he mean, saying he doesn't know?

He says a name and tries to get the man to understand that this is not the correct name.

'You know it's wrong,' he says. 'Why do you keep saying the same thing? Can't you give us a different name? You were their driver . . .'

The soldiers come back down the stairs and sit down on the boxes around them in the room. They wait. It has to happen now – doesn't Khaled understand that Jonathan is his saviour?

'I don't remember,' he says, shaking his head.

He leans in close to him, almost crawling down to him on the floor and for a while he is almost level with the captive's eyeline and their eyes are right against each other. He can smell the sour stench from his mouth. What does he mean, he doesn't remember?

'I don't know any of them,' he whispers. 'I just drove a car. What do you want me to say? I'll say anything.'

The realisation that the man really doesn't know runs through him like a deep chill. He will never be able to provide them with the right answer. He is just a driver, a Syrian taxi driver from Raqqa who ended up in the midst of the whirlwind of destruction and madness that has consumed his city. Perhaps he thought he was lucky when – against all the odds – he got a job for the new regime leaders. They came from Jordan, Libya, Iraq, even the UK; he didn't know them, he just drove them around in his car. No, he then thinks. It is a difficult situation, but the man is the right person. The very thought that the man has no idea about what they are asking is intolerable. He refuses to believe that such a mistake could have occurred, because what salvation would that leave, what meaning? He refuses to allow the doubt to take hold. Furiously, he whispers:

'Don't you understand? We need the truth.'

The prisoner doesn't answer, sweat running down the tense furrows on his face. And in that moment, his perception of Pathfinder is transformed. It happens quickly, like a chemical split; from one second to the next the man is someone else, or perhaps it is that for the first time he sees who he actually is: a stranger. There is an enormous distance between him and the panting, skinny body on the floor. He thinks: What are we to each other? Nothing. And that is a relief, because he had been invested in the other man, but now that feeling is alleviated and he feels like he can breathe more freely; there is nothing between them, there never was.

He gets up. The pale body on the floor isn't his, it is here as a peculiar object on display – how was he ever able to identify with him? he wonders. He angrily says that he is disappointed, why won't he cooperate? And then, without thinking, he kicks the man's side. Not hard, but not softly either, and it is a relief for him. He is on the verge of tears. The soldiers seem to think he is laughing, and they holler, pleasantly surprised.

The darkness in the kitchen is like thick water as he takes in deep, gasping breaths. Then the darkness wants to leave him. He makes it to the sink before throwing up. Leaning over the basin, he waits while the cramps subside. Then he sits down on the floor and finds some respite; it feels good to sit there in the quiet, spacious kitchen – something like that assumes a strangely enlarged sense of significance.

When he opens his eyes again it is lighter in the room.

He starts when he sees the sergeant standing by the table, as if convinced that he too will be struck.

'Wake up,' says the sergeant. 'We need you.'

He shivers in the cool morning air as they cross the yard. The soldiers are sitting by one wall, a row of sullen figures. As they approach the door, he pulls himself together and tries to control his breathing because he doesn't want the sergeant to notice his anxiety.

The basement room is illuminated. The sickly-sweet stench of blood and shit immediately thrusts itself upon him. Nausea makes him belch and he pulls his shirt over his mouth for protection. In the harsh light of the fluorescent tube he can see the man lying spread out with his face against the drain and his arms splayed from his sides. The concrete is dark from urine and blood. The body is covered in bumps, wounds and large bruises. The face is swollen, with a fine web of burst blood vessels, as if they have burst through an eruption of internal pressure.

He immediately makes up his mind: he will never speak of this. He will carry it with him, remembering but never uttering a word. Because he already knows, standing beside the man's body, that if he tried, then the words would grow within him until something burst. He nods when the sergeant tells him that they need to clean up.

His entire being recoils at the way the man is lying there, naked and beaten to a pulp. How can he see himself as part of this? It isn't possible. But if he were ever to tell someone what happened, perhaps many years later, when life has moved on, when he thinks he is ready to talk and able to see himself as the person he thinks he is, despite everything, he would still describe how he and the soldiers helped to pick up the man's body and wrap him in rough tarpaulin. He lifted the body by the ankles and it hung between him and one of the soldiers like a sack. It was light – weighing almost nothing. And he thought: Dear God, what have we done?

He would say that they placed the bundle in the back of the van. Once the body was inside the rustling blue tarpaulin he became anxious that it might still be alive. It was a strange thought, but he couldn't let go of it. It was as if the corpse hated him for what he had done, and he was ashamed.

He would say that he and the sergeant and one of the soldiers had driven along the narrow gravel tracks in the half-darkness up towards the mountains on the Turkish side of the border. It was dawn when they stopped on a bend in the road in a place where the locals threw away their rubbish. The hillside below the road was strewn with refuse, plastic bags hanging from the shrubs and rustling in the wind. They dragged the bundle out and stood at the edge of the road, swinging it between them. He held on to the tarpaulin as best he could, but the body was cumbersome, he lost his grip and was afraid it would fall out. He just wanted to get away from there. The bundle flew through the air, they saw it tumble down the slope and come to rest on other bags of rubbish. Then they drove back in silence.

He would say that it had been awful, but also a relief. The matter was resolved. But he didn't know how to carry on living. He might say that it is difficult to explain the insight that what he had done would never leave him, only grow over time and

236

become an incident in his life that was so heavy that he would never be free of it. Because what he had done was unforgivable. But it is strange how one gets used to it, how the mind tries to make the best of everything. How the unbearable becomes liveable with, over time, like a callus, a tender bruise that he is careful not to touch.

When they return, the other soldiers have lit a barbecue. That is what receives him in the chill morning air: the smell of grilled meat.

They are driving into London. He can hear people asking him things, but he is too tired to answer. He sits silently reclined in the backseat. He can't stand the music playing on the radio, the beat makes him feel unwell. 'Turn off the radio,' he says after a while. A fine drizzle turns to steady rain.

He is back, but for a brief moment everything still seems foreign. He watches the evening traffic and the smooth onrushing movements of the cars. How is it possible for such a well-organised normal day to be happening under the same evening sky that looms above the House? There wasn't the slightest sign here of what had happened; he could claim to be innocent. It could be done with obscene ease – everyone would believe him.

He is received by the two handlers and Grandma, the coordinator, who unlocks the flat.

It isn't the same flat as the one he stayed in before he left. This one is different, newer, with shiny surfaces. He sees other people, there are so many of them around him. Exhaustion throbs through him.

One of the handlers shows him to his room and explains where everything is, the practical details. He barely has the energy to listen. When they leave, the flat is wonderfully quiet.

In the bathroom he catches sight of himself in the mirror, and at first he can't comprehend that it is him. The face is emaciated, the cheeks are slack and hollow. There are dark shadows around his eyes. An ugly scratch has formed into a scab on his forehead. He thought he was smiling, but no, the corners of his mouth aren't moving. His face remains serious.

The room is light. What time is it? He is lying in a bed. Then he calms down and closes his eyes. When he once again wakes up the light has changed.

'Hello,' he calls out.

The response from the other rooms is one of dense silence. He gets up, stiffly pulling on a dressing gown.

The flat is bright and tastefully decorated. A generous sofa and two armchairs that no one seems to have sat in are in the living room surrounded by bookcases filled with unopened volumes. The kitchen is clinically clean and well equipped, and even the fridge contains enough food for a substantial breakfast and dinner. This could be a home, but no one lives here. There is presumably no name on the door and no post ever arrives. The logisticians at Vauxhall Cross are careful about those kinds of details.

The digital clock on the cooker confuses him – it must be wrong. Has he slept for more than twenty hours? His thoughts move slowly and coagulate. He peers out of the thin curtains onto a narrow, neat street in Kensington. A well-heeled area where no one wants to be in view and everyone prefers discretion.

His legs stiff, he walks to the bathroom and after relieving himself and taking a shower he feels much better.

Few people know where he is. That makes him calm. He is once again just Jonathan Green, an employee of MI6. He doesn't need to pretend, doesn't have to claim to be the Trade Attaché, an aid worker or a patient. He is nothing.

Even within MI6 there are departments without the authority to know his true identity, who only know who he is by a code name or number. That is the fundamental principle behind a secret: it controls information, enveloping and protecting it.

He sits in the unused kitchen while it gets dark. Having just awoken, it is confusing to see day becoming night, as if time had left him half a rotation of the earth's axis behind. In that moment he has a diffuse but intense experience of standing outside of existence. What does it want of him? Does it really apply to him? Reality, he thinks, all this is just an ongoing flow of perceptions that he could leave, quietly and unnoticed, without it making the slightest difference. He thinks about Antakya. What they did there was bad, perhaps part of him will never be able to reconcile himself with what happened. Yet he let it happen. If that was the wish of the government, how could he have changed the course of events? He knows that isn't the right question. But he also knows the feeling will dissipate, his gaze will grow accustomed, because it gets used to even the worst things. Over time it won't matter, he tries to persuade himself.

It is only then that he discovers his mobile and real passport on the kitchen counter. He reaches for them and thumbs slowly through the passport. Someone has been here while he was sleeping and returned his real identity. He will be leaving the flat as Jonathan Green, but he doesn't know whether that is a relief.

He turns on his mobile and is surprised when it starts to vibrate in the palm of his hand. Ten missed calls, eight new messages. He would like to delete them because it is the ambassador in Brussels who has called him, and he can't stand that man's brisk, demanding whine.

'Jonathan, we've got a bit of a crisis here. Please call me as soon as you can.'

Then the ambassador again, but now in a sharp tone:

'Jonathan, I don't know where you are. This is important. It's regarding your assistant Heather Ashford. Please call me. Thanks.'

A shooting sensation of fear flashes through him.

'Where are you? This is urgent, Jonathan. It's regarding your assistant. She has been declared persona non grata. They're throwing her out the day after tomorrow.'

He closes his eyes.

'Jonathan . . .'

He puts down his mobile with a sinking feeling. He should never have trusted Heather, he thinks. She was too young, too inexperienced; it was madness to give her such a demanding assignment.

The thought hits him like a sinking feeling of nausea. Heather said she had dealt with the leak; she must have lied to him. Now he is in a labyrinth he can no longer survey. It's over, he thinks to himself. They'll crucify him.

'Hello.'

Robert is standing in the doorway.

'You scared me.'

'Welcome back,' says Robert, lumbering into the kitchen as if it were his own home, opening the fridge and helping himself to a bottle of mineral water that he drinks in deep gulps without taking his eyes off him. He feels the room shrinking, as if Robert's presence is forcing him towards its edges.

'I've got good news,' says Robert, leaning against the kitchen counter. 'You're looking at the new Assistant Head of MI6.'

Jonathan looks down at the table and smiles to disguise his

discontent. Robert, the new operational chief for all of MI6. The degradation hits him like a caustic acid. Then he realises he ought to say something.

'Then let me offer you my congratulations.'

Robert nods and looks at him in concern.

'This whole business didn't go well, Jon.'

He says nothing.

'You delivered a fat nothing. What you got out of Pathfinder is bloody worthless. I'm starting to wonder whether you even interrogated him.'

'I think it was the wrong man.'

'It was *not* the wrong man.'

Robert slams his hand against the kitchen counter; the sudden noise makes him jump. He can imagine Robert as an interrogator – how inexorable it would be. But he wouldn't have had more success with Pathfinder than he had.

'The Swedes have taken Heather.'

It becomes apparent to him that his former friend is now his superior. Second-in-command, Head of Foreign Operations. Perhaps he has already discussed the crisis in Brussels with their chief, C, perhaps he has already signed an order to get rid of him, to exclude him from the organisation he has committed his life to.

'Old boy,' says Robert with a degree of sarcasm, 'you really are causing problems.'

He says nothing.

'What does she know, your agent – about the House?'

He thinks. 'Nothing,' he mumbles.

'Do the Swedes still have the documents?'

'I don't know, Robert,' he says with angry obstinacy that makes him sound shrill. 'I don't know what the Swedes know.'

'You said you had the leak under control. That she had eliminated it.'

He spreads his arms out in an ironic, resigned gesture.

'That was the information I had. I was presumably wrong.'

Robert is immediately pale. His head drops, his face bloated and aged.

A cold joy begins to grow within Jonathan. He can see they are thinking the same thing. If the Swedes have the documents, then it will harm Robert. The House is liable to come tumbling down on top of him, burying both him and his career.

'You were supposed to take care of this,' says Robert.

His own career must soon be over, but if that is the case, then it should be for Robert, too. Over the years Robert has always pushed forward, taken all the adulation, got everything. If it is possible to ruin it all for him, then he wants nothing more.

'Bloody hell!' Robert bellows.

Gone is the indolent, superior crown-prince-in-waiting of MI6. Instead there is a raging, hard-pressed man who knows that his carefully calculated career plan may crack like thin ice beneath his feet at any moment. Robert leans forward, close to him.

'You are a disgrace to the service, Jon. This mess is your fault. Your poor judgement and useless management. If these documents get out, then Parliament will be competing to tear down our MI6.'

It is so unfair. He has always been loyal to MI6. He couldn't have stopped that cursed analyst from leaking. He has tried to do everything right.

Robert is wandering around the room.

'You will deal with this,' he says, pointing a finger at him as if it were a pistol. 'You will eliminate the documents immediately, otherwise I will blame you. You will take the blame alone. Believe you me, Jon. I will crush you.'

And he believes him.

Kate is standing in the doorway. She stares at him as he steps into the hallway as if she can't believe her eyes. 'Hello,' she says in a low voice. Then she regains her senses and moves backwards from the door to let him in.

Everything is as before. It seems completely absurd and simultaneously completely natural to be home again.

Kate turns around without saying a word and disappears into the house. He puts down his bag and saunters after her. He finds her at the dining table with her computer, absorbed by its blue light, and when he comes into the room she looks up hastily, as if she is surprised to see him there.

From the headphones he can discern the faint sound of shouting and noise. He makes to move around the table to see what is happening on the screen, but notices that she would rather be alone so leaves her. He is exhausted from Syria and is still unable to muster interest.

His thoughts return anxiously to what has to happen now, in Brussels. He has to make contact with Heather. But he doesn't know how; he has already tried calling her and her phone is off.

Kate, with her resolute seriousness, is encroaching upon the calm he needs. He had hoped she would be asleep when he came home. He can't talk to her about any of what happened in London or Syria – not a word – yet that is all he can think about. He is alone in all of this, and having her around just makes him feel lonelier.

The kitchen is a mess. Plates with food crusted onto them, dirty glasses and cups are scattered on the kitchen counter. He gets out a clean wine glass, finds an open bottle of white wine in the fridge and pours a generous glass.

'But is there someone who can give them a lift?' he hears Kate say in the other room. 'Okay, okay.' She is standing in the dining room talking on the phone. Indecisive, he stands still in the kitchen, but then goes into the living room.

Kate is standing by the dining table with her back to him, her arms around her small body as if she is cold, mobile to her ear.

He has killed a man. Imagine if she knew. If she knew that, his career and the whole life they have together might soon be over. It is so overwhelming that he forlornly does what requires the very least of him: he flops onto the living-room sofa and turns on the TV. Three sports channels are showing the same football match, with different commentators and slightly different shifting angles in the simultaneous flow of games. Barely ten minutes of the first half have been played. He drinks wine and watches the match, all while he can hear Kate's brief, low conversations from the dining room.

A Spanish team has possession. A rapid cross is followed by a forward on the offensive, the player bounding along the touchline. The battle is approaching. The players run about in their formations. An uncontrolled pass is intercepted by a defender for the French team and the attack is over just as quickly as it began. The rhythm of the game yields to a series of long, cautious passes. He looks up.

Kate is talking about the fact that they can't just wait, it is a family with a three-year-old, then he can't hear her over the chatter of the television. The French team go on the counter-offensive in a series of rapid passes. But he is no longer following the match, instead watching Kate as she paces back and forth on the other side of the sliding doors to the dining room.

As if she senses him watching her, she turns and looks angrily at him. She disappears into the kitchen.

He can't deal with her, but he can't get away – it is as if the whole house is enveloped in a dark gravitational field. He gets up to fetch more wine.

Her computer is standing on the dining table. A Facebook page is visible; he reads a few of the posts: a steady stream of appeals to provide clothing, medicines, questions about whether anyone can take in a family with a child. Kate has written a post. She is offering to give lifts, she has posted her phone number. It is careless – it might also lead to him.

Another page is open in another tab. A shaky video clip. Someone filming with a mobile phone. It is a district in central Aleppo. Despite the crumbling façades, he recognises the office block on the corner of Al-Mutanabbi Street. It should be taller – but the top floors have collapsed forming a piecemeal stack of destroyed offices. It is as if an angry giant has put its fist straight down through the building.

Kate is sitting in the kitchen crying.

'Kate?'

'Frances called.'

He is silent. He has always known that sooner or later his life would collapse under the weight of all the secrets.

'She told me . . .'

He wants to say something extenuating, that it wasn't serious, that he regrets it, but he doesn't manage to before Kate says:

'I can't live like this.'

There have been nights of paralysing anxiety that she will find out what he is up to, but now, instead, it is a tremendous relief. Perhaps he has longed to hear those words from her. For a brief moment he can see her and himself, as if looking at them in a doll's house, and then he thinks she is right – she is always right. They can't live like this.

'I'm sorry, Kate.'

The words feel awkward in his mouth, like sharp rocks. He isn't even sure whether they are true any longer. It is sad, he wishes deep down that this had happened a long time ago. That she hadn't sacrificed so much. Because he is a good person, he wasn't with Frances to hurt Kate. He was just doing what he wanted to do, he thinks to himself. It had nothing to do with Kate. He is used to separating things, everything in his life is compartmentalised. It is as if one emotion could just as well be another. He has loved Kate and now she is completely unimportant to him, which is strange.

'Who are you, Jonathan?'

'You know who I am.'

He waits, trying to determine the right thing to say. Then he stops himself, realising how strange it is to think like that: as if this were an interrogation or contact with an enemy intelligence service.

'You used to be open. You were considerate. I know you loved me. But I haven't felt that for a long time.'

He says nothing.

'Sometimes I look at you and think you're this person with me and someone completely different when I can't see you. Like now. You've lied to me.'

'Yes, and I'm very sorry . . .'

'What sort of person are you?'

'I'm a completely normal person.'

'Where have you been?'

'You know I can't talk about my work.'

'But you must be able to tell me *something*.'

She stares angrily at him until she realises that he really isn't going to say anything.

She turns around and reaches for her phone. But the movement is more of a pretext to avoid showing her face.

If he tells her what he works on and what he has done . . . A relationship isn't just based on what you say to each other, but also what you spare the other from having to hear.

'What should I say?'

She looks at him sadly.

'I don't know, Jon. What about the truth?'

'Okay. I love Frances. I have always loved her.'

She looks at him, her eyes wide open, her face hurt.

He knows he has crossed a line. A final line. But he wanted to shake Kate up and make her see that he isn't the impassive man she believes him to be and that deep down he is afraid he has always been.

Bente crosses the neat park in the Square de Meeûs in which office workers are eating their lunch as a light shower passes by. Her hip still hurts. She has been at home for two days to avoid surveillance. It's a relief not to have to see her staff.

A war is now raging. Sources in London say the British are turning all data from across the European continent inside out in their search for Heather.

Almost three hours after she silently left Fredrik and the boys at the breakfast table, she approaches the Section's shiny glass façade. First, she drove to the airport, before heading for the city centre. At Porte de Namur she had rapidly handed the car to an operative from Stockholm and hurried down into the metro station, going as far as Trône and then emerging into the clear sunshine, slipping into the lunchtime hubbub. She still isn't sure whether she is in the clear.

She crosses the bright lobby, but doesn't take the lift up as she would on an ordinary day. Instead, she inserts a key and selects level minus two.

The culvert is a slit of grey concrete. She follows it to the end and enters her code. The white fire door swings open.

A man leans his head out vigilantly, but he recognises her and relaxes.

Gustav's people are sitting at their screens in a small ante-room. They are working shifts around the clock to prepare material for the interrogation going on in the adjacent room, behind the next white fire door. Fears, hopes, dependencies, debts, every detail of Heather's personal history and work forms the raw material used by the interrogator against her.

'How's it going?'

Gustav grimaces.

They have been holding Heather in there for over twenty-four hours. They are already working overtime, because with each hour that passes they approach the moment when they must let her disappear into the clear autumn weather.

They are taking a short break. Heather needs to relieve herself.

Gustav appears to be maintaining a strict regime: she is not permitted to leave her cell.

'She admits that she works at the British Embassy and that she met Fredrik at a workshop, but nothing else. She knows she can wait us out.'

Stockholm has gone through her mobile, he explains. Everything points to her having worked alone. But they still don't know exactly what she did. And they need to rule out the idea that there might be more people like her – agents infiltrating the Swedish system.

'The Belgian Ministry of Foreign Affairs is going to declare her as a persona non grata as soon as we can demonstrate that she is MI6,' says Gustav. 'They'll throw her out immediately.'

'Can I go in?'

Heather is slumped on a chair in the small cell. Behind her is a mattress and in the corner a basic toilet and handbasin. The air is stifling; they have turned down the ventilation on purpose.

Heather looks at her in alarm. Her face is pale and washed out, she is exhausted, dried up. Bente stands by the wall and observes the slight young woman. She would like to crawl inside her like a parasite and comprehend how she managed to make her husband fall for her so hard. How was she able to exert power like that? After all, this is no demon before her but a completely ordinary woman with straight dark hair that she occasionally tucks nervously behind her ear.

Gustav is right: she hasn't cracked. Because when Heather meets her eyes she sees the stubbornness and the furtive expression. Heather knows that by keeping quiet she will win.

She wants to say that she doesn't care that Heather has slept with her husband, but that is irrelevant now. She still has to make an effort not to look at her mouth and think about the fact that those lips have kissed him, taken him in her mouth. The thought stings like a burn.

She puts her hand in her pocket and retrieves the flash drive.

'This is what you're looking for, isn't it?'

Heather can't hide her reaction; she stares at the small black object.

'You've used your own body to get at this information.'

Heather glowers silently at her.

'I'll show you.'

She puts the drive in the computer lying on the table by the door and quickly clicks through the documents. Then she sits down on a chair opposite with the computer on her lap. Heather can't help looking at what she is showing on the screen. She doesn't know, Bente thinks. She has no idea what the documents contain.

She pulls up a photo. The House. The courtyard. Then a beaten, swollen face. A string of the House's clients.

'Why do you think Jonathan wanted you to get your hands on this?'

She leans forward. Their eyes are level. Heather remains defiantly silent.

'Look,' she says, pointing at the screen. 'These are lists of people that allied forces captured and that your colleagues subjected to hard interrogation.'

She points at Jonathan Green's signature.

'Why are you showing me this?'

Her tone is calm and scornful; she doesn't understand what is happening. It is working; Heather thinks Bente is trying to shake her, frighten her with the documents.

Bente shows her the ten most important documents relating to the House and then to Hercules, calmly explaining how the operation is planned. Heather listens with a frown.

'Do you understand?'

Heather shrugs her shoulders.

The camera on the wall is filming everything.

'Are you listening? Do you understand what I am showing you?'

Heather nods. She drinks the poison without smelling a rat.

They sit there for more than an hour and when Bente closes the computer she knows that Heather will never escape her grip. The young agent doesn't understand yet, but she now knows a secret way above her rank. Heather shouldn't even be familiar with the code name Hercules, or the House, let alone what they conceal. The last unauthorised individual in MI6 who saw these documents was B54, who was found dead a few weeks earlier.

'Do you see the camera there?'

Heather nods. And slowly, the penny begins to drop. Her face is taut with fear. She tries to resist and shrugs her shoulders, but she knows she is caught in the trap, she is just unwilling to accept it.

There are secrets that tear apart everything that comes close to them and Heather has just swallowed a big chunk of one.

She thinks she can see Heather changing. She looks confused, as if she had just awoken from a strange dream. They will release her soon, but she will never be free because she knows too much. The knowledge she now possesses cannot be erased, it makes her a burden on those she thought would protect her.

'Jonathan Green is returning to Brussels this evening,' she says. 'I'm going to make sure he gets the video. He'll doubtless find it interesting.'

Fear turns Heather's face to a stiff mask.

'What sort of trick is this?'

'You mean tricks like sleeping with my husband. Coming into my home.'

Heather's face is covered in weariness. She looks furrowed and worn out, a woman caught in a system she will never escape. One of many women tricked into sacrificing themselves for a greater goal.

Heather dries her eyes.

'What should I do?' she says.

'Tell us everything.'

As Jonathan wanders up the stairs of the embassy he is remark-ably clear-headed.

He is early, the corridors are in a state of unusual and pleasant peacefulness. He has spent the night lying awake on the sofa as thoughts about how to resolve everything have bounced around in a confusing whirlwind. His thoughts destroyed all prospects of sleep and he got up early, before dawn, to get out of the house before Kate woke.

Heather has finally replied with a short message: *I have been released*. He hurries to the trade department and Heather's office, but she isn't there. She is still useful – overnight an idea has taken hold of how she might come in handy, and now he is worried she may already have left. He has to find her, find out exactly what happened before London gags her.

The door to the photocopying room is ajar. The machine is performing its lightning-fast sweeps back and forth. He pops his head in but she isn't there.

Then he spots her sitting on the floor.

He likes observing people who aren't aware he has seen them – something of an occupational hazard. The facial expressions of someone who thinks they are alone are often radically different from those of someone who knows they are being watched. Heather's is grimly absorbed. Her career in MI6 will be brief.

'Good morning,' he says, leaning further through the door. She looks up with a haunted expression. She has been crying.

The photocopier works quickly and rhythmically.

He picks up the bundle in the feed tray and thumbs through it. There are three top secret reports on Brexit.

Naturally she has yielded under questioning. Their threats have taken hold of Heather and now they are testing her to see whether she is useful to them. A sample, he thinks to himself with a sigh. He is on the verge of failure. The tiniest error ... It was fortunate that he discovered this, otherwise he would have had to handle another leak.

He pretends nothing has happened – she would only lie to him – and takes the papers out of the photocopier.

'Come with me, please,' he says warmly while heading into the corridor.

He plays the good boss and fetches them each a glass of water and, to be on the safe side, some paper hankies.

She has already started packing. The bookcases already have gaps, and the trinkets she used in an attempt to make her office more personal are in a moving box, together with folders and notebooks. There won't be a trace left of her tomorrow.

Once she is gone he will never know what passed between her and the Swedes. He has to make her realise that the only person who can save her is the sandy-haired, tranquil man in a grey suit in front of her. In London it will be too late – Vauxhall Cross will make her promise eternal silence and loyalty before casting her out.

'When is your flight?'

'This afternoon,' she says, fiddling with her glass. Then it is as if she can't hold back her despair. 'I'm so sorry,' she whispers, hiding her face behind one hand.

He makes a deprecating gesture, like any good boss should. But it is as if she were genuinely seeking absolution.

'I failed, didn't I?'

She is truly insistent; perhaps she wants to hear that everything will be okay. But he needs her bad conscience, so he tells it as it is: yes, she failed. He can barely stand her trembling face as she fights back the tears. He should never have given her the assignment.

'*We* failed,' he says.

Her sorrow and shame provide him with the opportunity he has been hoping for. Her feelings of guilt: he needs them. Guilt is a form of loyalty.

'But we may be able to resolve this,' he says, smiling at her. 'If you simply tell London that you found and destroyed the documents, but that we were then discovered . . .'

'Should I really . . . ?'

He nods. Yes; she should lie to them.

Then he slowly reviews the day she visited the target, Fredrik Jensen. She hesitates in embarrassment and tries to avoid the more awkward parts of the story. He calmly asks her to tell it as it happened. He is tempted to hiss, 'Good God, will I have to tear the truth from you?' But he knows that won't elicit the truth, so he makes an effort to maintain his usual calm. They will ask exactly the same questions in London, he explains; she must be prepared to answer precisely and without hesitation. So they are practising.

'What happened the day you visited Fredrik Jensen?'

The mineral water in the glass on the table in front of her ripples quietly. She is quiet. Or perhaps she is looking for the right words. Bubbles rise in the glass and emit a barely perceptible light whisper, as if the water already knows the answers.

Then she explains. She went to Fredrik's, well, to their home, on the Friday two weeks ago. They usually met at a hotel, Le Louise, or the apartment in Ixelles, but that day he invited her home. She clears her throat. And they slept together.

'Where?'

She looks at him in surprise. 'The bedroom.'

'And then what did you do?'

They talked, drank some wine. He asks which wine, but she can't remember the brand, just that it was white. She has to remember things like that, he says sternly, because in London they will ask her everything.

When Fredrik disappeared into the bathroom she searched the house. Thanks to surveillance directed at the house, she knew there was a study upstairs, so she began there. She found a safe. If the documents were anywhere in the house it was there. She looks proud when she explains how she installed two monitoring applications on the family computer; she was quick and had time to search the bedroom and living room as well as the basement. But she found nothing. Then he came out of the bathroom. They kissed. And he wanted to do it again.

She looks away.

They stood on the stairs and did it. And then, while they were standing there, the younger son came home.

'Their son?'

What he is hearing now is all new to him. Why didn't she tell him this before?

The boy saw them. She remembers the way he stood there staring. And then he stormed off and she heard him shouting at his father and she thought everything was over. But then, in the days that followed, nothing happened. She doesn't know what Fredrik did, but the boy kept quiet.

She wanted to abort, but it wasn't an option. It took a week before she managed to persuade Fredrik to invite her back to his home again. But that time she was lucky; she found Bente Jensen's mobile lying in the hall. He must remember? Yes, he remembers. She took the mobile and installed the malware they had been provided with by London. At the Swedish reception the same evening she put the phone in Fredrik's jacket pocket. It was risky, but it worked.

'And the documents?'

She hadn't managed to get into the safe, she explains disconsolately. She had brought a decoder, but hadn't had time to crack the code. She only ever had a few minutes while Fredrik was in the shower.

He looks quietly at his young, beautiful, but no longer wholly successful agent and wonders with resignation what the Swedes have told Heather to make her willing to cooperate with them. Sapping anxiety gnaws at his intestines.

'So where are the documents now?'

'Surveillance suggests that Bente Jensen still has them in the safe. But I don't know for sure.'

She twists the glass uneasily between her hands. But she is telling the truth. He concentrates, going through his thoughts for a dizzy moment, considering which possible risks and potential mistakes might occur.

The small lie he has come up with must now be grafted onto the events she has just described, and be allowed to grow.

'You can tell London that you opened the safe the first time you visited the Jensens. Then you were discovered by the boy. You fled and met your boss – me,' he says. 'You gave me the

258

documents and I destroyed them. That's the only thing you need to change about your story, nothing else.'

She looks concerned.

'Let that be your only truth.'

He gets up.

'Oh, and by the way,' he says, handing her the papers from the photocopier. 'Stop this straight away. You're not a traitor, Heather.'

She turns pale and he knows he has guessed correctly. The Swedes aren't stupid; it was lucky he caught her out. Now she is bound to him through guilt and gratitude, the strongest ties there are. She will tend to the small lie he has given her.

'Sorry.'

'Just tell London exactly what I asked you to. Then it'll all be okay.'

Sitting in front of his computer on the fifth floor, he visits the website of a modest company that makes databases. He finds their customer service page. He rests his fingertips on the keyboard for a short while as he weighs up which words to include in his next countermove. A brief message through the customer service page will have to do: *We have cooperated for a long time and need to discuss the continuation of our relationship. Would appreciate a prompt response.*

Everywhere he turns there are enemies. The abyss is tugging at his feet. He mustn't think about how close everything is to failure. He must forget the House and everything that has happened, he thinks, and look forward. If Heather just does as he has instructed her, he will win time, perhaps enough to get to the documents. Perhaps, he thinks with desperate hope, he can manage to make the Swedes see how deeply they are harming the relationship and persuade them to let the documents disappear. He won't fall.

Then he calls a number that he hasn't used once during his time in Brussels. It rings twice before a businesslike voice answers.

'Jonathan, it's a been long time.'

'I need you and your brother.'

She reads the message that arrived a few minutes earlier via their website and knows that it is Jonathan Green. She can hear the anxiety behind the words, and she knows she has the upper hand in the game they are playing.

Over the course of just twenty-four hours, ten new young faces from counter-espionage in Stockholm have noiselessly and politely appeared – as if they had grown straight out of the lino floor. They have quietly barricaded themselves into the conference room. No one is allowed in except her.

Gustav closes the frosted glass door behind her. Yes, he has seen Green's message. The fish, as Gustav refers to him, is on the move.

They released Heather to see whether the fish took the bait. The water is bobbing, the fish is swimming in big circles around the hook.

But she is aching with doubt. They both know how loyal Jonathan Green is to his own organisation. Jonathan means it when he says he works for Her Majesty's Government. He is under pressure, but is that enough to make him turn traitor?

'Gustav, are you certain about this?'

He shrugs his shoulders. Of course, 'certain' is a word people are reluctant to use in an industry of uncertainties and half-truths. Naturally he is uncertain. But she doesn't like his restrained elation. He wants this too much, she thinks.

'So what do you think?'

'We play high.'

Jonathan Green is vulnerable and open to influence, is the assessment. She can see that, but Gustav is too keen about the opportunity to haul in a shiny, rarely seen and valuable fish – one swimming deep inside British secrets.

Gustav goes to the table where his staff are sitting and asks them to listen. Everyone stops, quiet. This is what Gustav loves, she thinks to herself as she sees him surrounded by his team.

'I want to say a few words,' he says.

Then he talks about Jonathan Green. He asks them to remember who they are approaching. This is a man who has committed his life to working in MI6, the service that invented all the methods they are now using against him. Green is one of the most skilled individuals they have ever gone up against. If they are to tempt him, they must handle him with the utmost caution. 'He has no reason to trust us. That's why there will be no surveillance of Jonathan Green, except for tracking his mobile. During the contact itself there is to be no bugging, no microphones or cameras. And, since some of them are already wary, no physical surveillance throughout the operation. We will use the documents, turn the House against him, but we can't give him any reason to suspect it.'

A surprised silence spreads around the table.

No babysitters. No surveillance. Only the passive tracking of Green's mobile phone via GPS. And no one to be anywhere nearby except for him and Bente Jensen, he concludes, gesturing at her.

She is about to leave the room when one of the men from the

hotel approaches and gives her a three-digit telephone number. She recognises what it is: an emergency code. It only has to ring once for them to enter crisis mode.

'Only in emergencies,' he says with a friendly smile. 'We'll come straight in without knocking.'

A layer of low cloud is moving across the dark, wet city. Yet another evening shower. Gustav wants a cigarette and wonders where on earth he is allowed to smoke. They take the lift to the roof, walking the final bit up the echoing, clattering fire stairs and emerging into the gusting wind on the roof. They have stood like this many times, her shivering next to a smoking Gustav Kempell, in Stockholm, in Vienna, in Brussels. A raindrop falls from an incredible height and leaves a dark mark on the roofing felt. Standing in the shelter provided by a large ventilation duct, they talk in low voices. Gustav asks her how things are at home. What can she say? Things are terrible. She and Fredrik aren't talking. The EU Commission building looms before them like a fortress, seeming oddly close by. From where they are standing, it is also possible to glimpse the British Embassy in the swarm of buildings.

'Are you okay?' says Gustav, blowing smoke.

She nods. She is ready.

A beep notifies him of a new message on his mobile, and he is already holding the phone before the noise has stopped. For a second, he thinks it may be Robert, or by some miracle Frances. But the sender is unknown; it contains a link.

He looks at the picture. It is an advert on an auction site in the 'Home Electronics, Computers, Accessories' category.

There is a photo of an ugly black flash drive.

USB flash drive in perfect condition, reads the description. *For sale or will consider exchange for item of equivalent value*. The seller wants to be contacted by email. He quickly writes a brief message:

I am interested.

He waits. A minute or so later, a reply appears that confirms his suspicion that he is not on an auction site at all, but is in fact within an isolated, digital room controlled by Swedish counter-espionage:

What do you have to offer?

He snorts. They are so shameless; typical Swedes, boorish and no finesse. They have already drained Heather, and have the documents, but naturally they are trying to blackmail him. He gets up and paces anxiously around the room, tension making him feel empty. *No*, he thinks. He knows what they want from him. He can see the line of thought they are pursuing; nothing would be more valuable to them than giving himself up to them in exchange for their saving him by destroying or returning the documents. But a pact like that would hollow him out and transform him into the thing he hates the most: a traitor.

Let's talk about it, he writes, stopping to think. Perhaps he can still play this to his advantage. *I can come to B's.*

Hours pass. Then:

OK.

Shortly thereafter an address and time arrive. They want to meet tonight; it suits him well. The address is so familiar – he knows every room in the house, even though it has only been described to him by Heather.

At lunch he takes a long walk around the city, despite the rain. He wanders aimlessly through the centre and into the lanes around Grote Markt. No one is following him.

For a while he toys with the idea of telling them all about the House and pinning the blame and responsibility on Robert. It is a titillating thought – because the Swedes might report it up the chain of command, to their government, who in turn would sooner or later want to discuss the matter with his government, and if that happened, then the powers that be would back away from their new Assistant Head, even if Robert doesn't think so. All the warm hands currently holding Robert up would let him fall. Because, in any choice between sacrificing Robert or being forced to handle a political scandal, the government would dump the bastard. But if that is to happen, he must cooperate with the Swedes, and he is no traitor. Focus, he thinks. There is no room for sweet dreams of revenge.

*

265

Back at work, he opens the safe in his office and removes a worn-out black pay-as-you-go mobile. Then he replaces it with his normal phone, and locks the safe. The message that appears when he turns the mobile on is brief: *On the way*. The two resources landed at lunch, so why haven't they been in touch again? He can't stand waiting; he hates the feeling of his entire future being determined by unpredictable chance.

He paces the corridor, stopping for a while in front of a world map. Which country would be best to disappear in, if it became necessary? He drinks a glass of water in the toilets and tries to avoid his employees, hissing in irritation at an analyst when the mild-mannered man knocks on his door for a signature. He really must keep calm, even if he is tempted to kick things over in pure frustration. Immovable in his seat, he stares out at the roundabout. Occasional raindrops hit the windowsill like gentle hammer blows on a coffin.

When the phone rings he answers straight away.

Half an hour later he enters a hotel room. The two men are sitting on a large bed, yet another football match blaring on the TV. They get up, relaxed, and shake his hand. They are security-conscious and don't lower the volume. He looks around; they seem to be comfortable, and beneath the TV are two empty beer bottles next to several empty crisp bags. They shouldn't be drinking, he thinks in irritation. It has been a long time since he worked with this kind of resource. They have a laid-back, jokey manner that he struggles with. Their familiarity with violence means they have a marked lack of respect. He pulls out a chair and sits down in front of the TV. While they go over what will happen that evening, Anderlecht score against KV Mechelen and the joy rumbles from the TV.

Everything that is now happening is happening for the first time. She has never done this before – let a meeting with another intelligence service take place in her own home. But Gustav liked the suggestion; it was informal, it could be a way to make Jonathan Green feel safe.

She takes a gulp from her coffee mug, the bitter taste helping her to focus. Standing at the window in the living room she looks out onto the street.

'What do you think?'

'We'll see,' Gustav replies curtly.

He is sitting immovable on the sofa, as if transformed to a waxwork, except for one foot that is bobbing up and down. Even Gustav is nervous. If Green refuses to cooperate, then what happens? 'We try,' Gustav said. 'If the fish doesn't bite, then no harm done.' She isn't so sure.

It is eight o'clock, the agreed time. She shifts her weight.

Jonathan Green has been in the British Embassy all day, according to their tracking of his mobile, apart from a one-hour walk through the city centre. Ten minutes ago he had still been there – he didn't seem to be leaving his office, so far as Gustav's team could tell.

'Where are the boys?'

She replies that Rasmus is at a friend's house. Daniel is with his girlfriend. Fredrik has been given strict instructions to stay out of the way. He is at Petra and Mats's house.

Jonathan Green should feel like he is talking to them as an equal, Gustav is specific about that point. Gustav will make Green the offer: the documents in return for him working for them. If he accepts, they will have a long phase of interviews and cautious meetings, then an initial assignment. Possibly providing them with a report about Syria. Nothing big to begin with. A test to see whether he is cooperating and able to adjust to his new situation. And as a way of getting him dirty. Then the assignments will gradually increase, deepening the treachery. But she is uncertain whether Green will take the bait. If he doesn't cooperate, the leak will probably destroy his career and reputation, which he probably couldn't stand. But treason . . .

The doorbell rings.

The two-tone bell sounds fateful to her ears. Gustav gets up and nods. He is here. Wasn't he just at the British Embassy?

She adopts the calm, neutral expression she intends to maintain throughout the meeting, even if she hates the man who is now waiting outside her door. She will open the door and receive him. Gustav will wait in the living room, and they take their positions.

She goes to the door just as it rings for a second time, more impatiently now.

Then she hears the rattling sound of a key being put in the lock. Then a familiar, broken voice.

Rasmus is standing in the hall.

'Sweetheart, what are you doing back home?'

He flings off his jacket.

'I don't want to be at Sven's,' he mutters. 'All he wants to do is watch a film I've already seen.' He kicks off his shoes. 'Sven is such an idiot.'

She turns around. Gustav is standing in the middle of the living room merely shaking his head vigorously. She takes a step closer to her youngest and says calmly:

'But Rasmus, we agreed you would spend the evening at Sven's.'

Her tone isn't calm enough, because Rasmus glowers at her. He doesn't want to be at Sven's, he repeats with a slightly sharper, coarser voice and she knows exactly what the small step change means and what could happen if she doesn't stay very calm and gentle. They don't have time for this, but there is no other way.

'We agreed, didn't we?' she says.

'But I don't want to,' he exclaims. 'I want to be at home.'

Naturally, he doesn't understand. How could he? He is so absorbed in his own confusing life. A boy who has gone home without knowing that what he calls home has this evening been transformed into a secret meeting place, a platform for a kind of person he will hopefully never need in his life.

Rasmus has caught sight of Gustav.

'What's he doing here?'

She suddenly loses patience; she can't let an entire operation fail just because he wants to be at home playing computer games.

'You can't be here right now, Rasmus,' she says harshly. 'We need to be alone here.'

But, of course, that doesn't work. The boy is immediately affected by the aggressive underlying tone and his voice gets louder, shouting.

'Why can't I be at home? I live here too.'

She reaches out an arm to stop him, subdue him. She is on the verge of shouting back, but with a deep sigh manages to stop herself. With strained softness she explains that they are about to receive a visitor.

The boy glares at her, ready for battle, but at least he is listening.

'It's a man who is very . . . careful,' she says slowly. 'He wants to meet me and this man, Gustav. But only if no one else sees him. It's important that we meet him, Rasmus. We just need a little while. Do you think we can have a meeting with him on our own?'

'But I don't want to be at Sven's.'

'Perhaps you could go to someone else's house,' she suggests with a bright, encouraging voice.

'Can't I just go upstairs to my room?'

'No, sweetheart. Not tonight.'

Rasmus shakes his head. He is hurt; he can't understand his mother.

Every second moves them closer to catastrophe. But Rasmus remains resolutely where he is.

'Rasmus, leave now,' she says sharply.

The boy's face falls. Then something happens that she rarely sees these days: his eyes fill with tears. A sob trembles around his mouth.

'But I don't want to. Aren't you listening?'

Facing his unhappy rage, she is at a loss; no one seems to be accepting her words any more, and anyway what right does she really have to tell him that? It is his home, after all. She has promised the children that they should always feel safe there.

Rasmus tries to push past her into his home. She grabs hold of his arm, but he is strong and shakes himself loose.

'I live here too,' he shouts through his tears.

Then he is past her. He stomps up the stairs.

'You bitch,' he shouts from upstairs, and perhaps he is right, perhaps she is a bitch who doesn't care one bit about him. The door to his room slams.

'He's coming,' says Gustav sharply from the living room.

She hurries up the stairs. 'Rasmus,' she says. 'Please, Rasmus.' But the only thing audible from within is a moaning cry. She knocks.

'Rasmus, darling.'

She leans her forehead against the door. Is she a mother? Right now she is mostly part of the Security Service using the part of herself that is a mother to influence the boy inside that door, and she is disgusted at herself. She is letting them down. And this makes her hate the man who will soon be arriving. The hate is a hard, tensed muscle. She wouldn't have had to do this if it hadn't been for him, she thinks to herself.

'Bente,' Gustav calls from downstairs, and she knows it is too late.

She steps away from the door. Perhaps this can work. If he stays in there all the time, if Jonathan doesn't notice anything.

'Stay in there, Rasmus,' she calls through the door. 'And be quiet. Promise me?'

Strictly speaking, it is nothing more than an ordinary unforeseen event, a change to the situation, she thinks to herself valiantly in an attempt to shake off the quivering sensation that she has hurt her son, and will continue hurting him.

The doorbell rings.

Jonathan Green is standing in the evening darkness outside. He looks surprisingly worn out. There had been an aggressive tension to him in the hubbub of the Swedish reception – typical

Green. But the man standing at her door is hollow-eyed, has wrinkles and dark bags under his eyes. But the pale-blue, sharp eyes that almost never blink remain the same.

'Welcome,' she says, letting him in.

She takes his coat. He is wearing a jacket and a pair of jeans, as if he had been invited round to hers like an ordinary guest. Yes, who knows, perhaps in another life with different constellations they might have been friends.

'So this is where I live,' she says, and he nods, emitting an awkward hum.

Gustav emerges from the living room, and for a moment she can see the Brit is startled, as if he hadn't counted on the Swedish Head of Counter-Espionage being present. But then he greets him with sincere warmth.

'Gustav,' he says. 'It's been a long time.'

'Would you like something to drink?' she asks as they go into the living room.

He shakes his head and looks around the room. Then he asks them to take their mobile phones apart. She and Gustav get their handsets out and remove the batteries and SIM cards and place them on the coffee table.

'You know why I'm here.'

Gustav nods. 'Yes, naturally.'

'We're glad you want to meet with us.'

Jonathan says nothing, waiting.

'Recent events have done none of us any good,' says Gustav quickly, and a little drily. 'We need to deal with this and move on – isn't that right, Bente?'

Jonathan watches her.

'We're concerned that we've ended up in conflict with you,' says Gustav. 'To be honest, I just want to see you as a partner.'

272

'What do you want?' Jonathan asks sharply.

'We can help you.'

'Good,' he answers brusquely. 'Please hand over the documents.'

Gustav grimaces, his expression affected.

'That's the problem. We can't just give you the documents and pretend nothing happened. It would make it look like we were able to accept the . . . methods described in the documents. The fact of the matter is that we're surprised that your government has approved what you refer to as the House.'

'That was a long time ago,' Jonathan says sharply.

'But the site is still in use, isn't it?'

Jonathan looks unhappy. Before he has time to reply, the old spy hunter begins to slowly reel in his quarry:

'We'll have to raise the matter at a political level.'

'What do you mean?'

'We have to let our Ministers discuss the issue.'

Jonathan's lips purse, his pupils dilate. Gustav seems to have correctly guessed that the House has not been approved at the highest political level. She smiles to herself. In that case they have their fish on the hook.

Gustav says:

'We would like a more in-depth cooperation with you.'

Jonathan gives a low chuckle, and nods.

'Your career is over if you can't save it. You'll be dragged through the mud – you know that. But it doesn't have to be like that.'

Jonathan gives them a cold smile.

'You want me to betray my country.'

He looks at them calmly, as if he wants to double check he has understood correctly.

273

'So what did you have in mind?' he says.

Gustav starts to lay out their offer in a friendly tone of voice. They will hand back all material they hold, all the documents, and enter into a series of confidence-building meetings with London to repair the partnership. This process will help to bolster London's trust in Jonathan.

Jonathan listens with interest.

'If you cooperate,' Gustav concludes.

'And what form would this cooperation take?'

'We will need certain information.'

He looks at them and nods.

'You want to blackmail me. But our Minister is aware of the House and how we use it,' says Jonathan as if talking pleasantly to two children. 'We can deal with the leak simply through you giving me the documents and never mentioning the matter again.'

Gustav turns around. She too has noticed the muffled, familiar sound of car doors closing. It came from the street, just outside the house. She excuses herself and goes to the window to look out.

In the dark her own face appears in the windowpane, but she catches sight of two men crossing the street and walking towards her house. Then she hears crunching from the drive.

Jonathan looks at her seriously. And she knows – it is an immediate and desperately simple realisation – that they have underestimated their enemy.

'Gustav,' she says in Swedish, and she can hear the fear in her voice. 'We need to abort.'

Jonathan doesn't understand what she has just said, but the way he watches her as she hurries up the stairs tells her she is right.

'Rasmus,' she shouts. 'You need to get out.'

She tugs at the door. It is still locked, so she thumps it.

'Rasmus, listen to me. You need to get out.'

A familiar sound sings through the silence. The doorbell. She turns on her heel, a sinking sensation in her stomach.

'Gustav,' she shouts down the stairs. 'Don't open it.'

But it is too late: she can hear his steps at the end of the hallway, she can even hear the soft click of the door opening. The familiar noise sounds like the threatening ratchet of a weapon, a machine of death. Then voices: Gustav and another. She hears thuds, the muffled sounds of tumult. Shortly afterwards, there is a brief, juddery shout. It is Gustav; he is screaming.

She is quickly filled with fear, and parts of her are acting independently. Following a sequence committed to her muscle memory, she moves back and violently kicks the door just beside the handle. The door bursts open with a crash.

'You need to get out of the house *now*.'

Rasmus is curled up on his bed with his device and stares at her in fright.

'Darling,' she says. 'Climb out of the window.'

Through the window? He grimaces anxiously.

Good God, remember he's just a child! she thinks to herself. She has to make him understand.

'Do as I say. Hurry up.'

He meets her gaze and he understands – a primordial power has awoken within his mother, a sense of decisiveness so strong that he falls silent and gets up from the bed.

Quick steps move through the hall, up the stairs. He won't make it, she thinks to herself.

'Wait,' she says. 'Under the bed.'

Fear makes him move lightning-fast: she has never seen him

275

move like that; he practically falls onto his face, and crawls quickly under the bed.

The phone; she needs to call the emergency number.

'Give me your phone,' she says, and he digs out his mobile from his pocket and slides it across the floor.

Her hands tremble as she dials the number. It rings once.

She rushes onto the landing towards the safe where she keeps her weapon. She is barely thinking, driven on by violent impulse.

All she notices is the panting sound behind her before the stranger hits her. She falls headlong into a wall. He is on top of her. She manages to twist around, but she is helplessly weak when the man forces her arms, locking them down, forcing them behind her back so that she can feel her tendons and bones stretching to breaking point. He hits her on the back, two rapid, hard blows against one of her kidneys, and it is impossible to offer resistance to such pain, to the body's own defeat when faced with the skill of the man's silent violence.

He pulls her off the floor, and she sees another man coming up the stairs. It is so unreal and disgusting to see the men in checked shirts and chinos with their military-style haircuts here, in her home.

They drag her rapidly downstairs. This is how her operatives have moved through unknown houses and apartments, and she has always seen it as necessary, acceptable, but now this is such a level of violence that she doesn't want to believe it is happening to her.

Don't resist, not before it is possible, she thinks to herself.

Checked shirt, small tattoo on the right arm, hair colour, aftershave, the bodily odour of someone who wants to hurt you – she commits the details to memory.

Gustav is lying on the living-room floor on the thick rug by the coffee table. Jonathan Green is standing next to him with a pistol in his hand.

The men put on latex gloves. One of them lets go of her and grabs hold of Gustav, picking him up like a package and putting him on a chair, pulling out a roll of duct tape and with a ripping sound pulling off a long piece and wrapping it around the lower half of Gustav's face. Gustav begins to gasp, his breathing through his nose is weak.

'Bente,' says Jonathan. 'Where are the documents?'

She doesn't answer.

The man behind him pulls out the roll of tape again, and puts a large piece of tape straight over Gustav's nose and around his head. He tries to writhe away, opening his eyes and throwing himself about in his chair while he can't breathe.

'Stop it!' she shouts. 'Stop it.'

Jonathan nods at the man, who slightly loosens the tape. Gustav draws breath with a hissing sound through his nostrils. His eyes are watering, he stares silently.

Jonathan looks at her furiously.

'Can you see what you've done, woman? This is your fault. Now we're going to retrieve the documents. Where are they?'

'Upstairs. In a safe.'

'Give me the code.'

'There's a code and fingerprint scanner.'

She is certain that he knows she is lying. Perhaps Heather has told him how the safe works, perhaps he has been here before, they have been watching her for months . . . but she can't see any other way, she needs to buy time – enough for the others to get here.

Jonathan nods, pointing at the stairs.

She feels the men release their grip on her and they walk towards the stairs. He stops outside Rasmus's room.

Then he crouches, his weapon still aimed at her, and peers into the room.

'Come out,' he says. 'Come out from under the bed.'

He shouts loudly down the stairs that there is another person here, and that they need dealing with. The two men in checked shirts hurry up the stairs with heavy steps. The only thing she can think about is protecting Rasmus; she forgets that Jonathan is armed and tries to push past.

He immediately turns the muzzle towards her.

'Don't hurt him,' she says.

They pull Rasmus out and get him to his feet. He stares at her, scared out of his mind, and then is past her and heading downstairs. They are dragging his gangly body between them and it looks awful, their broad backs and cast-iron hands grasping her son's thin upper arms. He offers no resistance; they lift him like a rag doll, and he is silent, and it is heartbreaking because he ought to start shouting if anyone touches him like that but he says nothing. Something cracks inside her; this is her fault.

'Rasmus, darling,' she shouts after him. 'Try to stay calm . . .'

The study is cramped, he stands close to her, and she blocks his view of the safe, shielding it with her body so that he can't see that it is a completely ordinary safe without a biometric reader.

'Hurry up,' Jonathan chivvies her.

Her fingers are trembling; for a moment she actually forgets the code, and knows that if that happens, then he will probably kill someone – he will do that if she doesn't do everything he asks of her right now. Then she manages to gather her thoughts and enter the six digits.

She spots the letter opener. It is made from carved wood and is in a pen pot with a handful of pens; she can see the wooden handle sticking out, and the slender, shiny piece of metal ending in a sharp point.

'Move,' he says, and she turns towards him so that she is standing by the small cabinet. Her hand fumbles, her fingers brushing the slender outlines of the pens.

He makes an annoyed gesture with his head. The pistol – she constantly has it in her sights – is facing her.

She feels the square shape of the handle and closes her hand around the knife before quickly moving to one side.

'Sit there,' he says, and she sinks into the sofa, feeling the cool, soothing metal of the paperknife slide under her cardigan sleeve.

He crouches in front of her by the safe. There is her service weapon, and a spare magazine. Passports, an envelope filled with cash, papers in different files. And the flash drive.

He holds it up by its tip.

'This one?'

Yes, she nods. That one.

'Is this the only copy?'

'Yes, that's the only copy.'

He leads her before him down the stairs to the living room. She can feel the handle close to her wrist. With each step she tries to find a way out, just a tiny opportunity, a second of inattention would be enough. But he is sharp, professional, just like her. He keeps his distance and doesn't relax his guard.

Rasmus is on his knees in the living room with his hands on his head. He is absolutely silent and looking down at the floor. Gustav is sitting on a chair in the middle of the room with his hands tied behind his back and duct tape over his face, and next to them are the two toughs. It looks like a surrealist painting. She can't quite believe this is happening to her, and at the same time it is so intensely real that every detail sparkles in her mind's eye.

'Okay,' says Jonathan briskly, holding up the black flash drive. 'I'll ask again. Is this the only copy?'

'Yes,' she says. 'I promise.'

He looks at her in dissatisfaction.

And then she realises all hope is lost, because he doesn't believe her, even though it is true. One of the men in checked shirts steps forward and strikes Rasmus's face without any warning. Her boy falls headlong to the floor and curls up into the foetal position.

'No,' she cries out. 'Leave him alone.'

She turns to Jonathan.

'Jonathan, listen,' she says while Rasmus's hoarse sobs fill the room. 'There are no other copies. You can hit him as much as you want, but there aren't any others. I promise you ...'

The man looks self-conscious when he bends down over her son and pulls him up by the jumper, raising his hand and striking Rasmus again with the broad palm of his hand across his mouth. The cracking sound almost makes her vomit.

'Stop it, stop it,' she begs.

Rasmus is screaming, horror-struck, as blood bubbles out of his mouth.

Gustav jerks in his chair and tries to shout through the tape; one of the men strikes him across the face.

'No,' she shouts when the men straddle the boy's ribcage and press him down into the rug. She tries to get to him to stop them, but one of them holds her while the man leans over her boy and wraps his hands around his neck. Rasmus falls silent and begins to struggle noiselessly.

'All the copies,' says Jonathan.

He's dying, she thinks.

And with resounding clarity she realises what she has to do.

'There is another copy.'

'Where?' Jonathan roars.

'In the basement.'

The man loosens his grip. A horrible rasping sound emerges from Rasmus as he gasps for breath.

Jonathan nods, as if he had known all along she would admit this.

Initially, her boy lies there, immobile, when the man who has been sitting on him gets up. Then he quietly rolls onto his side and vomits onto the rug, and stays lying like that, still, curled up, as he had once lain inside her, completely safe. She just wants to hold him, protect him from all this pain, destroy it, erase the memory of it. If only she could.

Jonathan pushes her from behind down the narrow basement stairs. 'Where is it?' he says. It is more than impatience; he is upset. Perhaps he is going to kill me, she thinks to herself while looking around; where should she lead him? Then she makes up her mind: there is only one spot where she will be close enough to him.

'Here,' she says.

She opens the door to the sauna. He is too agitated to think; he is also afraid, she realises. This is an obsession for him, too, and he doesn't know how to get out of it. She glimpses his sceptical expression when she holds the door open for him. But the gesture, so deceptive in its ordinariness, makes him react the way she had hoped he would: instinctively. He steps carefully over the threshold.

'Wait.'

She bends over the unit and pretends to search behind it. She has imperceptibly begun to control the situation: he is waiting for her, and doesn't notice how she discreetly positions herself to be in the best spot. Nor does he notice, when she bends forward, how she shifts the weight in one leg, leaning with her upper body and carefully raising her free knee.

Then she kicks. A hard and fast blow, straight out, with her foot against the hand holding the weapon. The move is unfamiliar, but she still knows what to do. His hand flies up towards himself and for a brief moment the muzzle goes up and away towards his head and he reels in surprise. The knife slides out of her sleeve and is in her hand. With a small cry she flings herself at him.

She stabs him in the stomach, in and up, and feels the wet warmth running over her fingers as she pulls out and stabs again. He sighs, gasping as if he had run up the stairs. The explosion when he fires his weapon is painfully loud in the confined space; she anticipates a sharp pain, and for her body to give way, but instead the bullet hits wood. She presses his arm up towards him and he struggles against her.

Jonathan lashes out one arm to defend himself, a wild gesture, but weakened. The pistol falls, rattling, onto the clinker floor. He bays like a slaughtered animal. Blood is running out of him, a dark and bubbling sludge. It seems odd that such a cold person can have so much blood in them.

She turns around. He has collapsed by the lower bench in the sauna, as if in prayer.

The man lying there has had a power over her like no other. Behind him is an expansive organisation that he has been able to shape into a weapon against her. But lying there, it seems incomprehensible. How has *he* been able to penetrate so deeply into her family's life?

Jonathan pants. His hands clasp at the bench, smudging blood onto the pine.

She bends down and picks up the pistol, and then rummages through his pockets until she finds the flash drive. He offers no resistance.

With a rapid step she is out of the sauna and leaning against the door. Then she sees the mop in the corner, the one she usually uses to swab down the sauna. It will have to do. She jams it under the door handle and peers through the small window. Jonathan is still on his knees, he is too badly injured to break down the door.

She can hear them upstairs in the house, their rapid steps on the creaking hall floor.

She turns off the lights. She is enveloped by protective darkness. She peers up the stairs, the door forming a rectangle of light. Once again, she hears a familiar creaking sound: steps on the parquet in the hall. Closer now.

She crouches and raises the pistol.

'Sir?'

A round silhouette slowly appears at the edge of the door.

He doesn't have time to see what is happening before the bullet hits his head. The bang is painfully loud as it echoes off the stone walls. The whole world whines and screams as she runs up the stairs, quickly, but not so fast that she doesn't have time to take aim at the living room and the other man staring at her. Her second shot misses. The powerful explosions tear through the air of her home.

She hurries at a crouch through the kitchen and waits, leaning by the fridge. It is quiet . . . but not entirely: she can hear Rasmus making a strange, juddering noise, as if a sob were stuck inside him. And she can hear the other man panting. This is her home and it is familiar terrain for her. She knows every mark on the herringbone parquet in the living room, she knows where the hall creaks and which of the steps make a noise.

She can hear the enemy moving in the living room, quick steps with the final one muffled. He is at the edge of the Persian rug, probably two metres inside the room, close to the coffee table and the TV.

A creaking sound. The threshold.

She waits. Then she hears another creak. She moves with the utmost caution to the kitchen door. Three metres away: she can't see him, but she knows he is standing there in the hall, next to the stairs. She wheels out, but lowers her weapon and throws herself back when she sees her son, a pale, shocked expression on his face, standing next to the man.

The shot reverberates downstairs, and her face stings from the splinters thrown into the air from the tiled wall. Rasmus. She can hear his terrified panting as the man drags him upstairs.

She glances into the hall. The man she shot is lying there like a bloody sack, still alive, trembling, twitching, in shock. She has no intention of saving him. She quickly bends down and twists the weapon from his loose grip before aiming up the stairs.

'Release my son,' she bellows.

She takes a few steps backwards. Gustav is lying in the living room next to the coffee table. He has crept under it, his hands still tied behind his back and his mouth covered in tape. He glares at her as if he doesn't recognise her, panic etched deeply into his face. She had been intending to free him and give him a weapon, but she can now see he won't be of any assistance at all.

Her mobile is still lying there, on the coffee table, in pieces. Her hands are shaking terribly as she attempts to assemble it.

The SIM card seems absurdly small; she covers it in blood, but then, finally, her mobile is switched on.

The seconds trickle away until it connects. She quickly writes a text message and sends it to the emergency number. It is as if part of her were a numb machine, the fighting part of her. *Man with pistol upstairs. One hostage. One wounded.*

She creeps, crouching, up the stairs.

'Rasmus,' she calls out in a low voice. 'Can you hear me?'

From upstairs she hears a drawn-out, sobbing reply. '*Mu-u-m.*' The impulse is so strong – he is just a few seconds away – that she wants nothing more than to rush up there. But she can hear where the sound is coming from, and knows that the man is at the end of the landing. It would be like stepping onto a firing range.

'*M-u-u-m,*' Rasmus calls out again, mournfully. She can hear him crying with his mouth open, like a prolonged, horrible laugh. '*Mumm-m-m-m-m.*'

'I'm here, darling,' she calls back but can't say more; her voice breaks. 'I'm here,' she whispers.

She is now standing just below the final step to the landing. She quickly raises her head, just enough to see the TV corner with the sofa, the hallway, and Rasmus's room. A shot breaks the silence, one of the slats exploding into splinters beside her. She presses herself down, huddling up.

'Let him go!' she shouts in English.

She can hear them moving.

She rushes up the stairs, because her son could die at any moment; she can't just sit there waiting.

She ducks into a small window bay as two shots fly past. She catches sight of the man in the bedroom, together with Rasmus sitting on the bed.

Then there is another sound that catches her attention. Through the window she can hear a scrape against the outer wall. At first, she can't understand what it is, then she hears a footstep against the wall. Help has arrived.

A detonation shudders up through the floor from downstairs. There is a violent crash as the glass in the landing window splinters, and then, before even glimpsing it, she sees the grenade come sailing through the air.

Time slows down. Every second is transformed into flickering, shining details. She sees the grenade and thinks *Cover my head* as it traces an arc through the air. Then she too is in the air, throwing herself at a shelf of board games.

The blast is so loud that her ears suddenly feel blocked. It seems to suck up all the oxygen, all the life in the room. She can smell the acrid, bitter smell of gunpowder. Three masked men clad in black rush past her – she sees them take up positions around the doorway to Rasmus's room – she sees the machine guns and the heavy vests. A Belgian Federal Police Special Unit.

They are shouting but she still can't hear anything; her ears are ringing. Then she is on her feet. One of the team turns around and aims his short-barrelled machine gun at her, eyes white and wide open beneath the black hood, surprised, frightened. '*I'm the mother*,' she cries out, not altogether sure why she chose to say that. She crouches beside the tactical unit. They shout down the hall:

'Show us the boy. Show us the boy.'

She can't understand how he gets free, but suddenly Rasmus comes rushing out of the bedroom. She throws herself at him because it is her child, and you will do anything for your child, even die, especially die, if it would save their life, and they

286

meet in the middle of the hall in a tight embrace. She wraps her arms around him, then bundles him through the bathroom doorway, where they fall, tightly entwined, onto the hard tiled floor. 'Darling,' she whispers over and over. 'Darling. Darling.'

Volleys of fire boom on the landing. A series of rattling explosions is followed by several dull blasts. She waits, lying absolutely still on top of Rasmus's body to make sure that he doesn't rush out onto the lethal landing in a panic. Bullets crash into the walls, plunge through doors and windows. Curled up, they wait for the war to reach its conclusion.

Then, suddenly, the shooting stops. Shouts are audible. Then silence.

After a while she gets up slowly, listening. Then she peers out of the doorway.

The walls have been hammered to pieces. The wallpaper is strewn with large holes exposing the skeleton of the house, brickwork. The air is grey and has the sour smell of gun smoke.

A member of the tactical unit crouches beside them. He speaks calmly to them in French and asks if they are hurt. She looks into the masked face. It's over, she thinks to herself, reaching for Rasmus who is lying beside her. She sees more of them appear and stop next to Rasmus while they talk calmly to her. It is peaceful. She has no idea what will happen now, what the future will look like, nothing. But it is unimportant. All that matters is that they are alive, she can put her arm around her son and feel that he is alive.

Rasmus stares at her in terror. And when they get up she sees in the mirror above the sink why: her face is smeared with blood. It has spattered and run all over her hair and hands and throat.

She is shaking, numb, as if outside of her own body. Yet she tries to think in a level-headed manner, looking forward. She goes to the study. The dead body in the checked shirt is visible through the bedroom door, lying spreadeagled across the bed. She turns her gaze away, but catches sight of the rigid face and the blood that has flowed onto the quilt, and can't stop the thought that it is sinking into the sheets on her side of the bed.

The safe is ajar. She quickly grabs the false passports inside and hurries back to Rasmus. Three paramedics have surrounded him, attaching a thick brace around his neck, placing him onto a stretcher and picking him up.

Cool evening air wafts through the ground floor. Two Belgian police officers put a rustling foil blanket over her shoulders and lead her downstairs; she hurries after the stretcher to keep up with Rasmus. She would prefer not to let go of his hand, but she has to.

She passes the living room and glimpses the gaping hole where the veranda door should be, the curtains being sucked into the darkness by the breeze. Where is Gustav? she wonders.

The other man is lying in the hall, dead, curled up in a pool of his own dark blood. A blue light flashes through the windows, making the interior of the house seem unreal.

The house and street have been transformed into a dark scene of light and shadow, fitfully illuminated in blue. Heavily armed police are moving around the garden.

Someone leads her towards the police cars and ambulances. She can see a large gathering of neighbours who have come out onto the street and are now watching her and Rasmus with a mixture of curiosity and anxiety.

As if strobe-lit, she sees Fredrik and Petra, their neighbour, together with her daughter Julia, their eyes wide open, and their mouths saying something to her. 'Mum,' she hears a familiar voice shouting, and she squints into the lights and manages to catch Daniel as he throws his arms around her.

Hands quickly lead her towards the illuminated interior of an ambulance. The paramedics work quietly to lift in the stretcher carrying Rasmus, then close the door and shut out all noise.

Gustav is sitting on a stool inside the ambulance. He is huddled under his foil blanket, a thin and pale old man. When she gets into the small space, he lifts his head and looks at her vacantly. She sits down next to Rasmus and holds his hand, all the while stroking his forehead. His eyes rest calmly on her, the drugs already taking effect.

And it is perhaps only now that she truly grasps that they are alive; that death, which penetrated the other bodies in the house, hasn't touched them. But they were so incredibly close to the power that will one day destroy their flesh. She grimaces at this, the chilly stiffness in her muscles suddenly representing the horrors of that sapping eventuality. She knows that Rasmus will live with the feeling of having come excruciatingly close to his own death, that he will carry death in him, like frost damage, for a long time to come. They are alive, but it will be a long time before he has any faith in life again.

Rasmus is asleep. She is sitting next to his bed, illuminated by a small night light, talking to him in a low voice, gently stroking his head until the medication drags him down into bottomless, dream-free sleep. She feels his fingers relax, and sees the tense expression on his face slacken. It scares her to see him disappear like that, but she knows she's just imagining it – it isn't death, just death's brother, sleep.

Darkness covers the shiny windows in the small room he has been allocated. She looks at his face, framed from below by the large brace that he will wear until his neck has healed. When they examined him earlier, she saw the purple-black marks all over his ribcage and throat, and it took all her strength not to cry and frighten him any more. Her beloved boy. The self-reproach burns through her with astonishing force. She is his mother, but also a strange, silent being he doesn't know; a danger. At that moment she wishes she could simply extract herself from the secret organisation to which she belongs and become one person among many.

'Is he asleep?'

Gustav has come into the room. He carefully draws up a chair to the bed and sits down. He is tired, dead-tired, grey and dishevelled like an old crow.

He asks her for her phone and she passes it to him, watching as he picks out the battery and SIM card and then hands her a new, identical device.

'Jesus Christ, Bente,' he says in a low voice, looking at her with a grim expression of amazement, as if he can barely believe he has survived. 'Fredrik and Daniel are in the safe house,' he goes on. 'The police are on guard. Don't worry.'

They sit quietly beside each other, watching the sleeping boy.

'You'll need to tell people about what happened this evening,' Gustav says. 'What you should tell them is that three armed men broke into your house. You were at home and they were taken by surprise. You defended yourself and called the police. Rasmus was taken hostage. Nothing more.'

He has already spoken to Fredrik, but she will need to steer the boys on what they say.

'And Jonathan Green?'

Gustav looks at her testily.

'He is alive. Barely. He's still in surgery.'

'You underestimated him, Gustav.'

Gustav looks at her sharply.

But he knows that she is right. He was responsible for the wrong judgement call on Jonathan Green, not her. She should have trusted her instincts and not listened to Gustav; it's a long time since he'd been her mentor. But she, too, wanted to catch the fish. And how were they to know that Green would attack with such murderous rage?

Rasmus is breathing deeply and calmly.

'He really was prepared to kill us.'

'Perhaps,' says Gustav. 'Perhaps he just wanted to threaten us to get the documents, and then it all went wrong.'

His judgement must have been impaired by his panic about the leak, she thinks to herself, and the disgrace to which his career in espionage was heading. But even if he had obtained the flash drive, he could never have been certain. His position could have been devastated at any moment by the click of a mouse.

'Do you think Green was working on London's orders?'

Gustav shakes his head.

'I spoke to London a little while ago,' he says. 'To their new Assistant Head, Robert Davenport. He explained that the operations against us by Jonathan Green, the surveillance, the infiltration and this attack, were never signed off on by them.'

According to Davenport, Green was suspended following the leak a month earlier, Gustav had been told. Green had begun drinking, MI6's new star had explained. London considered him a liability. Apparently, there was a history of violence stretching back to a posting in Damascus. Davenport had apologised for what had happened.

'Do you believe him?'

Gustav shrugs his shoulders.

'I think they need someone to blame everything on,' he says. 'Perhaps they tasked him with infiltrating us and, when that failed, making contact. Perhaps London needed a useful idiot to take the blame for the leak and infiltration and lots of other shit. He was recently in Syria – we don't know what happened there.'

Green is alone, she thinks. When he wakes up after surgery, he will be out in the cold. The perfect scapegoat, because whatever he says, no one will believe him. No one believes a spy who has gone berserk.

'I think he was working alone,' she says.

'We'll never know what MI6 thinks, Bente. Regardless, our relationship is damaged. It will take a long time before London looks favourably upon us again.'

He falls silent. Then:

'We're going to have to close the Section.'

She can't stop a small cry. *No.*

Then she is afraid she has woken Rasmus, and falls silent immediately. But the boy sleeps on, expressionless.

Gustav has already received notification from the powers that be. 'They have been considering it for a long time,' he explains, 'and now that the Section is unable to work in secret . . . It's simply impossible to continue with a vulnerability like that.'

'It's not fair.'

'It's in everyone's best interests, Bente.'

She doesn't want to believe it is true. She wants to say that she did nothing wrong when she accepted the British leak. It was an achievement, something everyone ought to thank her for. But she knows that what Gustav is saying is right, because they won't be able to work in secret like before. Some secrets have such gravity that they tear everything apart that comes too close; she underestimated the risk when she agreed to meet the Brit on that rainy day an eternity ago. It really is over. She thinks about Mikael, about everyone who trusts her, everything she has fought for. She has failed, she thinks to herself. It was her responsibility to lead and protect the Section. But it is as if it no longer matters. She looks at Rasmus and is glad he is alive, and that she is alive to be there with him. She can't understand how she had thought she could ever bear to lose him. She loves him, just like she loves Daniel. Compared with the relief of seeing her boy sleeping soundly, the Section doesn't matter one little bit.

It is her fault that he is lying there. She has used him, they have both used their boys – she and Fredrik. She wonders what she has been up to all these years, and whether the boys will ever forgive her.

'So what happens now?'

'You're going home, my dear.'

Home. That means Stockholm.

'For good?'

'For good.'

She strokes Rasmus's hand. It is warm and doesn't react to her touch. He has barely any memories of Sweden; to him it is a foreign country. A new life. She can barely imagine what it will mean for the boys. Daniel has been ill at ease, but has now found his feet here, and has a life with friends and a girlfriend. Will Rasmus cope with a move? It might exacerbate his anger and confusion. Or it will be okay? she thinks to herself. A new start for them all?

Gustav gets up. Then he remembers something. Is there anything in their home that he needs to take care of? She stops to think. She took the passports, but her computer is still there. He nods and says he will fetch it.

'And the documents?'

She has forgotten. They are still in her pocket. She pulls out the flash drive, the black scarab, holding it between her thumb and forefinger. Such an ordinary thing. She never wants to see it again.

A grey, rain-filled sky looms above the fields around Waterloo, shaking the scrubland along the motorway. She is driving, and he is sitting quietly in the passenger seat. Fredrik has also learned the art of silence and is currently engaged in it. They have left the boys in the temporary apartment, just for a few hours, even though they were reluctant. She didn't want to, at first: what if they die while they are gone? She is more affected by what has happened than she wants to let on. She has experienced a level of violence that has dislodged and distorted normality. It has hit her in recent days, this sense of lassitude. She suspects that the chasm that she feels opening within her at times like this will close with time, and form scar tissue, a dark memory.

The house is the same as ever on the outside. An ordinary detached house in the leafy suburbs. The only thing that hints at anything different is the Belgian police tape fluttering over the gravel path.

The front door is still missing. Instead, there is a piece of chipboard covering the doorway. In front of it is a police officer in a thick coat. He gets up and approaches them as they reach the garden.

'This is a restricted area,' he says. 'You can't come in, there's an investigation going on.'

She explains and he looks at them sadly, carefully examining their ID cards and nodding with approval. After a while, a police officer emerges from behind the chipboard. He is wearing rustling white protective overalls and a mask.

Standing outside on their own front step, they each pull on an overall, rubber gloves, forensic galoshes and masks. This is no longer a home; instead, it's a place contaminated by violence.

Returning is almost unbearable. She sees the thick patch of blood caked onto the tiles in the hall. A technician in white overalls stands up and nods.

The living room is simultaneously strangely intact and destroyed: the books are still on the bookcase; the TV is untouched by the sofa. But the rug has absorbed a black stain the size of a tea tray. Chairs have been smashed to smithereens, but lie there untouched, carefully marked with small flags, frozen in the moment. Broken glass, splinters, wallpaper riddled with bullet holes; a war has taken place here. A billowing plastic sheet covers the large hole where the veranda door used to be. This violence is from her world, she thinks to herself.

She follows Fredrik upstairs. She stops in her tracks on the landing, astonished by the destruction. Walls and doors have been torn apart by bullets. Everything is tipped over and ruined, as if a raging wild animal had applied its claws to the walls and furniture. The floor in the hall and bedroom is smeared with blood.

We survived this, she thinks. Fredrik turns to face her, the eyes above his mask wide open.

The police watch as her latex-covered hands gather some of the boys' clothes, games and books. Soon it will all be gone, she thinks. Someone will come and pack up their stuff and ship it off, and their lives will change completely. In the bedroom, a large patch of blood has dried onto the quilt. She rummages for blouses and trousers, skirts and tights and underwear. She isn't thinking, and in a clumsy gesture she straightens the pillows at the head of the bed as the technician quickly asks her not to. Of course, it is no longer a bedroom. They silently leave the house.

The boys like the temporary apartment. After an evening with fingers clasping devices and remote controls, they go to bed, turning off the lights one after another and leaving the rooms in darkness. But they sleep restlessly. Daniel is awake. Rasmus is dreaming, whimpering in his sleep. She is woken by his cries in the small hours.

Fredrik disappears early. Whenever they happen to be in the apartment at the same time, they move in a painful dance through the rooms to carefully avoid each other.

In the mornings and evenings, the seams between waking and sleeping, she feels blurred grief that Fredrik's presence is gone. It is like a memory in her body. Her body misses him. She doesn't want him to be part of her life, but an equilibrium has been disturbed and everything is unfamiliar.

One morning she hears Rasmus shouting at his brother in the bathroom.

'What are you arguing about?'

Daniel explains: Rasmus thinks their father is moving with them to Sweden, but that isn't true.

'Because he isn't, is he?'

They quietly eat breakfast before she drives them to school. A shower of rain has passed over Brussels. The streets gleam black in the overcast weather. 'Bye, Mum,' they shout to her before hurrying across the playground, and she waves in despair, as if it were their final parting – she isn't sure why. She just wants to call them back and tell them she loves them, and to ask them for forgiveness, for everything.

When she gets home, she sees him sitting on the sofa looking out of the window: his familiar neck, and the hair thinning on the crown of his head. If they stopped remembering, would they be able to rediscover each other? Because the strange thing is, that when she sees him like that, she misses Fredrik; not the man sitting there, but the person he used to be, before. She doesn't want to remember.

They drink coffee, and talk in grown-up, sensible terms about relocating and separation, about moving companies and furniture. An existence turning into household goods. The words float above an unspoken chasm.

He says: 'Bente.' Then he starts crying. She strokes his shoulder. Perhaps he finally realises it is happening.

After he has left, she sits by a window and cries. It is as if an all-consuming cramp had finally loosened. She finds herself at the beginning of a new era, the days of a prolonged farewell.

If Fredrik disappears from her life, she will carry on living. But how? She has never been here, she doesn't know which direction the future will take her. If she leaves him, she will become someone else, or perhaps herself, and the painful thought strikes her that he might feel better when he is no longer with her. It is as if he were now appearing clearly, that she can see *him*: the man she fell in love with, the face she has loved, the eyes that were so happy when they saw her. All that will disappear; she can't understand how it is possible, how it can happen so easily. But one of the few people who knows her is leaving her, and she is leaving him. She wants to go, but at the same time is turning around and holding on to him.

If only time could pass. Then perhaps her exhaustion and despair and longing could be subdued. Then she thinks. A cold winter's day might bring to mind a memory with melancholic clarity: his birthday. A year later, she might pause in a new kitchen in a different apartment and remember what it was like: Brussels, the house, their lives. The memories form a shooting pain that will eventually abate. She already knows that, with time, all these days, all these violent and confusing emotions, will become less important. Everything that is their shared life, and everything she wanted to say but that remained unsaid, will, over the years, lose significance and disappear.

But it doesn't have to be like that. One day, months later, she might be sitting in her new office, sharp spring sunlight slanting through the window, reading a message from Fredrik. Short and hesitant. *Do you want to meet?* On a whim, she might say yes. Perhaps they will arrange to meet in a wine bar, and when she arrives she will realise it is the kind of wine bar they had planned to visit after the Swedish reception in Brussels long ago, in her former life, and she will be hit by the strong feeling that things would have been different then, without knowing why. She doesn't have a clue what is going to happen. She wants it, and she doesn't want it. She is close to the boundary where silence stops and something unknown takes hold.